An Actress Of Repute

RONAN BECKMAN

Cover Image – The Duchess of St. Albans by Thomas Lawrence

Creative Commons License Courtesy of the Indianapolis Museum of Art at Newfields

All images are Creative Commons License

Copyright © 2020 Ronan Beckman

All rights reserved.

ISBN: 9798663967327

DEDICATION

Dedicated to my wife -
for having such a fascinating lineage and her invaluable editorial assistance.
And to my daughter –
May she continue the legacy of the strong women in her heritage.

LONDON

INTRODUCTION

Looking at my mud-caked hands and feet, I put them to use in order to hoist myself up into the foliage of the sturdy, tall tree. The rags on my body were stained and threadbare. Rips and tattered openings revealed glimpses of my dirty flesh underneath. I sat silently, waiting with heightened senses for the opportunity that was coming my way. Gazing down below from my safe perch on the tree limb, I spied upon the village woman placing her wicker basket full of fruit, bread and cheese, and a filled ceramic jug of water onto the ground. She was carefully arranging the items, as if she were expecting others to join her in eating this specially prepared feast. Suddenly, I let out a blood-curdling scream which sent the startled woman scrambling away in a panicked state – as quickly as her legs could take her. I dexterously swooped down from the branches and ravenously shovelled lumps of food into my mouth. Fruit juices oozed down my soiled face. Overcome by thirst, I greedily raised the jug to my parted lips and felt the rush of liquid gush into the cavern of my mouth, the excess trickling down my jawline.

Hearing angry barking dogs and frightened villagers, I curled my back into a protective, hunched arch and grabbed a huge lump of wood to use as a makeshift club. Some of the men were carrying lit torches and sharp pitchforks – shouting indiscernible syllables at me. The women followed behind timidly, curiously gawping at the strange sight of this beastly creature. Instinctively, I gave out a hiss of warning as I wielded the heavy club above my head. The men of the village hesitated – holding their arms out to shield their wives and daughters from danger.

I gazed out at all the staring, shocked faces that were entranced by me. Spellbound, it seemed as all were incapable of any movement – except perhaps a gasp of breath to recover from the shock of my appearance. I let out a piercing shriek and hobbled towards the arboreal safety of the mighty tree, dragging the club to ensure the villagers were kept at bay. One of the men then dramatically walked up to a rope hanging near me and pulled on it with great determination. Church bells began to peal loudly. From above, a cloth banner unfurled. Written in bold lettering were the words "La Belle Sauvage". I screamed once more, looking to the assembled audience sitting dumbstruck in their seats all around the auditorium as I dropped down from the branch once again. I caught a glimpse of Papa with a most curious but endearing look upon his face. It was a blend of astonishment and pride in his daughter's accomplishments. Memories of mirror-gazing with him suddenly rushed into my thoughts. His directions and commands came flooding back and I began to respond reflexively in anticipation of the music. The orchestra in the pit struck up the tune. I took my position and began my fierce, savage ballet dance. The grand spectacle had begun.

CHAPTER 1

St. George's on Hart Street, Bloomsbury

September 1803

His hand firmly grasped my chin and lifted it, forcing me to stare directly at my own image. I tried hard to suppress my giggles, but Father was in a stern, serious mood and quickly losing patience with his student's lack of dedication. This made my efforts all the more impossible.

"Elizabeth, you must direct your gaze at the audience. Connect with them. Your countenance conducts your grace and attitude every bit as much as the steps of your dance or the poise of your repose."

I could not help myself, but whenever I glanced towards the full-length looking glass my gaze fixated on the huge crack creaking its way from the upper corner down to the centre, as if it were a lightning bolt frozen mid-strike. The mirror was a present from one of Papa's clients. It was really more of an afterthought than a conscious gift. Father noted on an instructional visit to an aristocratic family that they were about to discard the damaged piece. He happened to overhear his rather odious pupils - a particularly tiresome and uncooperative brother and sister of adolescent years, discussing the impending removal of the offensive room accessory. Being a luxury far more than we could afford - even in its broken state, father took the courageous step of enquiring as to whether he might be able to purchase the mirror from the squire. To our good fortune, the Lord was a kindly man who would consider no such transaction and insisted upon Father taking the item at no cost. Indeed, he even arranged for his own footmen to deliver the magnificent, damaged treasure to our humble terraced home. I remember well when it first arrived. I was a young girl, just six years old, and could not resist the lure of my reflection as I imagined myself as a lady of great means - so very important and beautiful. I would stare at my image for hours on end, fascinated by every characteristic movement that I could make myself create. How different then to the present moment when I could not bring myself to look at my face without bursting into helpless laughter.

Seeing the futility of his efforts, Papa tried another tactic. I could see that he was actually beginning to enjoy the challenge of trying to increase my concentration and dedication to the task at hand. I glanced at him in the mirror furtively with the side of my eye, and noted a sly grin forming on his lips, as he too, I suspect, was attempting to resist the swelling air of mirth and merriment being conveyed through the power of our most magical looking glass.

"Lizzy - attitude!" he shouted sternly, with a clap of his

hands.

Immediately, I responded by reflex to the command - posing in the way I imagined the Greek goddess Athena would present herself. Staring into my own blue eyes, I closed out all other thoughts except imagining that these were deep pools of azure water, leading me hypnotically towards the warm seas as I brought my thoughts to diving and swimming towards the wisdom of the fair goddess. My trance-like state was soon interrupted as my father leant in close and whispered mischievously into my ear.

"Now, take great care not to take notice of that hideous boil on the nose of that dainty lady in the box." I could sense him wiggling his nose, trying to entrap me with his range of humorous faces. "As well as the romantic inclinations of the corpulent Duke sitting beside her..."

Papa puffed his cheeks out until he resembled the Prince of Wales, and proceeded to make smacking, kissing noises. "Or the cross-eyed sailor in the pit, so besotted by your great air of elegance!" Papa crossed his eyes, but I persevered with my stance - counting on Athena's grace being able to overpower my father's comedic talents.

"And of course, never...ever...let noises from the audience distract you from your main purpose!"

Papa leaned as close as possible to my ear. I squinted in anticipation of what torture was yet to come, holding firm to my pose with a stiff grimace. Papa then proceeded to torment me by making the slight, tiny noise of someone making a most indecorous sound emanating from below the waistline and set it delicately adrift – then followed that with complete silence. I could only maintain my repose for what seemed half a second, before bursting into hysterical, uncontrolled laughter. Through my tears I could see the beaming smile of Father as he relished the delight of breaking down my resistance.

"I detect far too much joviality being conducted in this room. Space is at a premium in this household and should I have known that no good use was being made of one's time in here - I would most certainly have procured the room for myself! I have a considerable amount of sewing to attend to." Mother announced this in mock disgust, as she entered the room, with a hint of glee in her eyes. "Besides, the light is failing, and you will damage your eyesight if you continue to stare at yourself dancing the hornpipe."

"Ah, you have much to learn yet, Little Liz. Now, as mother mentioned it, I do feel it is appropriate to practice your hornpipe steps." Father clapped his hands and hummed a Celtic ditty, as I held my dress up and danced my memorised steps of a proper Scottish jig. I was smarting slightly from the condescension of my pet name 'Little Liz'. Perhaps mother felt the same about being 'Big Liz'. But I had to push the thoughts aside as I focused on my poise whilst dancing. This is something Father had been drilling into me continuously, so I aimed to excel. I pasted on a fixed grin of imaginary delight, giving the air of carefree frivolity and ease as I manoeuvred through the tricky, energetic steps. On completion, I curtsied in a well-rehearsed manner that reflected a lady-like disposition of grace and elegance. And whatever I felt deep within my soul, my expression would never betray my true feelings. Being an actress, a dancer, or a performer meant that you had the power to transform yourself into whatever the situation required. Applause from my little brother Tom, Father and Mother grew in my ear as I turned to the magical mirror and imagined the roar of approval of my adoring audience. I fixed my eyes on the reflection and saw not the fourteen-year-old girl with curly chestnut brown hair that I was, but the image of Athena, full of wisdom, bestowing opportunity upon me. Something unavailable to most girls, I realised only too well that I had a chance to achieve more than my current station in life. This was a gift not to be wasted. Yet it was almost too much for me to contend with. It frightened me. However, I knew it was a destiny that I was born to fulfil. How could I know such a thing? To feel such a strong inclination so thoroughly and intensely? I suddenly looked away and re-joined my family as we proceeded together to the kitchen.

I looked around the table as we dined and thought of my life being on the cusp of change: childhood not long behind, and the enticing, yet frightening world of adulthood and marriage lying in the ever-closer future. I wanted to remain where I was - right there, in the comfort of this moment in time. Papa, the experienced dancing master - providing us with scandalous titbits and insights into the elegant world of the Bon Ton, or the Beau Monde. These were the fabulously beautiful and wealthy set – the aristocracy that lorded over those of us who were born much less fortunate. Papa would regale us with his tales of the well to-do; and dealings with their spoiled, petulant offspring as he sought to drill some rudimentary skills at Cotillion, or the Scotch Reel, all within the opulent surroundings of the empty ballrooms of the privileged. Mother, the devoted, hard-working wife; ensuring that our household kept the appearance of a higher station in life than we possessed in actuality. During the day, fitting in chores and our education, while trying to sew period costumes for the various non-patent theatres, such as Sadler's Wells, for which she would receive some small monetary reward to add to our meagre household coffers. Steadfast, dependable, and calm, she was the foundation on which we all depended upon. Yet she was undemanding and seemingly content with this role, bearing only the slightest hint of melancholy about her nature the source of which I was unsure of. I would find such a situation infinitely stifling, myself. It is a woman's lot in life yet I wished and hoped for there to be so much more in store for me. And then there was little Tom - who could be annoying, amusing, and affectionate; all in equal measure. The perfect recipe for a little brother. A loveable rogue, and a reminder of the joys of childhood that were passing me by at this very moment.

Our dwelling on Hart Street was a handsome brick town house, equidistant from Bloomsbury Square and the British Museum. With three large sash windows facing the street on each of the four floors, light and sound would stream in from the road outside. The Duke of Bedford went to great lengths to prevent traffic, so the area had a rather peaceful air about it. The neighbourhood was occupied mainly by professionals - solicitors and surgeons, with a few merchant men sprinkled through. We were most fortunate to be renting the house at a reduced rate, as a favour from a connection of my father's Aunt Harriet. Two doors away was the grand, brilliant white spire of St. George's. There was many a time as a child that I would stand staring at the Grecian porticoes of the church; transporting my thoughts, I'm rather ashamed to say, to the gods of mythology rather than to the faith that the building was actually intended. Peculiar in having the main spire located to the side of the church, rather than the front or back; it was an inspiring setting to set my imagination free. The statuary on top of the tower particularly sparked my imagination, as I ran up the steps and played between the great columns of the porch. I would find myself dreaming of riding on the unicorn's back, escaping the fearsome lion baring his gruesome teeth at me. And I would curtsy to old King George staring down at me from the very tip of the pyramid-shaped apex, then proceed to perform the latest dance steps that Papa so lovingly taught me - oblivious to my surroundings and the bemused stares from passers-by.

I had fond memories of pretending to be a grand lady, prancing in front of Montague House as learned men made their way to the great library and museum to pursue their studies. In my mind, they were my footmen and servants, scurrying about to fulfil my latest whims and requests. I took note of all the grand carriages with their fine horses, considering most earnestly which was to be mine. The gardens of nearby Bloomsbury Square afforded me the window to the natural world. Looking skyward toward the stretching branches of the trees, I could temporarily forget the ring of exceptionally fine terraced houses that surrounded me and imagine myself in the midst of an enchanted forest. I had many freedoms as a child, and the realities of the world of responsible adulthood were now facing me in a most fearsome way. And soon, I would no longer have recourse to the magical unicorn of St George's steeple galloping to my rescue. I looked to little six-year-old Tom seated before me - rolling bits of his bread into cannonballs and firing them into his mouth. I give him a look of warning, glancing towards my distracted parents to ensure that he escapes censure - this time. And deep inside, I found myself envying his youth.

CHAPTER 2

*Elizabeth Searle
by John Young, after John Opie*

On most Saturdays, I was in charge of watching my little brother Tom. I must admit that this was no drudgery or chore, as we had the good pleasure to visit my father's dear Aunt Harriet every week. A visit to Great Aunt Harriet was almost always a guaranteed adventure. She lived in a rural idyll. She had been appointed to a small, rustic cottage near a delightful little pond to live in. Nearby was a barn, where she kept a few cows and goats. Fresh produce grew in her garden, ensuring an abundant crop of fruit and vegetables that we were welcome to harvest for Mother to prepare our meals from. Late summer would provide the spectacle of her abundant roses in bloom, their sweet smell permeating everywhere - with the ability to overpower the unpleasant odour of her livestock. This all would have made for an enjoyable outing enough on its own, but there was much more to the setting than this description suggests. For this farm was located at the end of the Queen's Promenade in Green Park - right here in London! She was there at the behest of His Majesty, King George III. The rooms of her quaint home were decorated by none other than the Princess Marie herself!

Despite this royal connection, my great aunt held no airs and graces. She was most amiable, and the humble beggar felt equally at ease in her company as those from the ranks of the nobility. Aunt Harriet would matter-of-factly regale my brother and I with stories about the high and mighty that others would be spouting to prove their importance and valuable place in society. But these were all just the characters that she happened to encounter in her corner of the world. She was not name-dropping to impress. She would never even contemplate such a thing.

We were more than happy to embark upon the chores with her - from milking the cows to sweeping the stables. For we knew we would be privy to stories from another world…the world of royalty, palaces, and privilege. And our great aunt was amongst their midst! I remember her story of her nephew George Brummell's first meeting with the Prince of Wales, which took place in the farmyard. Yes, that is correct…I am speaking about the well-known dandy and man of fashion George 'Beau' Brummell. Though I never have even laid sight upon this distant cousin of mine, I could feel the tangible excitement of knowing that he, when but a mere adolescent young man about my age, had stood right here in this spot and had a pleasant chat with the Prince of Wales himself just ten years previously. It was unfathomable to me, yet Aunt Harriet would recount her stories about the great and the good with the same enthusiasm as one would relay an account of listening to the morning's church bells peeling.

"George told the Prince he wished to be an officer in the army. I suppose His Highness was impressed, but we all know now that he just liked the look of himself in uniform. I believe that in my nephew he could sense a kindred arrogant spirit. I am led to believe that with the passage of time my nephew has transformed himself into a rather vain, self-important man. He no longer has time for his Aunt Harriet... I do hope it won't be the same with you two little dears!"

Great Aunt Harriet dressed as a relic from another age; and in some way was a gatekeeper to another world and time, just as she served as a gatekeeper to Green Park. She wore a tall bonnet that looked most curious, sporting a pink satin bow on the top. I could imagine this being an item of fashion back in the days when my father was born. I tried to imagine her holding my father as an infant whilst wearing that same bonnet. Her dress was very old-fashioned and seemed rather impractical for farm work; but she did not let it impede her. She thought nothing of lifting her skirt and getting down to the labour at hand.

Perhaps the greatest oddity of our visits was our role in satisfying the curiosity of those who came to better acquaint themselves with the workings of agriculture. It was difficult for me to comprehend, but it seems that many ladies of great means and wealth have no opportunity to witness the process by which food is placed on their tables. These city-dwelling women of fashion: wives of wealthy merchants, daughters of bankers, even maids-of-honour to Queen Charlotte herself, difficult as it may be to believe - actually have the desperate desire to experience (in the most delicate way possible) the life of a humble milk-maiden. As Auntie is infinitely discrete and well-connected, she found herself receiving a steady stream of ladies of the fashionable world wishing to play at being a farmhand. My brother and I were enlisted to help Aunt Harriet accommodate and instruct these most peculiar tourists in the ways of rural life.

Tom would instantly be the recipient of great adoration from the moment of his first, well-rehearsed appearance.

The immaculately dressed ladies laughed and cooed at his innate charm and infectious smile. He would then proceed to go about his various duties: collecting eggs, churning butter, pushing a wheelbarrow greater in size than he, sweeping animal manure out of the way of the visitors. Whatever he did, he ensured that he stopped mid-flow to glance at the observers and flash a beatific, angelic smile and an adorable tilt to his head. This - coupled with his expressive blue eyes and curly brown locks melted the hearts of his adoring fans. Only I knew all too well the insincerity of his actions, and I would try to discretely give him remonstrative looks when he stuck his tongue out at them as they turned away to admire the next item of agricultural interest.

I carried out the role of teaching the ladies about the intricacies of the cow udder. I felt it was very good practice for the stage, as I had to maintain my genteel deportment and unflinching support as these rather silly ladies squealed with shrieks of manic hysteria whilst one by one, they dared each other to attempt the milking process. Patiently and expertly, I would demonstrate the correct technique, all to no avail - as my poor bovine friends had to endure the amateur attempts of my dithering students to bring forth the prized liquid. I must admit that I seized these sessions as opportunities. I took note of these women - their speech, mannerisms, affectations. I would try to sear these memories deep within my very being, so that when I returned home, I could race to the full-length mirror with the crack and practice each and every characteristic of those I had met that day. I would work carefully to perfect the accent, tone of voice, vocabulary; in short - to capture their very essence and claim it as my own.

Aunt Harriet was protected by a most fearsome goose named Goldie. No guard dog could provide greater protection! Occasionally, one of our touristic guests would wander away from the main group. Suddenly we would become aware of the missing party due to the screams of alarm from some fashionable woman cornered by the fearsome, hissing Goldie trapping them in their place. Tom and I would then come to the rescue, sticks in hand as we tried to prod the goose away from the target of her ire.

Our guests were always rewarded with an invitation to Auntie's simple kitchen. Here they were treated to her delightful scones, fresh butter, and home-made jams. I do not believe Auntie charged any fee for these visits. But she would often be amply rewarded some days later with kind gifts from her esteemed patrons. These would include items such as delicious cuts of venison, whole pheasant, or even some fine tea to brew. As this was far too much for a lone elderly lady to consume, much of this bounty was packaged up for Tom and I to take home. Therefore, our salary was amply paid in kind through the provision of generous helpings and portions of unwanted food items. We would labour back to our home; heavily laden with meats, cheese, milk, fruit, and vegetables from the cornucopia that was Aunt Harriet. This, coupled with gifts from the fine families of my father's dance pupils, meant that we were never wanting for food in our household. Our household budget could then be spent on other luxuries that might not be otherwise affordable. In my case, a considerable portion of this windfall was spent on singing lessons for me. Unlike dancing, my musical talents were considerably more modest and in great need of nurturing.

CHAPTER 3

Theatre Royal Drury Lane

One benefit of living near the theatres in Covent Garden and Drury Lane is that sometimes Papa would be in the mood for the entertainments that these venues provided. He felt it was part of his duty to keep abreast with the latest music and dance steps that were presented on stage, for he knew that his charges would be requesting these dance moves from him in future lessons. As Mother was often tired from her chores and had to see that Tom was sent to his bed at a timely hour, I was frequently the lucky companion to my father as we embarked on the magical journeys provided by the theatrical world. Our usual procedure was to procure some fruit and a playbill from one of the hawkers outside the entrance. There was nothing to compare to the joy of huddling up to enjoy a warm, roasted apple on a cold winter's night as we studied the evening's playbill. Most evenings consisted of a 5-act dramatic performance. Many would choose to come after the interval when prices dropped by half. The afterpieces performed were immensely popular – often with a strong music or dance element – such as a pantomime; or adding a touch of comedy with a farce.

After paying our entrance fees, we would scurry to find some seats. Those of the Beau Monde, where price was no concern, sat comfortably in their beautiful boxes – paid for by seasonal subscription and ensuring prime seating and access to the spacious saloons and anterooms. Our budget meant that we usually had to settle for the faraway heights, being seated in the gallery. But it meant that we avoided the scrum of the rabble fighting for seats down in the pit. From where we sat, it could be a struggle to hear dialogue and the view would often be obstructed. The compensation was that we had the grand scene of the spectacle provided by the audience members themselves. It was most entertaining to view the range of humanity present: the pompous gentry, the elegant courtesans fluttering their fans and trading furtive glances towards potential new admirers, military officers dressed handsomely in their uniforms - the great diaspora of humanity all seated before the stage in anticipation of an evening's entertainment. The rowdy spectators often provided a far more amusing divertissement to what was being offered on stage.

But there were some performers that particularly captured my attention, and all the audience was spellbound by the enchantment that they conjured. The incomparable Mrs. Jordan was a case that particularly comes to mind. I remember marvelling as she took to the stage, playing the part of Peggy in *The Country Girl*. She commanded the attention of the crowd before her with her wit and talent. The effect she had was mesmerizing, and I too fell under her spell. Oh, how I longed to have her air of utmost confidence; gliding across the stage in her breeches without the slightest hint of being daunted or embarrassed. I would have been petrified myself, but Dora Jordan had the ability to make each and every one of the 3000 audience members of the vast theatre succumb to her air of lightness and put them at complete ease. All in Drury Lane were hypnotised and gave their rapt attention whenever she appeared.

I must admit that I preferred Mrs. Jordan to the highly esteemed tragic muse, Mrs. Siddons. Dora Jordan's pieces were full of fun and frivolity. Her comedies provoked mirth and laughter, with sweet music and jolly dances to further enhance the mood. One left the theatre in a most buoyant mood. Sarah Siddons, in contrast, brought a sense of respectability to the stage at Covent Garden. She had a gravitas about her that would compel the audience to hang on her every utterance and look to her countenance in complete empathy of the deep emotion she was conveying at the time. Her performances were an investment. In return for your attention, you became embroiled in the range of deep emotion that she was imparting. I would feel completely drained, and quite tearful at the end of her performances. As a young girl, I found this most disconcerting and a bit daunting at the time.

What inspired me the most was that many of the most celebrated stage talents in the nation were women. These magnificent, gifted ladies were not admired solely for their great beauty, but also for their incomparable talents. They had the means to attract fees that ensured their independence and security. Furthermore, they received just plaudits for their considerable acting virtues. By means of the stage, they had found a door to self-determination. They were not dependent on the whims of a fickle husband. This was a rare opportunity of escape that was not available to the vast majority of those with the misfortune of being born female. The feminine realm was a world of limited options. One was primed from an early age to use one's name, connections or beauty to charm and snare a suitable gentleman to ensure a fortuitous future. It seemed to me that this was all some frighteningly silly lottery. The consequences were potentially disastrous, and this was not a game that I wanted to consider playing. Could the theatre potentially open the door to opportunities I could not possibly contemplate otherwise?

On reflection, I wonder if Papa was gently guiding me towards this chance. Mother was always the sensible thinker of our household, censuring me if I dared to dream beyond my station. My study of the arts was all well and good, but in mother's mind it all served a purpose: to increase my charm and raise my prospects of securing a favourable spouse. She was never encouraging of the idea of my entering the world of entertainment. I suspect she harboured some great disappointments from her experience as a dancer on the provincial stages. But I could never press her to relay any stories of her theatrical past – it was as if I were tearing open an old wound. And so, she primed me inexorably with the skills to secure matrimonial success. With some luck, she thought it possible that I may attract the attentions of a clergyman, an army officer, or even a wealthy merchant. Yet never once did I hear Papa speak of marriage prospects for me. But on the topics of theatre and dance, there was no stopping either of us in our enthusiasm!

"Miss Decamp is a most exquisite dancer!"

"Oh, and Mrs. Mountain has the sweetest voice; does she not, Papa?"

It was the ladies of the theatrical world of which we spoke the most. Papa loved to critique the moves of the dancers in precise detail. No minor slip-up or error escaped his expert gaze. He would advise me of the finest qualities and attributes of each performer, then suggest that I study them carefully in the hopes of my absorbing some of their talents. He found it so difficult to sit still in his seat when the music started, and I often noted that he was tapping his feet to the rhythm or waving his fingers in time to the tune. I often found myself lost in this dream world as well, transported to the lands depicted before the curtains. At that time, I had little reason to suspect that there may be other girls in the not-so-distant future who may be sitting there in the theatre's vast audience; gazing at me, entranced by my graceful movements on stage, my expert recitation of dialogue, the tone of my maturing singing voice. I would never be able to fathom the notion, but there would come a time that I would be able to command the respect of those who gazed at my appearance before them and be an actress of repute. Feted, admired, applauded, adored – all words that seem to be an unreachable dream. If only I had a magic crystal ball that could have portrayed this vision of the future that I could never foresee. Unbeknownst to me, I soon found myself embarking on a career that would have me placed on the very same stages of those women I so admired. How was I to know?

CHAPTER 4

Circumstances sometimes thrust us onto the precipice of decisions that we would not ever had dared to contemplate otherwise. Sometimes fortune smiles, or it could be misfortune making an unwelcome entrance. In my case, it was a misbegotten combination of the two. I would never have imagined that I would have been as courageous as I was about to become. One day, I awoke to find I was a resourceful, talented young woman; having been merely a playful teenage girl just the day before.

It was late September, and the air had a taste of the impending autumnal gloom about it. The sky had a heavy greyness which the sun seemed unable to penetrate through. I awoke early - or should I say that I was awakened early by the awareness of some presence about my person. I felt aware of a weight on the side of my bed and heard what sounded like a rasping, rattling wind. Wearily, I pried my tired eyelids open, only to be started by the sight of two beaming blue eyes located just inches away from my own. This revelation was accompanied by the maniacal giggles of Tom as he stroked the side of my face with a feather. I arose with a start, causing Tom to fall off me into a laughing heap on the floor.

"What in heaven's name do you think you are doing?! How dare you!"

He just babbled "Coochy-coochy-coo-coo!" before erupting into another fit of hysterical guffaws.

"Tom – you are not amusing! This is...just...ohhh!!!"

Words were failing me and having no effect upon Tom. He was weeping with joy at having caused me so much consternation, and having great difficulty breathing. I picked him up by the neck of his nightdress and marched him out my door.

"You do not have permission to be in my room, EVER!" I had to hold the door shut, as my annoying little brother persisted in trying to re-enter my bedchamber. His noisy squeals of delight sounded as if he were a maniacal resident of Bedlam. This irritating romp was interrupted suddenly by a piercing cry from my mother.

"ELIZABETH!"

I could tell from the tone of her voice that the matter was serious. I feared that I was about to be punished for the transgressions that were caused by pesky Tom. I pushed past him as he threw a stupid smile at me, relishing the idea of the scolding I was about to receive from my perturbed parents. I walked into the room in a very contrite, apologetic manner.

"Mother, I am so sorry to have woken you. You see it was Tom who..."

"Never mind that! It's your father...I can't seem to wake him, and he is all feverish."

Her face was riddled with worry. I put my hand on Papa's pale, sweaty forehead. He acknowledged my presence with an unintelligible murmur as he struggled to open his eyes. I looked to mother for a signal as to what course of action to take. It was incomprehensible to me to consider that my strong, lean, charming father was rendered completely incapable so very suddenly. I could sense that it was causing my mother some considerable distress which she was trying very hard to quell for the sake of us all.

"Fetch some water – and some clean towelling."

I did as I was told. Even little Tom sensed the urgency of the situation and tried to help as best he could with simple household errands. None of us spoke, we only reacted to the current demands of the situation. Much of the morning was spent mopping father's brow and providing small amounts of barley water and meat broth in an attempt to restore some of his strength. When it was approaching noon, mother realised that it might be prudent to notify father's clients of his current indisposition.

"Elizabeth, go through father's appointment book. I will need you to go to each customer's address and make them aware that father is feeling unwell and will not be able to conduct lessons for the next few days. I need you to be less than forthcoming should they ask you any details as to his condition. Be sure not to reveal the seriousness of the situation if you are pressed for information…"

This command alarmed me considerably, for I could sense in Mother's voice an uncertainty with regards to his prognosis.

"Mother, how could I answer otherwise…I know not what is happening to him. Will he recover? This is all so sudden! Do you wish me to go to the apothecary for medicines?" A doctor was something far beyond the reach of our limited finances.

Mother cried out with a hint of despair in her voice - "Elizabeth, I beg of you – please just do as I say! There will be more time to review the situation when you return."

And so, I did as I was told, with great worry and a troubled mind. And yet at every stop I had to put on a false front. Acting very nonchalant and rather glib, I reassured each client that father's indisposition was a trifling affair, and he would most assuredly be on the mend soon. We would notify at the earliest moment when his return was imminent. And as I made the rounds, I fought back my tears. It was important that I maintained the confidence and trust of Papa's customers, lest they seek a new dance master. I disassociated myself from my fears and panic of the current situation, and focused on this new, temporary persona that I had just created. But when I eventually returned home, there was no review of the situation. I knew not to press mother for her thoughts, and I quietly, subserviently provided whatever help and assistance was requested of me.

This charade continued. Day by day, I delivered our sincerest apologies to Papa's clients. They had no idea, but I was aware that his progress was quite slow. Aunt Harriet, when she received news of father's condition, arranged for a medical acquaintance of hers to come and attend to father. The process of bleeding and blistering Papa was horrendous to witness, but it did elicit some reaction from him. The fevers and sweats were gradually abating, but he remained bed bound. Most disconcerting was the developing paralysis that was becoming more pronounced on the one side of his face. His diet remained extremely limited, but we began to introduce bread that was softened by dipping into his soup. He still needed us to spoon feed him, as he was still too weak. He was able to mumble short phrases from the side of his mouth occasionally, but we encouraged silence and rest from him – reassuring him that all was well and there was no cause for concern.

The truth was far different, however. On entering the second week of my father's illness, I was beginning to discern a bit of disquiet amongst his clients. It was becoming more difficult to placate them with my practised excuses and reassurances. They were wanting more information as to the nature of his illness and how prolonged it may be. I had to change my tactics and began to report that he was experiencing a bit of a relapse.

"It is such a nuisance, this illness – but please do bear

with us and his return to instruction will be imminent, rest assured."

To their credit, Papa had endeared himself to his pupils to such an extent that they almost universally expressed the utmost concern and a fortuitous amount of renewed patience. We received kind gifts that helped to keep our spirits up – if only temporarily.

Mother spent most of her time attending continuously to Papa. I could tell that she was exhausted and drained with worry. Yet I was frustrated that she refused to share her concerns with me. I was left with increased household duties, trying to fill in the voids left by Mother's current preoccupation with nursing, and nearly as much in the dark about the facts of Papa's situation as my little brother. Poor Tom, who was by now my charge and responsibility, was certainly no trouble to me at all. Sensing that everyone must do their utmost to help, he was on his best behaviour and voluntarily undertook a number of additional chores completely upon his own volition. He made himself scarce and was never in my way. When I did spot him, I noted the look of melancholy as he methodically swept the stairs or polished the silver – deep in his thoughts.

On the morning of the eleventh day after Papa first fell ill, Mother called me to her room. I remember the day well as it was the day my entire future changed course forever. That sounds overly dramatic, but it is indeed the truth. Father was still asleep as Mother sat at her writing table, sealing a note with hot wax. She turned to me with a serious look on her face and gazed at me with an almost apologetic look. I sensed that she was working hard to compose her thoughts, and she seemed very considered - almost reticent, as she spoke to me.

"Elizabeth...I am not certain how to say this, so please forgive me if what I am about to say sounds abrupt in any way. I have been hoping and praying for your father's speedy recovery. The truth of the matter is that I am not sure when...or even if...he will regain his full capabilities to fulfil his duties as a dance master."

My heart dropped there and then. I felt my hand reflexively form into a fist, as I pressed it firmly against my lips to prevent me from sobbing audibly. Tears were welling up in my eyes, as the severity of the situation was becoming clearer – a reality that I had been trying to suppress for all these days. There was a long, perceptible silence as Mother looked away – then with a deep intake of breath she continued.

"I am sorry to say that if this situation continues, we as a family will find ourselves in a considerable financial predicament. Kind Aunt Harriet has offered assistance, but I feel it is best not to be continuously dependent on the charity of others. Somehow, we must find some means to bring an income to this household. I have been at odds thinking as to how this can be accomplished. Tom is so young, and he needs my attention, as does your father. I was considering working more formally at one of the theatres in making costumes. But I think it is far too much responsibility for someone as young as yourself to take on all the household duties, oversee Tom's education, nurse your father..."

"Mother, please know that I am willing to undertake any task that will assist our current situation – no matter what that might be! I am more than able to watch over Papa and..."

Mother grinned slightly in appreciation and tilted her head slightly as she gently brushed the side of my face.

"I am so very ...vexed at having to make this decision – and yet I think this may be a better plan for us all. From the moment of your birth, I was determined to see that you had access to a better life...an easier life than I had to endure as a young lady. I wanted you married and securely cared for by a sensible, professional husband who might whisk you away from this wicked city to a beautiful home in the countryside. But now...now, I find that I am being forced to consider that you will follow in my footsteps. And I pray that you may be able to avoid the pitfalls and traps that challenged me...in the theatrical world."

I fixed my gaze on Mother, hanging on every word. I did not feel that I was fully comprehending the language that she was trying to convey. I had to take great care to remain standing, as my knees suddenly felt as if they were made of jelly. I had always thought that my mother had just tolerated my forays into dance as a way of communicating and sharing in my father's skills. She had, in fact, always actively discouraged my pursuits whenever I dared to share my interest in the studies required for a career in entertainment. Indeed, I never forgot being scolded at the mere age of seven when she caught me dancing, singing, and bowing to my imaginary audience on the porch of St. George's church. It was quite humiliating for me, as she reproved my vanity in seeking the approbation of others. How sinful too, on the steps of the house of our Lord God! And now...was she really proposing that I pursue this career? One I never secretly dared to dream of? Was this true, or a mere dream? Mother continued to explain herself – very methodically and thoughtfully. She took extreme care with her words, and I could feel that the situation was exceptionally difficult for her.

"Listen carefully to my proposal, Elizabeth. An old acquaintance of mine has returned from an extended tour of America. I hear that he is directing a new ballet at Drury Lane. His name is Mr. Byrne. I want you to take this letter to him at the theatre. When you get there, do not hand this message over to anyone other than Mr. Byrne...do you understand?"

I nodded, slightly dumbfounded.

"To whomever answers the stage door, I want you to tell them you have an urgent letter to deliver personally to Mr. Byrne, and do not leave until you can do this. Tell Mr.

Byrne discretely that you have a message of importance from the former Miss Elizabeth Siddenham. I am not certain that he will have work for you, but I am hopeful that he may be of some assistance to us in our plight. Now take heed of what I am about to say, Elizabeth. You are a beautiful young woman. The theatre attracts many unsavoury characters who relish the opportunity to charm the gullible and unwary. Be on your guard at all times. I have seen too many naïve and innocent young fools become victims to those who prey on the unsuspecting. Promise me this! You must protect your virtue, for I still do have sincere hopes for you to be able to find a favourable marriage at some point in the future. Hopefully, times are beginning to change, and actresses are less likely to be looked upon as women of a disreputable status. Miss Farren left the stage to marry the Earl Derby, and Mrs. Siddons has demonstrated the respectability that women in the profession can possess; so there is some hope that a young lady can improve her circumstances through her skills and talents in the performing arts. However, do not let some buffoon from the Green Room tempt you to let down your guard. Maintain the decorum of the ladies you have met through your Aunt Harriet. And do not forget all the hints and lessons from your father. I have always managed to listen in on his lessons with you, and he has taught you well." Mother's eyes were watering, as she was on the verge of tears.

"I assure you Mother that I will do my best to make you proud. Please do not worry after me. I am a sensible girl and I would never contemplate doing anything to bring shame upon you and Papa."

I clasped her hand to mine as she presented a soft, sad smile my way. And with that exchange, she pressed the fresh letter into my hand, and bid me haste.

CHAPTER 5

Scene from Cinderella

I felt myself shaking as I was suddenly overcome with fear. What was Mother asking of me? I could not believe that my carefree days of youthful bliss had come to an abrupt halt. Now I was expected to enter the adult world of work. It was all so abrupt and sudden. I felt completely unprepared. Before setting out with the message, I had the urge to stand before the cracked mirror. I hoped it would impart the confidence that I was going to need as I embarked on my duty. I hoped that it could convey the wisdom of my father from all the times we gazed together at the reflection before us. Slowly, I drew a breath for strength, and looked directly at the young girl before me. I directed my gaze directly into the eyes that were facing mine. I needed a miracle, a transformation. I could recall all the commands of my father in our dance lessons:

"Grace! Deportment! Countenance! Every movement conveys meaning...communicate to those before you. Enlighten them with the very essence of your soul through the expression contained within your physical articulation."

Without realising it, I had been posing various attitudes reflexively. I felt a powerful force within me that was indescribable. And as I looked ahead, I saw not myself - the mortal Elizabeth Searle. I could see the wise Athena conveying her powers through me. And for the first time, I saw the woman that was me in my reflection - no longer a meek, silly girl. In my eyes I saw the azure blue of the great skies of the heavens and the turquoise hues of the seas. The chestnut brown locks of my hair rippling like the winds parting the golden waves of grain in the summer fields. The luminous incandescence of my skin radiating as if I were the harvest moon. In my figure, I could see the ideal of feminine beauty as portrayed by the great classical sculptors of the ancient world. I curtsied before the looking glass the same as I would do were I before a king in his palace. The evil of doubt had to be pushed aside. My mind had to be cleansed of all the worries that troubled me. I must be completely secure in my talents. My journey had begun.

As I stepped out the door onto Hart Street, my mind began to focus on the document within my hands. What message did it contain? I had such a surge of near insatiable curiosity, but I knew I had to repress the feeling and not succumb. I stopped briefly to hold the iron rails outside the church of St. George's. I followed the mighty Grecian columns with my eyes until I could see the brave lion at the top, beseeching me to carry on with my travels. As I turned left onto Bow Street, I glanced at the traders and shopkeepers busily selling their wares. And my mind drifted off into the range of possible employment that this Mr. Byrne may be able to procure for me. Just because I was to meet him at the theatre was no indication that I might be deployed on the stage. Perhaps I was merely to be his scullery maid. I scuttled past a ragged woman selling loathsome meat scraps and offal for feeding to pet dogs and cats. How fortunate was I to be able to avoid such disagreeable employment. Or would my future fate require that I join her? Maybe the intention was that I could be a governess to the theatre manager's children. Looking at the fruit vendors, I thought perhaps I may become an apple seller - roasting the fruit to tempt theatre goers with the rich, sweet smell. Passing the drapers, I supposed that I could be involved in the wardrobe in some way - a seamstress, a dresser or seeing to the face powders and wigs of the actors. Seeing the newspaper hawker, I thought I may be shouting at passers-by in order to entice them to buy the evening's theatre playbill. Dodging the brooms of the street sweepers and the cries of "Dust-o!" from the dustmen collecting cinders from all the street's fireplaces in their carts, the notion entered my mind that I too could be mistress of the broom - sweeping the grand steps of the Theatre Royal.

And there before me was that very door - the stage door at Drury Lane. I had always marvelled at this grand building on my entertaining excursions with Papa, but never did I suspect that I would be here on a matter of urgent business. Churches aside, this was the tallest building in London. The imposing edifice consisted of mighty archways on the ground level, with grand windows gradually receding as you followed up 3 more floors. I took a deep breath and tried to steel myself for the task ahead. Somehow, I had to find the courage within myself to accomplish my mission – our lives literally depended on it. Climbing the steps outside, I reached for the door and quickly knocked before my resolve weakened.

I watched the door creak open slowly, and I leapt into action. The doorman was taken aback slightly as I entered before speaking. I wanted to ensure that he could not simply slam the door on me, leaving me with no further course of action.

"Forgive me, kind sir; but I have been entrusted with a letter of the greatest urgency for a Mr. Byrne - whom I believe is currently in the theatre's employ." I knew that I had to try to muster up an air of supreme confidence. I needed to convey an air of slight superiority to the man before me. Perhaps intimidate him slightly by making it appear that I was a member of the upper classes. If not that, then at the very least to portray a character before him as someone in the employ of the great and powerful. This would increase my chances of getting my message through.

"Certainly, Miss. I can assure you that I will get it to him straight away." To my dismay, he was seeing through my guise and taking me for just an unimportant, troublesome girl wasting his time.

"I am most sorry for my impertinence, but I am under strict orders by the author of this document to ensure that he is given it directly. It is imperative that I actually witness him receiving this envelope." I surprised myself at the imperious tone of voice that I was able to employ.

"I am afraid that is not possible, young Miss. Mr. Byrne is in the midst of important rehearsals on the stage at this very moment and is not to be interrupted. You have my word that he will be in receipt of your letter at his earliest convenience."

The door opened fully behind me, and the doorman was gently trying to steer me out - but was blocked by the person making their entrance. I continued with my entreaties to him.

"Please sir, I beseech you...I must get this message to Mr. Byrne personally with the utmost haste! It is a most pressing matter, and I will be held personally culpable if he does not read it!

"I can escort the young lady to Mr. Byrne, if you like." The person in the doorway spoke. She was a radiantly beautiful lady with a kind smile, and hints of blonde curls peeking from her bonnet. And at that very moment, I thought she had the sweetest voice that I had ever heard - unmatched by any imaginable heavenly being. "I'm on my way there at this moment - it will be no trouble whatsoever."

"Miss Bristow, it is highly irregular for someone to walk

straight off the street and disturb..."

Miss Bristow interrupted with a reassuring grin. "Nonsense! The responsibility will be all mine - I assure you, and I will be the one to blame if Mr. Byrne sees this as an intrusion. On the other hand, if the message is of such great importance - what would he think if he were to know that you were the cause of the delay in receiving that letter?"

The doorman was visibly flummoxed and could only manage to stutter a mumbled reply. "Er, uh...very well then..."

The doorman glared at me as I entered the theatre victorious. I gave him a slightly condescending, triumphant smirk as I moved past. Miss Bristow took me by the arm and guided me through to a small dressing room.

"You may leave your coat here if you like. Place it on top of mine!" Both our coats were piled onto the back of the nearest available chair back.

"Thank you so much for your kindness, Miss Bristow! I don't know what I would have done had you not come to my rescue."

"Well, let us not waste any time worrying about what hasn't happened! Now, firstly - what is your name? Secondly, and most important...what are the contents of this most urgent letter?!" Miss Bristow's eyes widened in mock gossipy delight. "Are you a bailiff in disguise, trying to seize the bankrupt Mr. Byrne and cart him off to Fleet Prison? Or are you to tell him that he has been infected with the dreaded Yellow Fever? It is all he talks about, you know. That is the very reason why he and his family did not settle in Jamaica. They were stacking the bodies at the quayside when they arrived at Kingston from Philadelphia, apparently. And he made the courageous decision to bravely hop back on the boat and scurry straight over to London, as quick as the sails could take him!" She had an infectious laugh. And despite my nervousness about the whole situation, I found myself joining in - adding my own giggles to the mix.

"He does like to complain about his travels - the backward provincialism of the theatres in America, the prospects of a plantation in the West Indies unfulfilled, the unhealthy air of London...what a misery! But he is a genius at choreography. Which is precisely why he is here, of course!"

"My name is Miss Elizabeth Searle. I am afraid that I do not know the exact contents of the letter, but I suspect it may be a request for some form of employment for me. Apparently, my mother was a friend of the family in the distant past."

"Ah! Not that urgent. But of course, urgent for you! We need to ensure you have the best opportunity then. Follow my lead. I will introduce you. We are beginning to work on a pantomime ballet, based on the story of *Cinderella*. Initially it was to be ready before Christmas, but I think they will be lucky to have it ready for the New Year. Mr. James has added elements of Greek mythology to the story so that the adults do not feel their time has been wasted on a mere fairy-tale. And Mr. Kelly has composed the most delightful music to accompany the performance. If you do not mention travels to Mr. Byrne, he actually is quite an amiable family man. You know he works here with his wife and his little sons - all dancers, and extraordinarily talented. So many of us are family here. My sister is married to Mr. Grimaldi, who performs here in comical roles. And my other sister is at Covent Garden. You had best call me by my first name - Charlotte, lest you get us all confused. I perform with Bella Menage and her sister. Her brother and father are theatre people as well. And, of course, there are all the Kembles. It seems one cannot find a stage anywhere without a Kemble of some sort making their presence known. One, in fact, constantly pursues our very own Cinderella, Miss Decamp. Apparently, his family do not approve. She has been waiting for him for what seems like an eternity to make her a Kemble by marriage."

She led me to the stage and discretely pointed to Mr. Byrne, who was discussing scenery and stage mechanisms with some other men. The stage was dimly lit from the few windows that had the curtains drawn back, and the theatre seating was completely dark - but I could perceive the enormity of the place in the blackness. Charlotte waited patiently for him to finish, holding my arm in hers. Then, as the moment approached, she looked at me reassuringly and moved forward.

"Mr. Byrne, I have someone who has been waiting eagerly to meet with you. May I introduce Miss Elizabeth Searle. She has brought with her a letter which I believe her mother has written to you, which may be of some consequence."

At that, Charlotte slipped away imperceptibly into the shadows leaving me in privacy with Mr. Byrne. I could tell at once he was a dancer, with his tall, lean build and the elegance of his airs. There were hints of grey climbing up the sides of his dark hair. He looked at me somewhat distractedly as I spoke.

"Sir, I apologise for disturbing you. My mother insisted that I deliver this written message to you and await your response. I believe you may have been acquainted in the past - she was known as Miss Elizabeth Siddenham."

The name registered a definite recognition upon Mr. Byrne's face, as evidenced by his expression. He fixed his gaze firmly upon me at that moment, as if seeking further clarification as to my purpose. He held out his hand, and I placed the letter in his grasp. He seemed to hesitate momentarily, staring at the red wax seal; then quickly tore the letter open and began reading. There was a moment where he looked almost startled and he gazed at me. He then placed his hand upon his chin, rubbing it as he continued reading. He folded the letter and put it in his waistcoat. He looked at me and forced out a rather insincere looking smile as he spoke to me.

"Miss Searle, your mother informs me that you are a dancer of some merit. You have been under the tutelage of a Mr. Thomas Searle, the well-respected dancing master of Bloomsbury, who recognised your natural born talents at an early age. I am informed that he instructed you well, nurturing your knowledge of ballet and various country dances. I would be most interested in seeing what you can manage and how quickly you can learn a step."

My heart was racing at this point. What was he going to ask of me?

"Let us consider this an audition of sorts. Miss Bristow, would you be so kind as to join us? Now Miss Searle, Miss Bristow is about to undertake the role of one of three Graces in our new production, along with the ever-absent-minded Miss Menage. Where is she, pray tell - can anyone inform me?" He looked around the stage with a perturbed air. "Now, I shall fetch one of our violinists to accompany you. Miss Bristow shall teach you the steps and movements. If your performance meets to my satisfaction, then I shall see to it that you may appear on the stage as the third Grace. And so, I shall see you in, say, fifteen minutes hence. Ladies, do excuse me as I enquire as to the whereabouts of Miss Arabella Menage."

Mr. Byrne bowed his head slightly and glided off the stage. Charlotte looked at me with an enthusiasm and excitement that was hard for her to contain.

"That was most remarkable! I don't think I have ever seen an audition appear out of the ether like that before! Come, let's make sure you get this...I so want you to get the part! The moves are actually quite simple. The main thing to remember is that you are to convey the very essence of grace...by being one! Follow my lead...you do this...and don't forget your arms. And your face - look serenely at the audience...like this..."

Charlotte demonstrated the movements, and although I felt a bit too self-aware - they were indeed simple enough to pick up. Having the backing of the violinist helped me keep in time. In my mind, I imagined Papa clapping his hands and humming to help keep me in time. In what seemed no time at all, we heard a clap from one of the boxes in the semi-darkness. Mr. Byrne's voice drifted through to the stage, commanding us to perform. I was aware of where he was, but I could not see his face distinctly- and therefore had no indication whatsoever as to how he was feeling about my performance. Charlotte nodded slightly and mouthed words of encouragement as we took our starting stance. To steel my nerves, I tried to pretend that the vast, darkened auditorium was merely my cracked mirror at home; and here I was just practising one of my father's many lessons. The violinist repeated the sequence of music, as he had done for us before. And, hard as it is for me to believe, I felt truly transformed into one of the three graces. I do not recall making any significant errors, and with Charlotte's guidance I was able to mimic her moves to my satisfaction. If this were not sufficient enough to secure my place within the production, then at least I knew my efforts were the utmost that I could have produced.

After the completion of our brief two-minute segment, there was silence. And this stillness continued for what seemed like an eternity. All the while, Charlotte and I were maintaining a pose not unlike the statuary one would see at Ranelagh Gardens. It was becoming frightfully difficult to remain so fixed and still. To my great relief, I heard Mr. Byrne clear his throat slightly and he then proceeded to speak.

"Thank you, ladies. Miss Searle, I would like to see what you are capable of on your own. There may be times when a large audience becomes unruly. Or perhaps a performer has become ill, and we need a quick performance to fill in and buy the management some time until it becomes more clear what action we may take. I want you to imagine that this is the case right now. On the spur of the moment, what would you be able to perform? The management need to have the complete confidence that those in their employ can behave calmly and professionally; and provide entertainment that is so seamless, that it would not be apparent to even the most seasoned viewer that there was any difficulty backstage whatsoever. And so, Miss Searle, that moment is now upon us...how will you fill our time?"

Before I had any time to think and let the sheer panic of the situation well up inside of me, a series of words seemed to reflexively emanate from my mouth.

"I shall perform a Scottish Hornpipe for the audience's pleasure, sir."

I almost immediately felt a twinge of regret, as the clothing I was wearing was not the most conducive to the energetic movements required of the dance. But on the positive side, it is a dance that I feel most at ease performing. I cannot help but radiate joy from all my limbs and set free a beam of glee from my face when undertaking the Scotch dances - I do love them so.

"Very well then, step forward and deliver to the audience around you. Remember that during a performance there will be 3000 sets of eyes gazing upon your every move. If you make a mistake, hide it well and continue on, lest the mob eat you alive. They do not miss a trick. Violinist, may we have some musical accompaniment? And... Begin!"

Mr. Byrne clapped his hands once. The fiddler immediately played a tune that I was not altogether familiar with. Oh dear! I knew that I would have to improvise then. I curtsied, and on the next bar my feet carried me through the intricate leaps and kicks that would make up my performance. One hand was incapacitated by the need to hold my skirt up slightly, ensuring my legs had the freedom of movement that was needed. My other arm I was able to raise and lower in keeping with what one would normally expect to see in this regional dance. I maintained my composure throughout. I hoped that I was able to convey sheer bliss and delight, rather than the sickening anxiety that I was feeling in reality. I looked straight out - then left and right, panning the audience with a confident smile. This is what Papa had always taught me to do. As I continued, I came to the realisation that I had no idea how long this performance was to last. In mid-thought, the music stopped rather abruptly. I did the best I could to make it look that I was completely aware of this. I landed from my jump and rather awkwardly attempted a finishing curtsy to the imaginary crowds before me.

Despite my breathless state and knees that felt as if they would give way at any moment, I held my pose until told otherwise. Out of the corner of my eye, I was aware that we had been joined by another woman on stage. Mr. Byrne began a brief, measured round of applause that Charlotte and the violinist joined in with. The newly arrived lady looked rather bemused. At this moment I had the realisation that this was perhaps Drury Lane's most renowned dancer, Miss Bella Menage. She glanced at me with a somewhat puzzled look. Petite, with amazingly round, hazel eyes; she stepped over towards Charlotte. She undid her bonnet, releasing waves of luxuriant, startling bright red hair. Mr. Byrne spoke with a scarcely disguised tone of disapprobation.

"Ah Miss Menage! How delightful you have decided to come and join us! And what has kept you so very long from our company?"

Seemingly unperturbed, Bella immediately replied coquettishly. "Was this not the appointed time for my arrival? I do apologise if I have caused any delay in rehearsals. That would never be my intention, of course." She paused slightly, before continuing - feigning surprise. "I must say, I had no awareness that we were adding a scene of Highlanders to the pantomime. Do tell, how will this fit in with the scenes of Greek mythology? And do you intend to wear a kilt as the fair Prince, Mr. Byrne? It does confuse me so..."

"Well let me put that pretty, little mind of yours at rest, Miss Menage. I was just putting our newest dancer through her paces. May I introduce to you Miss Elizabeth Searle. She shall be joining you and Miss Bristow as one of the three Graces."

I could scarcely believe what my ears had just heard. But my sudden rush of delight was tempered by the continuously unfolding antics of bold Bella. I must say that I was most taken aback by her disrespectful demeanour towards Mr. Byrne. I was to learn that this was not a behaviour that she reserved solely for him, but one which she freely shared amongst all of those she encountered professionally. Holding her hand to her heart, she looked to me sweetly - and yet spoke with such stinging insincerity.

"How enchanting! I am so very delighted to meet you. I had thought that we would be acquiring our third Grace from the ranks of our current roster of distinguished dancers. But that is not a matter for me. Mr. Byrne knows best - for he is directing the pantomime. When James was writing the play, did he have you in mind? He was very remiss in not mentioning that to me if he did! Oh, silly me! Of course he didn't, for you are new to this theatre." She flashed a false and sarcastic smile at me, then pretended to have a puzzled look - as if she were deep in thought. "Searle...Searle....I cannot say that I recall ever hearing that name in London. Are you from the provinces?"

I shook my head slightly. Mr. Byrne was making his way back to the stage, and Bella continued with her unwelcome diatribe, gesturing towards Charlotte.

"The Bristow family toured the provinces, and now have established themselves as successful performers in London - is that not so, Charlotte? And my family have a long tradition in the theatre here as well."

Charlotte quickly quipped "Yes! You may know of Bella's brother - he is well known for mimicking a monkey at the Sadler's Wells. He looks the part exceedingly well. Did you help him practice the part? Or does monkey-business come naturally to the family?" I was very heartened by Charlotte's retort. But Bella paid her no heed, and continued in a faux sincere manner, as if Charlotte had never uttered a word.

"I for one think that new talent is necessary. It is the lifeblood of our theatre. We cannot be expected to stick with old millstones around our necks - holding us back in the tired, old ways of entertainment. It seems as if we are all surrounded by the disciples of the long dead Mr. Garrick." Bella looked pointedly at the returning Mr. Byrne.

"James, do tell me what the starting salary for a novice dancer is these days. I am afraid that is a phase I do not recall ever going through. You see, Miss Searle, when I started at Drury Lane - Mr. Sheridan knew I had a certain, shall I say... quality... that would endear me to the audience. I was fortunate to be offered prominent roles from a very early age. In fact, I've known nothing else..."

"Miss Menage, I do advise you to address me by my surname. We are not on a first name basis. As to the salaries of novices, we can always see to it that your salary does match that of a beginner to help satiate your curiosity. Now Miss Bristow, would you be so kind as to take Miss Searle to Mr. Wroughton and have her sign the necessary paperwork to get started. Miss Searle, they will inform you of your duties there and fill you in on the details of your payment. I am most pleased to have you join us. I am sure you will need to make arrangements at home, so let's see you here tomorrow. Miss Bristow will inform you of timings and show you around backstage. In the meantime, Miss Menage, I believe we have a considerable amount of rehearsing to catch up on."

CHAPTER 6

Dorothy Jordan, by John Hoppner

I could scarcely believe that this was truly happening to me. Was this all a dream? Charlotte took me to the stage manager, Mr. Wroughton and delivered the message to him from Mr. Byrne, informing him of my new role within the theatre.

"Very good then. Welcome Miss Searle. We will have you on contract for the season, at a salary of 15 shillings a week. I need to remind you that if you should miss a rehearsal, other than through a genuine indisposition, you will forfeit sixpence of your salary for the scene missed. If you are absent from an entire rehearsal, that will be two shillings and sixpence forfeited. Any performer who should refuse to study, perform, or rehearse any part in an actual theatrical performance when requested to do so by the managers, shall forfeit a fine of five pounds. If you should pretend sickness or wilfully absent yourself from the theatre..."

Mr. Wroughton continued listing in minute detail an ever-increasing litany of fines that might be incurred – far more than I could ever hope to repay. In that way, I suppose his speech had the desired effect. I noted to myself that I must never be absent from any of my theatrical duties – not that I ever intended on doing so. I had to admit that I began to wonder whether Bella Menage had ever incurred such fines. Her insolence and rudeness irked me even more as I thought about it in retrospect.

He then informed me that I was to play minor parts in the chorus and background of plays until my appearance in *Cinderella*. I was to start on the Saturday in a musical production of *The Camp*. I was to be one of the country women who mingled and sang onstage. I must have looked slightly alarmed at the prospect, but Miss Bristow quickly piped in – "Oh you'll find that easy! You will be joining my sister, Mrs. Grimaldi, and I, along with about a dozen other ladies as your fellow country folk! Not to worry!" I sighed in relief.

"Any questions Miss Searle?" asked Mr. Wroughton.

Startled back into the present time, I meekly shook my head. Mr. Wroughton smiled, assured me that I was welcome to find him if I did have any enquiries at a later date, and bid me farewell. Charlotte was still there with a big, beaming smile.

"I am SO pleased Elizabeth! I would wager that you can scarcely believe it all!" She looked to Mr. Wroughton as we departed, then looked back to me as we navigated the corridors backstage. "If only Mr. Sheridan adhered to the rules of the theatre as strictly as his employees."

I was a bit taken aback by Charlotte speaking of the theatre's owner in such a negative way. I didn't really understand what she meant, but I was a bit too timid at this point to press for details. I was also preoccupied with absorbing information as we toured the interior of the great theatre. At first, I thought the highlight for me was to be seeing the dressing room – with all of the tightly packed range of costumes squeezed within the confines of the limited space available. I could imagine it being chaos on a performance night! We met Miss Rein, who was designing and creating the costumes for all the female performers in *Cinderella*. She was very friendly, and immediately set to taking my measurements in order to make a start on mine – which would match those of Bella and Charlotte's.

Our last stop was the famous Green Room. This was where the performers could unwind after a performance and mingle with the privileged, well-heeled supporters of the theatricals – eager to meet the stars of the stage and shower them with approbation and gifts. Charlotte smiled as she opened the door and I gazed inside admiring the elegant décor. I was aware of a woman's voice reciting dialogue, which stopped suddenly upon our entry.

"Oh, Mrs. Jordan – my apologies!! I was just showing our newest cast member around the theatre. May I introduce to you Miss Elizabeth Searle. She will be one of the three Graces in our winter pantomime, along with Arabella Menage and I."

As dumbstruck as I was to be seeing the greatest comedic actress the stage has ever known standing before me, I was to be receiving a further shock. Charlotte glanced over to a gentleman who had been intently staring at what I was to presume was Mrs. Jordan's prompt book. Charlotte suddenly looked flush with embarrassment, and quickly curtsied.

"My sincerest apologies, Your Grace! I did not notice you sitting there. Forgive me of this indisposition, I..."

Mrs. Jordan and the gentleman laughed heartily. I could detect that there was a very sincere bond between the two. I made a feeble attempt at curtsying in the man's direction, then did not know quite what to do about Mrs. Jordan.

Poor Charlotte was looking a bit aghast, as if she had committed a serious faux pas. But the delightful Mrs. Jordan soon put the entire room at ease. The gentleman gazed at her adoringly as she spoke, as if hanging on her every word. Although a bit short, with a slight plumpness that was common in women in their forties; she radiated beauty – her charisma charming us all.

"Miss Bristow – leave your airs and graces at the door! We are all family here! And I was in need of a break from all this tedious memorisation of my lines. Please, do come and join us for a drink. Come! I insist. Would you care for some barley water?"

The gentleman stood up, with some effort, and proceeded to pour out drinks into glasses for all of us.

"Ahhh..." Mrs. Jordan was the first to take a sip. "My throat gets so dry during these long recitations. That was just what I needed. Now, Miss Searle – I would like to welcome you to the great Theatre Royal. How old are you dear, and where are you from?" I detected that Mrs. Jordan's accent had shifted from the theatrical, plummy voice she used for her lines into her natural state – a hearty, inviting Irish brogue.

"Thank you, Mrs. Jordan. I am 14 years old. I am from London...Bloomsbury! My...my father and I watched you perform several times! He is a dance instructor. He taught me how to dance. I love your dancing!" I could not believe the foolish words coming out of my mouth. How could I be so tongue-tied? She would think me an idiot if I continued in this way!

"Why thank you, my dear! I'm amazed I can walk after all the children I have brought into this world, much less dance!" She clasped her stomach, while she and the man laughed – looking at each other.

"And recently delivering unto me a beautiful princess." The gentleman's eyes and smile demonstrated all the joy and pride that he was feeling. There was such a strong bond of affection between them both. He continued "Her name is Augusta. Born on the 17th. And now here is this incredible lady, ready to tread the boards again!"

Dorothy laughed. "Never mind all that. I am quite used to all of this birthing business. My audience awaits, and I must not disappoint. Now, do tell me what is your theatrical experience? Have you been working in the provinces?"

"Uhh. Err...no. This is ... will be my first time on the stage."

"Well now...the provincial theatre is a bit like a schooling ground, where we can learn our trade before attempting the stage in our nation's capital city. I started myself in Dublin. In fact, I think I was close to your age. You must be exceptionally talented, indeed, to have bypassed the usual way of entry. I will give you some advice: do not be daunted. Just become your character. You will be portraying a Grace - then be Grace personified!" She held my hand, and smiled sweetly at me, conveying genuine affection and kindness - so much so that I could almost feel tears welling up in my eyes. She stared at me, and then curtsied in very exaggerated fashion – as if I were a sovereign. "Your Grace!" she said to me, as if I were a royal princess.

She soon continued. "When they rebuilt this theatre, it was with the thought of getting the maximum audience in. No account was given to the experience to be had by the poor old audience member. Or the performer, for that matter. Mrs. Siddons has called it 'a wilderness of a place'. It is not the easiest or most intimate of venues. Therefore, it is vital that you accentuate and exaggerate your movements and amplify your voice at every opportunity!" Mrs. Jordan gesticulated rather wildly and increased the volume of her speaking voice in her last sentence to me.

"It is quite ridiculous, is it not?!"

We all burst out laughing. Charlotte then interjected that she was afraid that we were not helping Mrs. Jordan with resting her voice, and perhaps we should be taking our leave now. We gave our thanks and farewells, as Mrs. Jordan and her companion wished me success as I embarked on my new career. Charlotte took me by the arm and careened down the stairs excitedly. Her face was beet red as she grimaced and squealed with excitement.

"Eeeeee! Do you know who that was? I have met with Mrs. Jordan many times before – she is absolutely lovely! But that was the first time I have seen her with the Duke of Clarence! I did not know what to do! I nearly died of shame! Did I address him correctly? I didn't even SEE him, until..."

"YOU were embarrassed?! What about me? I was so tongue-tied...I looked a fool! And... the Duke of Clarence? A PRINCE? The King's son?! Pouring us BARLEY WATER?!!!"

We both laughed so hard, falling to the steps as we could scarcely breathe! This was to be a day that I would never, ever forget!

CHAPTER 7

Maria Theresa Decamp by Samuel De Wilde

Racing home, I was so excited to relay the good news. But upon entering, I was reminded that this was a sombre time. It was perhaps a bit selfish of me to be full of glee and hopeful joy. Mother was pleased to hear that I garnered a position in the theatre. But it was tempered somewhat by my low starting wage. It would be difficult to maintain a household with my meagre salary. Mother had less time to spend on theatrical embroidery and costume mending, as she had to be near Papa and attend to his needs. Without me at home, there would be no one to support her - aside from our next to useless scullery maid, Maggie. She was downright simple and could scarcely empty a bedpan properly without supervision. But at least it was an extra pair of hands - though we were now rather worried as to how long we could afford her to be present. We were even more dependent on the handouts from Aunt Harriet, and little Tom had the added responsibility of making daily forays to gather food packages from her. The thought of this small, young boy making the journey across the big city on his own filled us with trepidation, yet we had no choice. Tom was undaunted. In fact, he was pleased that he could contribute to our family in this time of need. And having reduced time to spend on his lessons and studies with Mother was, no doubt, a further enticement for my little brother.

I sat next to Papa at his bed, and lightly stroked the thinning hair of his head. In contrast, he was developing quite a thick beard. His appearance was altering - no longer the suave, sophisticated gentleman. Before me was this almost mute, invalid version of what my father once was. I refused to let go of that dear Papa I knew and loved so well. And so, I leaned over and whispered in in his ear my exciting news. I knew that any conscious part of his bearing would be enthralled by this success. For I was his daughter, and it is only through his meticulous, loving instruction that I was able to secure this role in the finest theatre in all of Britain. I told him of the audition, and dancing before Mr. Byrne. I divulged about the kindness of Charlotte Bristow. I spoke of the sheer insolence of the dreadful Bella Menage. I relayed all the terms and conditions of my employment as set forth by Mr. Wroughton, and the excitement of meeting Dora Jordan and her prince in the Green Room. All the while, I had been so engrossed in releasing my information into the air around me that I had not taken the time to notice my father. To my amazement, Papa was looking directly at me! He had a half grin, and he winked at me with the eye he was able to close properly.

"Oh, Papa!" I threw my arms around him and gave him a kiss on his forehead. "I knew you were listening! Mother come here - oh, this the best day! It truly is!" And with that, I gave my father a big hug. I could detect a slight wheeze of laughter from him, as Mother came in and witnessed this encouraging sign of activity from him. She clasped her hands to her chest and burst into joyous tears. This was what we needed. A sign of encouragement. A ray of hope indicating that there was a chance for improvement, and perhaps - by some miracle, a recovery.

I felt relieved that Papa was beginning to feel better. It alleviated somewhat the sense of guilt I had in leaving my mother and brother behind to care for him as I set out for my rehearsals. I was well aware that at some point, my working day would shift - demanding my presence at the theatre in the evenings. Somehow, as a family we would have to adjust to these changes that were facing us. But for the moment, we felt blessed that we saw bright spots within the gloom of the adversity we had experienced. I was fortunate enough to be able to have a life outside of Hart Street, with experiences beyond Papa's convalescence. The theatre offered me another family in many ways.

Rehearsals of *Cinderella* were just starting to take place as the production development was still in its infancy. Meanwhile, I was joining in on other productions in a very minor capacity to help develop my confidence on the stage. It was such an excellent opportunity. I could scarcely believe my luck! It was most interesting for me to watch the other cast members and learn their particular quirks and characteristics. To think, only a few short weeks ago I was watching them from the audience, and now I was to be gazing upon them from the vantage point of the stage. Most remarkable!

In the days of rehearsals, I grew to become more familiar with all the performers at Drury Lane. Shocking as she could be, Bella Menage did provide me with a great many stories to disclose back at home. I met her older sister Mary, who honestly could not have been any more different from Bella. She was modest, unassuming, and rather sweet natured. She tended to hover in the background of various performances, playing minor roles. In fact, she was one of my fellow country women in *The Camp*. Despite Mary's ability to act, dance and sing; she never excelled in any particular attribute to the extent that would lead her to have any particular notoriety. That is one concession I had to concede to Bella Menage - she was exceptionally talented, and she exuded an unforgettable presence when on the stage.

Charlotte introduced me to her brother-in-law, the well-known clown - Mr. Grimaldi. Full of nervous energy, he was amazing to watch. It was such a shame that his role in *Cinderella* was so negligible. He was playing Pedro, servant to Cinderella's wicked sisters. I remember seeing him perform at the Sadler's Wells Theatre with my Papa one summer. His acrobatic antics were nothing less than astonishing. He did have an air of sadness about his person at times, a genuine distractibility. What thoughts hid behind those pensive, brown eyes and dark, curly locks of hair? Charlotte told me that her sister was actually his second wife. He was greatly devastated when his first wife died in childbirth, and there were times that it seemed he could not get over the grief. He worked at two theatres simultaneously in an attempt to not think about his tragic life. Her sister Mary was hired to nurse him back to health after a serious stage injury, and they developed a mutual admiration for each other. This resulted in marriage and an infant son, which must be some small consolation to poor Mr. Grimaldi. How difficult life could be for some. Her participation in *The Camp* helped to add a few meagre shillings to the family coffers. It seems it was not only my household that had experienced suffering.

Another new member of Drury Lane was the delightful Miss Tyrer. She was so incredibly short - I am certain that she is nowhere near five feet tall, despite being in her mid-twenties. Yet her stout little frame commanded one of the most powerful singing voices I ever had the pleasure to hear. She had an infectious smile, and she was like a glowing light of positivity wherever she went. I liked her immensely. In *Cinderella*, she was playing the Nymph, who was commissioned by the goddess Venus. Venus was portrayed by another great voice, the incomparable Mrs. Rosemund Mountain. When these two women sang, it was as if the angels were parting the heavens. Mrs. Mountain had a wealth of dramatic experience and was a consummate professional. Nothing daunted her - a change of direction, a criticism from the composer. No matter what the issue was, she was adaptable and took it all in her stride instantaneously.

Joining the cast of 'immortals' on the stage were the youngest members of the cast, Mr. Byrne's two little sons. Adorable little Edmund was Hymen. Barely four years of age, it was fortunate that his role was brief and involved no lines. Eight-year-old Oscar, however, was simply remarkable as Cupid. An elegant and assured dancer at such a young age, he instantly helped me to feel at ease. If someone as young as he could perform, then surely, I could! His parents routinely had him on the stage from the time he could walk. Dancing was his forte, and I could see clearly that his father was moulding him in his own image. Mr. James Byrne himself was performing as the Prince. He was not only the choreographer, but one of the lead characters as well. And Mrs. Byrne, joined by a Miss Vining (of yet another hard-working theatrical family) served as Cinderella's unkind sisters. Perhaps we were witnessing a new dynastic family of performers being created: a stage full of talented Byrnes.

And speaking of stage families, all of us were wondering if our dearest Cinderella, Miss Maria Theresa Decamp, would one day enter the great acting royalty known as the Kembles. Charles Kemble was the brother to the highly respected thespians - the acclaimed actress Mrs. Sarah Siddons and John Philip Kemble (now manager of Covent Garden Theatre). Charles and Miss Decamp have been engaged for nearly four years now, yet he still cannot persuade his family to allow their formal union. Miss

Decamp is a most accomplished actress and singer. With lovely brown eyes, olive complexion and luxuriant black wavy tresses, it is obvious that she has some French blood in her heritage. Yet from her early teens, upon the tragic death of her father, she was forced to become the breadwinner for her family. It was a story I could relate to. Charlotte told me that Miss Decamp used to have lessons under Mr. Grimaldi's father. He was the most dreadful, frightful man, by all accounts. It is difficult to believe when meeting his kind, gentle-hearted son. But Grimaldi Senior had a reputation for beating his students ruthlessly. I even heard a story that he had a boy locked and rigged in a cage suspended from the ceiling in the performance room as a punishment for some minor infraction. Unspeakable cruelty! No wonder he was called "Grim All Day"! I dread to think what torments he meted out on his poor son. It seems that the delightful Miss Decamp came through unscathed however, and she is now one of the most admired performers at Drury Lane. She was playing the role of Nancy in *The Camp*, affording me the opportunity to admire her great talents regularly before I would be working more closely with her.

Miss Decamp insisted that I called her Maria and went out of her way to make me feel at ease. She was so terribly busy, rehearsing several productions at once. She rarely attended our practice sessions for *Cinderella*; and when she did, she performed the part with such perfection that there could be no question as to whether she was ready to step into the role at any given moment. I marvelled at how she was able to remember all her lines from many the plays that were being performed almost simultaneously. Did she not ever get her words muddled up? Forget who she was and stare out at the expectant crowd like a startled deer? She assured me that the danger of such an occurrence was greatly minimised, thanks to the prompter just offstage - ready to help ensure the show ran smoothly. I had no experience of this, as my role involved no lines. A few mere lyrics sung and some elegant footwork - it really was the least stressful introduction to a career in the theatre that one could imagine. With just one significant exception.

The dreadful Bella Menage was astoundingly unspeakable and beastly to me at any and every opportunity. She took to calling me 'peasant girl', after my role as one of the country women in *The Camp*. To my chagrin, I discovered that I would be taking part in the chorus of peasants in this production. Of course, she had a plum dance performance with Mr. Byrne in the play to further enhance her ego and feeling of self-importance. Other cast members and crew tried to reassure me that this was just typical of her behaviour towards newcomers. This was but a mere initiation of sorts. Yet her criticisms seemed so very pointed and full of an intense hatred directed towards me personally. Suffering her barrage of torments, I was oblivious to the minor digs and insults she dropped on others almost continuously. And as comforting as everyone tried to be, it amazed me that no one was willing to confront her. It was as if she had some mysterious, magical power over the entire theatre. I am absolutely certain that many at Drury Lane had witnessed her cruelties towards me, yet they turned a blind eye - perhaps relieved at the reprieve from having any personal conflicts with her themselves.

From the very moment of my first rehearsals, Bella began her incessant unpleasantries towards me. I was absolutely astounded by the sheer talent and finesse she was able to exert in order to make a painful encounter look accidental, or to deflect the blame on someone else - most often me. I was smarting from bruises on my very first day from her flailing elbows, stepped-upon toes, and 'unfortunate' kicks that all seemed to land in my direction. Charlotte Bristow was unable to come to my rescue, lest she become the target of Bella's wrath. She confided in me later that she had been much in the same situation that I was in now but warned me not to try and complain to management. It would be to no avail, and it would most likely make the situation much worse.

"I don't know how she does it. It is as if she has some hold over Mr. Sheridan himself. The only person I have ever seen her show deference to is Mrs. Jordan. I was in the Green Room once when she insulted Miss Mellon. Can you believe the audacity? An actress of such high acclaim as she! Bella mentioned to some wealthy visitors backstage that they may wish to ask Miss Mellon for banking advice, and perhaps she could put in a good word to Mr. Coutts should they be in need of a loan. Miss Mellon was livid! You see, she has been trying to carry on a discrete relationship with the banking gentleman for some time now. His wife is terribly ill, and he may be in need of a new spouse at some point in time in the near future. She had been working so hard to secure a good respectable life away from the theatre. This was terribly embarrassing for her, as in no time the theatre - indeed the whole of London, became aware of her most private, personal relationship. If she can get away with such an insult as that - who is to stop her from these more minor incidents that you are having with her now? Perseverance is the answer…do be patient, it will get better in time, I assure you."

I was a bit taken aback by Charlotte's shocking revelation. Not just Bella Menage's horrid antics, but the thought of the lovely, beautiful Miss Mellon having such a relationship with a married man. I didn't care what the circumstances were - the vow of marriage was to be obeyed and respected by all parties. It was a contract with God that needed to be adhered to, in my eyes. And then I thought about Mrs. Jordan. Had I been shocked by her unofficial royal union? Indeed, I must admit that I had been. And with children out of wedlock! I was in the midst of a world of low morals. I was beginning to understand the concerns that Mother had for me here. Yet the person of low moral character that concerned me most was the spiteful Miss Menage.

Charlotte's tactic was to try and appear kind, helpful and supportive to Bella - to her face. Bella is no fool, and I am sure she saw through that ploy - but played along to some extent, because it suited her for the moment.

"Ow! You imbecile! You keep bumping into me!" This was a rather mild rebuke from Bella towards me. She was just getting warmed up for worse.

"Oh, do take care Bella! We mustn't injure ourselves. All of London is waiting to see this wonderful spectacle!" Charlotte offered, in a sweet, contrite tone of voice.

"A spectacle indeed! *The Times* and *The Morning Chronicle* will be full of stories about the spectacle of this amateur spoiling the entire performance! Why on earth could Mr. Byrne not provide us with an actual dancer; instead of this ragged, pathetic apple seller that he must have taken pity on and dragged in from the streets?"

Charlotte giggled cautiously. "Now, now Bella! This is easily overcome. Let's start again and I'm sure it will come out fine with a bit more care and effort on Miss Searle's part." I could see the nervousness in Charlotte's eyes - willing me not to succumb to Bella's taunts. I had to fight very hard to keep the tears back. Each of her vile words stabbed me to the very core of my being.

"You had better get it right this time!" Bella spat out at me, with an evil glint in her eyes.

"I am sure with your expert guidance and instruction I will perform much better, Miss Menage!" I managed to state aloud, with a quivering voice.

Sensing my vulnerability and weakness, Bella stuck the knife in deeper. "Ha! It speaks!!!" Bella burst into a seemingly uncontrollable fit of laughter at my expense. But I was aware that it was all too deliberate, and not funny in the least. "Why should I give over my precious time and waste my efforts to try and transform a little dullard like you into something approaching respectability? You are a pathetic little mouse!"

"Ah, Miss Menage!" Mr. Byrne's voice carried from behind Bella as he entered from the darkness.

"I think you will find the roles of the evil sisters have already been taken by Miss Vining and my wife. However, if you wish, I shall have a word with them and see if one of them would be willing to trade places with you."

Bella briefly looked as if she was taken aback by this reprimand, but quickly regained her composure.

"Well, Mr. Byrne! I am so honoured to think that I could possibly take the place of your wife!" she replied flirtatiously. "But at this late stage, I suppose we will just have to make do with the roles we have all been cast." Bella looked at me pointedly, implying that I was a weak link in the chain.

"No one is irreplaceable, Miss Menage. Do keep that in mind."

"As I am sure that you yourself always do, Mr. Byrne. Why, I do believe that I have heard Mr. Sheridan himself utter those very same words to you if I am not mistaken. In fact, I am sure that I saw Mr. D'Egville meeting with him. He was my dance instructor as a child you know. Perhaps he is looking for a change from the Haymarket Theatre. He would make a most sensational ballet master. Would you not agree?" Bella was unwavering in meeting his sharp stare.

As rehearsals carried on, similar insults and injuries flew at regular intervals. It did amuse Charlotte and I that, despite being one of three Graces, Bella seemed determined to carve out a star role for herself. When we danced arm in arm in a circle, Bella pointedly stared out to her imaginary audience vivaciously - leaving us looking as if we were mere supporting characters. She was always managing to linger for just a moment or two longer in the light, to leave a lasting impression whilst Charlotte and I faded into the background. As much as I truly despised her, I had to admit that she was exceptional in her ability to do this. Not only in our pantomime, but in every performance that I saw her in. And though she never wanted to give away her trade secrets - especially if it were to assist me in any way; I was looking and learning.

I officially began my theatre career on a busy Saturday. On the 8th of October, I would appear on the stage briefly with my countrywomen. On the day, Drury Lane Theatre was bustling - a hubbub of activity. A new drama by the name of *Deaf and Dumb* was to be performed for the first time, before the performance of *The Camp* was to take place. Such debut nights could provoke a considerable amount of interest from the theatre going public. I was almost giddy with excitement but tried to contain myself. Fortunately, my role was so small and in the company of many others – thereby taking away any sense of nervousness I may have felt. Many of the cast members kindly came to me to wish me good luck. I was feeling especially fortunate as Bella Menage was not working this evening, sparing me any of the awkwardness of having to endure her evil stares.

Before the curtains rose on the evening's first performance, the lovely Maria Decamp came to me and gave me a piece of paper which she had rolled up and smiled. "Here – I think you should have this! A little something to treasure…" She whisked herself away quickly before I had the chance to say anything. Unfurling the paper, I saw that it was a playbill from tonight's performance. Towards the bottom, in large lettering equal to all my colleagues was a list of the country women: BUTLER, WENTWORTH, GRIMALDI, KELLY, MENAGE, WELLS – and there, starting the next line was SEARLE. On the same line as my wonderful mentor and confidante, Miss Bristow. It sent shivers up my spine to see my name there in print, on the same parchment as the great names of the theatrical world – Mr. Cooke, Mr. Wroughton and so many others. Simply amazing! What a treasure this memento was, and so very thoughtful of Miss Decamp.

This was to be a most memorable day, and not just because was this the evening of my theatrical debut (although I was feeling a considerable amount of pride about this achievement). Reflecting back on this time, my thoughts instantly adhere to the sight of seeing a heavenly vision in the form of the character of St. Alme striking me virtually "Deaf and Dumb". From backstage where Miss Bristow had pulled me to watch the evening's performance discretely, I stood entranced at what was before me. The event of note was that this was when I first laid eyes on perhaps the most beautiful man I had ever seen. Henry Erskine Johnston was a Scotsman, though one would be at great pains to notice his origins - as he had taken painstaking care in being able to mask and disguise his accent. Indeed, his voice was soft, sweet, and gentle to the ear. Yet if the role needed it, he had a forceful, piercing quality to his timbre, lending an air of power and authority. His background was quite humble - the son of a hairdresser, and an apprentice to a linen draper in Edinburgh. He demonstrated a flair for dramatics at a very young age, and his innate talent led to him being given the opportunity to hone his craft on the stage. Maria Decamp filled me in on many details about his background. She had some second-hand knowledge of his history, as one of the Kemble family was instrumental in discovering and nurturing his talent from when he was only 17. His chances were much enhanced, no doubt, by his handsome looks and fine figure. I have to say that his appearance has been seared into my memory permanently: rich waves of jet-black hair and luxuriant sideburns framed his most magnificent face. Rich brown eyes, a perfect nose leading down to his full pink lips. His square jaw punctuated by a strong dimple set in his chin. His physique resembled classical Roman statuary – strong, muscular, firm. Over the next few weeks, just merely being in his presence was having a serious affect upon my constitution and mental stability.

Later in the evening, I stepped out and performed in the comfortable anonymity of my fellow 'country folk', and I have almost no memory of what took place. I marched about, moved my lips as if in song and then traipsed offstage at the required time. It was as if I were in some dream-like state. A final bow from all the cast. Applause. Moving perfunctorily backstage at the finish. And then I was astounded beyond words, as Mr. Henry Johnston came up to me and spoke. I not only heard, but felt his words being projected and directed towards me. It felt as if his eyes were burning straight into my soul. I imagined I was feeling a searing heat that was melting my skin like candle wax. My face felt flushed. Was all of this peculiar energy due to the presence of this angelic man? I had never felt anything like this before in my life. I was most certain that I was going mad.

"Miss Decamp told me this was your first performance at the theatre. I just wanted to congratulate you and say, 'well done'!" He smiled a sweet smile exposing perfect ivory white teeth. Everything about him exuded beauty. I was dumbstruck, but he had already turned to walk further backstage before I could have been expected to elicit a response. As my eyes followed him, I realised the full extent of my foolishness. His destination was the vivacious and stunning actress formerly known as Nannette Parker. Current name: Mrs. H. Johnston. Stupidly, I had not made the connection until this very moment. My heart sank and I felt a bit sick, despite the futility of my admiration for Mr. Johnston. What a beautiful couple they were. And what a silly girl was I to even contemplate romantic notions – that such a man could possibly even take the slightest interest in me.

Various production rehearsals carried on through November and December. Word was out that Cinderella in particular, was going to be a most-notable, spectacular production. No expense was being spared. The costumes were sumptuous, the backgrounds and scenery ornate and detailed. Complex mechanisms and stage trickery were being planned, designed, and constructed. I had the feeling that I was taking part in a momentous theatrical event. In the meantime, all my minor choral parts in The Camp and November's production of The Wife of Two Husbands gave me amble opportunity to admire the astoundingly handsome Scotsman that mesmerised me so. Anyway, all the theatrical goings-on gave me more fodder to relay to Papa when I returned home; minus details about my infatuation with a certain Mr. H.E. Johnston of course.

Time progressed swiftly, and I was most bemused to report back to Papa that the biggest December star of Drury Lane was a canine by the name of Carlo. He appeared in a musical afterpiece entitled The Caravan, and his run was having tremendous success. It was a rather predictable melodrama – Don Gomez, the Governor is trying to force his unwanted affections upon the Marchioness of Calatrava. He tries to increase his advantage by kidnapping her husband, the Marquis, and her young son Julio. The moment everyone in the audience was waiting for was when Julio was thrown in the watery depths, triggering the quick-thinking actions of the magnificent dog Carlo. Truly a spectacle! The whole town was talking about Carlo's heroic actions as he jumped into water onstage to save the drowning child (who was replaced by a stuffed dummy at this point) every evening to rapturous applause. An actual cascade of water had been set up on the stage – careening down into a real pool of water for the dog to dive into. 'Carlo' was actually two dogs. The talented, diving and swimming Newfoundland hated the bright lights of the stage almost as much as he adored the water. For all the other scenes, Mr. Bannister's mastiff was disguised as Carlo – and performed with aplomb for his master before the audience. Many of my fellow performers were a bit miffed at being upstaged by this dog wonder. And Master West's mother complained of the bruising her boy was receiving from the overbearing pup in his nightly interactions with him in the role of Julio. But the owner of our theatre was having none of it – the dog was filling up the theatre's seats with every performance. We had a lot to thank this canine marvel for. He was an absolute gold mine for Mr. Sheridan. Unbeknownst to me at the time, the theatre was in extreme financial difficulty, and the antics of Carlo had managed to steer Drury Lane back to some fiscal stability.

I was now in the chorus of 'villagers', still singing in the safety of a crowd. Miss Decamp was performing an amazing dance in the play whilst playing the castanets. She was a joy to behold each time she appeared. The play took part in Spain, not far from Barcelona. She played the part of Rosa, the Spanish girl, exceedingly well. So much so, that the audiences always demanded an encore. She was utterly amazing! But the real draw of the show was, of course, Carlo the dog. Especially as no one could predict exactly what the dog would do on the night. This air of uncertainty led to people returning again and again, evening after evening, to see what would exactly take place – often with the expectation of hilarious results. For example, Carlo was supposed to share his food with the imprisoned Marquis – but it was often the case that the dog would devour the whole meal, growling if the Marquis attempted to take anything off the plate. And there were times that the dog refused to jump in the water after the mannequin representing the boy Julio was thrown in. Mr. Bannister had to resort to giving him a shove once or twice to get in the water. Carlo would get overexcited from the audience reactions, barking and howling at the most inopportune moments. It truly made for a grand farce!

CHAPTER 8

Henry Erskine Johnston in the role of Norval in Douglas

The most abiding memory in my mind from that time was not of the silly dog, however. At each performance I was almost within touching distance of that certain devastatingly beautiful actor by the name of Henry Erskine Johnston. The world of the theatre was often populated by rather odd-looking gentlemen – character actors with distinctive, quirky looks. This amplified the comedic effect of their stage presence. Short men, skinny men, elderly gents, fat men, men with lisps or other distinctive affectations all seemed the norm for Drury Lane. Mr. Johnston was a most notable exception. I found that he was occupying my thoughts at almost every spare moment, driving me to a near frenzy of distraction. I could not repel this innate reflex within my very being. It was almost absurd! I often caught myself in an almost giddy state of mind, incapable of sensible action. I had never felt such a peculiar feeling before. It certainly lightened my mood when having to deal with my sinister villain, Miss Menage. His mellifluous voice and powerful presence acted as an armour against her cruel taunts. She was unable to reach me, for I could withdraw into my fantasy world and imagine my hero coming to my rescue. I could easily envisage Athena giving Henry – my Perseus, a mighty shield and sword to slay the evil Medusa that was embodied by that viper Bella Menage.

However, there was to be no hope for my besotted heart. I was constantly having to remind myself that the gorgeous Mr. Johnston was accompanied in his work by a stunningly beautiful Mrs. Johnston. They usually worked as a pair, performing in the same theatre as each other – and quite often in the same play, as was the case with *The Caravan*. She was the Marchioness to his Marquis – putting paid immediately to any girlish romantic notion that I may have harboured regarding Mr. H. E. Johnston. And as she was a picture of loveliness herself, I could see the attraction. There were countless times that I was treated to the tortuous vision of this ludicrously resplendent couple as they made the rounds backstage. The loving gestures, the intimate gazes, and the constant intertwining of hands – these were all actions that I was a witness to. Each occurrence felt like a brutal stab to my heart. Onstage, their matrimonial bond ensured that they worked together seamlessly, with an authenticity that would be nigh on impossible for most thespians to replicate. Despite my guilt over my secret desires, I was completely helpless in trying to resist my thought processes. I found myself calculatedly devising opportunities to be within the close proximity of his presence. Was it not shameful? What was wrong with me that I cannot find the moral wherewithal to resist these temptations? I was truly nothing but a weak little girl. Yet, as much as I despised my wanton behaviour – I continued on with my singular mission to seek him out.

My first genuinely extended encounter with Mr. Johnston was, without a doubt, unforgettable. The dogs were always about the theatre during these performances of *The Caravan*, and I loved their cheerful presence. Not only did they remind me of fond times at my Aunt Harriet's farm - but to my wicked delight, Bella Menage absolutely despised them. And as we all know, dogs are especially drawn to those who try to avoid them. During one rehearsal session, I was watching with glee as the Newfoundland was incessantly sniffing at Bella's bottom. I was trying to hide my giggles as she shouted in distress "No! Bad dog! BAD! Go AWAY!!! Mr. Bannister – get your wicked mongrel away from me! NOW!!!" In the midst of my mirth, I nearly jumped out of my skin at the sound of a hound's barking right beside me. I turned around, expecting to see one of the naughty 'Carlo' dogs as the source of my fright - only to see Mr. Johnston laughing in hysterics and giving me a flirtatious wink. I held my hands to my chest and gave him a remonstrative look that I usually reserve for my little brother, then burst out laughing. Bella Menage caught sight of us and presumed that our merriment was at her expense. She stormed up to us and hissed directly at me "Go ahead and laugh - silly little tart! You think it amusing? We will see who is laughing when you have to actually perform in front of a demanding audience. You'll think it funny when the crowd is jeering at you – tripping over your weedy little bandy legs!"

"How very presumptuous of you, Miss Menage. Believe it or not – the world does not revolve around you. We were having our own discussion which was quite independent of your doggie woes. Neither of us take any notice of hounds sniffing at bitches in heat."

Mr. Johnston's commentary left Bella momentarily mute. I could almost palpably feel the disbelief of some of the cast members at the words that they just heard. I could visibly see the tides of absolute rage welling up in her eyes – but she was too stunned and shocked to actually formulate any words. I too could not fathom what I was hearing. It seemed that Mr. Johnston had the courage and conviction to deal with Bella that everyone else lacked.

"Oh, what bliss! I do believe the cat has your tongue... all while the dog has your arse!" Mr. Johnston was dealing a verbal death blow – whilst his delightful Scottish brogue was making a guest appearance; slipping back over his highly practised, affected English accent. The scene was beginning to cause a bit of a stir amongst the Drury Lane crew present. With his most perfect timing ever, the Newfoundland returned to sniff at Bella's backside. All present were hooting with laughter, soon joined by howls from the naughty 'Carlo' himself. At first, Bella was aghast. In fact, I very nearly felt some sympathy for her predicament. But then the red face of embarrassment began to give way to fuming, incandescent rage.

Someone amongst the bystanders half-heartedly made an attempt at remonstrating Mr. Johnston. "You are showing your base origins, Henry! How very insulting. It is no way to be speaking in the presence of a lady!"

Bella was beginning to formulate a witty put-down to add, but she was sabotaged by the quick thinking of Mr. Johnston. "Aye! You are right sir!" he replied. Then, to my utmost surprise he turned towards me, bent down on one knee, and took my hand. He then began speaking with mock sincerity. "Miss Searle, I do beseech your kind forgiveness. I was so distracted at having to speak to that tiresome cow Bella, that I forgot I was in the presence of a lady!"

Roars of laughter ensued. I glanced at Bella, who was now in floods of tears. She turned away – speechless, as she escaped towards the dressing room. In the ensuing moments, several cast and crew members came to Henry, patting him on the back and congratulating him. Charlotte came to me and asked if I was alright. This all came to an abrupt halt as Mrs. Johnston walked over in consternation. "Henry, what on earth is going on here? Are you responsible for Miss Menage weeping inconsolably backstage? Why...why does this happen? Everywhere we go, you make a scene. Cause upset. Is it any wonder that you never get those lead roles that you so desire?"

"Oh, that's right Nannette! Take her side. Take anyone's side except your husband's. He has got to be wrong! Why don't you ever take a moment to be supportive of me for once...to hear my side of things?"

"I have and I do. And where does it lead me? To here. The same place, the same story. This happens time and time again. I am always having to intervene on your behalf when your temper goes beyond boundaries. You just have to say what you think, all the time. Can you not keep it to yourself? Are you proud now, having bullied a young woman to tears? What a man you are! I suppose apologising to her would be out of the question. You are far too cowardly for that."

Everyone was feeling decidedly uncomfortable and began to make themselves scarce - averting their gazes and quickly moving away from the ever-escalating row. I would have done the same, but I was in the most awkward position of still being attached to Mr. Johnston by the hand. All through the congratulatory moments and Miss Bristow's conversation, he had continued to hold my hand in his. Henry's grip on me grew tighter as his anger rose. Mr. Johnston's voice rose to a boom which echoed off the stage so that I am sure even pedestrians on Bow Street could hear. The emotions behind his response made me tremble so. I felt as if I might faint. I was absolutely petrified by the forcefulness of his diction.

"YOU NEVER even deign to consider MY position – not FOR ONE MOMENT!! EVER!!!" He was screaming the last words, spittle from his lips and sweat pouring from his brow. He pointed the forefinger of his free hand at her accusingly. I was trembling from the forcefulness of his emotion and the feeling of his firm hand reflexively and unconsciously clinging onto mine. I could make no escape and stood there helpless – a front row observer to the domestic altercation taking place. "Every little mishap is my doing. It is completely inconceivable to you that for once my actions may be justified. That vixen Bella does nothing but tread on the feelings of all of those around her, belittling them as she parades about, flaunting her self-importance. She deserved ALL that she got from me – I have no regrets. But who am I to have such opinions? My wife...MY INSOLENT, DISOBEDIENT..."

"Choose your words judiciously, husband! You have an audience here..." Nannette looked towards me and continued. "And you may come to experience those feelings that you only mimic on stage. Regret. Remorsefulness! SHAME! Look! Look everyone!" Nannette called out to all who had tried to slink to the background and busy themselves with imaginary tasks. Henry realised himself suddenly and let go of my hand – looking at me sheepishly and apologetic, then gazing towards his wife. He shut his eyes and grimaced as if he were about to receive lashings from a whip. His wife continued to administer her punishment verbally. "Behold! The golden couple!" Nannette commanded the attention of all around; compelling them to listen to her soliloquy. "The Johnstons...what a handsome pair! Well, the mask has slipped somewhat, has it not – dear husband? Perhaps they have a glimpse of what I have to contend with away from the stage. Your rages! Your wandering eyes transfixed upon the latest beauties!"

"I have never, EVER been unfaithful to you!" Henry countered – alternately whispering, then crying out. He was beginning to look weary and absolutely drained of his will.

Mrs. Johnston was relentless, and her words were like daggers. "But you and I both know that you very much wanted to be. And continue to do so!"

I could hear several audible gasps from the bystanders. With her retort still lingering in the air, Mrs. Johnston turned and walked towards the dressing room, maintaining the haughtiness of the Marchioness that she would soon transform into on the stage in a few hours' time. Mr. Johnston looked to the floor, gathered his composure, and sighed. Quietly, almost tearfully he continued to gaze downward as he softly spoke. "You...I...and now everyone. Our souls are bare, naked for all to see."

I, and no doubt all those around me, were frightfully startled as Henry's let out an unearthly wail and fell to his knees on the floor. Suddenly, he half ripped his shirt and was frantically flailing himself like a madman, hurling a pewter tankard from the nearby prop table angrily across the space - all whilst sobbing loudly and his body shaking violently. Some of the stagehands grabbed him and pulled him backstage to protect his decency and try to calm him. As they did so, he let out a cry that seemed to escape from his very soul. This completely unnerved 'Carlo', who began barking and howling. I stooped down to pat and comfort him, whilst feeling very rattled myself over the unexpected proceedings. I looked to Charlotte, who seemed to be completely aghast and totally unnerved by the events that had just unfolded.

I was most certain that the evening's performance of *The Caravan* would be cancelled. Yet, to my utmost surprise, the show carried on as if nothing had occurred previously. Indeed, the Johnstons seemed more affectionate towards one another than ever. Not only on the stage, but behind the scenes as well. Had they made amends? Or was this just an exceedingly well-played masquerade? The secret stage magic persisted, and no one spoke of the incident again. But I could never, ever forget. Henry's emotional pain, his scarred soul and deep distress moved me so. Coupled with his thorough rounding of Bella, it only served to endear him ever more to my heart. And it made my desire to comfort him all the more apparent, with no possibility of denying this fact to myself any further. I ached and yearned to console him.

AN ACTRESS OF REPUTE

CHAPTER 9

The Dance - engraving by Francesco Bartolozzi

Fortunately, at home things were becoming more settled. Papa was improving. Although his recovery was slow, there was certainly a discernible increase in his constitution daily. Aunt Harriet insisted on having Papa recuperate at her cottage. The fresher air around Green Park would be more conducive to his recovery. So, mother relented, sending Tom to stay as well to provide practical, physical help as needed. Father was able to move and walk very short distances now. Some speech was returning as well. Curiously, he was almost completely fluent in French now – a language he had not studied for years. So, whenever he thought of something to say, out it came 'au Françoise'. No matter, as we were just pleased that he was speaking again; and we were well aware that he was no agent for the Emperor Bonaparte. The extended stay was giving Mother the opportunity for a brief respite from her arduous traumas of the past weeks. She needed the chance to regain her health as well, after all this time of putting everyone else's needs before her own. A quiet household without having to attend to Papa was a blessing for her, enabling her to take on more sewing work. She was also able to speak directly with Papa's clients, trying to ensure that he would not be replaced in his absence. His students were fond of him and continued to wish him well. Even if they hired a new dance master in the interim, we hoped that they would be kind enough to consider engaging Papa once again when his health permitted.

With Christmas nearing, all of us were counting our precious blessings that helped to see us through this difficult year. Mother and I attended services at St. George's on Christmas day. My prayers were full of thanks for the sparing of my Papa from death's heartless grasp, and for the good fortune of my new position at Drury Lane. We had the whole family together on Hart Street for a proper Christmas celebration. Aunt Harriet and Tom prepared our feast, featuring a nice, fat roasted goose (*not* Goldie, I hasten to add). Papa was now making more use of his limbs. Although not ready to dance, he was in fine fettle and in a most jovial disposition. It was indeed such a gift – the finest one could ask for.

I had not shared with my family any of the antics of Bella Menage or the Johnstons. I did not want them to worry about me in such an environment. All of them had enough troubles of their own to preoccupy themselves with – without adding my problems to the equation. Father was far from being ready to return to his pupils, and we had no way of knowing if he would ever truly be fit for instruction again. Mother was busy trying to economise and run the household. She was considering whether to ask some of

Papa's clients if it were possible for her to instruct their daughters. It would be a daring thing to do, and she was not certain if it would offend the propriety of these families of great wealth. It would be something she would need to discuss and consider with Papa in the coming new year. Tom was missing out on his education – instead, learning the life of a farm hand as he did the chores at Aunt Harriet's, freeing her to attend to Papa's needs. I certainly should be able to cope with an ill-mannered dancing girl and the dashing good looks of a fellow performer. In comparison to each of my family members, it was a trifling issue.

Overall, we as a family were feeling a bit more optimistic about the approaching new year, as we bade a farewell to horrible 1803. Although Bella Menage had tried to instil fear in me with regard to my theatre debut, I have to admit that I was feeling a quiet confidence about the show. There was an initial setback. The show was originally set to debut on the 29th of December. However, due to the magnitude and the intricacy of the scenery – it was not yet in a state of suitable forwardness for representation on that evening. The show was cancelled and replaced by the ever-popular dog drama, *The Caravan*. The 3rd of January was now set as the first night of *Cinderella*. Much the better, I should think for avoiding 1803 altogether. I did not want to be superstitious, but I felt it would be a most appropriate start to the new year. And yet it would entail another week of waiting, building excitement and anticipation for the grand spectacle to start. Drury Lane was beginning to feel like my home away from home, and I was most comfortable there. Whether that comfort would remain when I faced the crowd of thousands remained yet to be seen. Announcements and advertisements were beginning to appear in the newspapers, and word was spreading about the lavishness of the production.

During my last two nights of 1803 I experienced the

most delicious torment. A gut-wrenching close to the year, in fact. And yet I seemed to enjoy this torture I was putting myself through. Both evenings I was to continue with my less than vital role as one of the villagers in *The Caravan*. As my part was so undemanding and well-rehearsed by this point, I had ample opportunity to watch the first evening's performances from backstage long before my play was to start. And who should I most wish to see? It would be most remiss of me to not witness my favourite actor in his finest and most notorious role. Henry Johnston was portraying Norval in the tragedy of *Douglas*. Mr. Johnston was feted across the land for his portrayal, and this was his showpiece. I am afraid to admit that my thoughts during his performance were leaning more towards the impure. The words of his dialogue melted away as I found myself staring at the armour tightly gripping his chest and biceps whilst his muscular legs were naked and free – exposed to all as he strode onstage with his native kilt. These evil, sinful urges washed over me as if it were the ceaseless tide, rendering me helpless to my wanton desires. I wanted to be able to compare his physique to the fine examples of Greco-Roman antiquities that I was able to furtively glimpse at in the British Museum, near my home. Oh, to be able to admire his exquisite form at leisure! Why could I not keep these thoughts away? I wanted them locked safely in the deep recesses of my psyche but seeing him before me unleashed lustful thoughts as if Pandora had just opened her box.

Saturday evening, the final night of the year was no better. I had the chance of dressing up as a peasant girl yet again. Certainly, I was no enticement for Mr. Johnston as he performed in *The Wife with Two Husbands*. Listening to the magnificent quality of his singing voice was like a siren's call – luring me to the rocky shores of unrequited love. I could not but help to stomp and sing miserably through my choral piece with the squawking simple folk, all whilst I deeply yearned for the play to be a true-life story - but with the title changed to *A Husband with Two Wives*. I longed to be fortunate enough to share Mr. Johnston with his fair wife Nannette. It would be a compromise that I would be most willing to make. Of course, in my sick imagination I was to be the favourite of the two. I even contemplated the three of us all in one matrimonial bed, before immediately sideling the carnal whim away to the cellar corner of my mind reserved for unspeakable thoughts. Silently, I begged God for forgiveness and a reprieve from these wicked urges. I had to stop. What an evil creature I was! Lowly worm! If only Mrs. Johnston knew of my innermost thoughts I would die of the shame. And then, suddenly I would catch sight of him, and the feelings flooded back – rendering me weak at the knees and scarcely able to stand upright. I was worried that I was teetering on the edge of hysteria, a descent into madness. I resolved that this had to stop in the new year and my sensibilities returned to the forefront of my mind.

On the Tuesday morning, mother prepared me a wholesome breakfast that my stomach butterflies were preventing me from eating. Mother looked a bit worried and reticent, as she spoke about the impending performance. I thought she was going to scold me for not eating properly, but I noted that she seemed as nervous as I was about tonight.

"I'm not entirely sure that I should share this with you Lizzie, I don't want to distract you as you have so very much on your mind at this moment..."

I looked at her with anticipation. As she did not continue, I was beginning to worry that something very grave was at hand. "Mother – please! Whatever is the matter...is there something wrong?"

Mother flashed a huge grin, yet tears were running down her face. I was most perplexed and finding the situation extremely disconcerting.

"Mother...?" I pleaded.

Mother put her hands to her lips. "I'm sorry! I'm being such a fool! It's just that...Papa...and I, we...we are just so very proud of you. And what you have done. Whatever happens, we want you to savour every moment that you have tonight. I am so amazed that my daughter, my own daughter will be on stage at Drury Lane! Never in my wildest dreams! Lizzie, you are living my dream. I never made it past the provincial theatres – Margate, Norwich, Birmingham. But there you will be, in the greatest theatre in the land!"

"I only wish that you and Papa could be there. It would mean the world to me."

Mother had an even bigger grin on her face, and it looked as if she was trying her best to suppress childish giggles. I looked at her imploringly.

"Mother! What is it exactly that you want to tell me?"

"Well, you do know that Aunt Harriet has acquaintances in high circles?" Mother then paused. She was drawing this out painfully for me. I suspect that she herself was relishing this whole process.

"Yes. And?!!"

"Well, some of those people happen to subscribe to their own private box in the theatre. And being terribly busy people, they sometimes are unable to attend some performances. When that happens, they are sometimes kind enough to pass on those tickets to some friends who may wish to see the performance."

I stood up excitedly, clapping my hands and squealing like a little girl. I nearly wept with unbounded joy as mother laid out four tickets – before me on the table.

"It seems that there is a ticket for Aunt Harriet, Tom, your father and I. Now, I don't want it to affect your performance. I want you to carry on as normal, and do not even attempt to try and look for us when you step out on stage. But be assured that we will be there watching your every move, our hearts dancing along with your feet!"

Like doves being set free from their cage, I felt all my worries and troubles flutter away. I gave Mother a big hug, and then sat down to the breakfast that would need to provide me sustenance through this momentous day. Later, she helped me to dress – fussing over every little detail. I had to remind her that I was to be wearing a completely different outfit on the stage. I reassured her that the dressers backstage would see to me, and additionally ensure that my hair and make-up were perfection. We both stared at the cracked mirror. In it I saw the fusion and melding of my mother and I. It felt as if her wisdom, experience, hopes, dreams, and disappointments were all being imparted and blended into my bearing. Little Liz was no longer gazing back at me. It was the debutante ready for the ball. I closed my eyes and gathered my thoughts for reassurance that it was not to be a façade, like Cinderella's coach and horsemen - all to be whisked away at midnight, leaving only tattered dreams and wishes. I opened my eyes, my mother squeezing my shoulders for reassurance; having sensed the reoccurring trepidation that was happening. But there was no need. I looked before me, and the mighty vision of Athena was there before me. With the strength and confidence of the goddess herself, I stepped away from the looking glass, and made the familiar journey to the theatre.

I arrived at Drury Lane in good time, perhaps a bit too early. The theatre was abuzz with the hubbub of the workers behind the scenes, trying to ensure that stage magic was delivered to the audience this evening. There were many tricks and devices that had to be performed perfectly, especially with this – the opening evening performance. Writers from the newspapers would be present to critique every fault and flaw of the show. A favourable review could ensure the success of the play and result in a long run. Of course, *Cinderella* was an afterpiece, which meant that the primary play of the evening had to be endured before I was to go on the stage and dance. This made the wait seem like an eternity. I had watched the rehearsal of *The Jew* just yesterday. I was told that it was an unusual comedy, in that it was portraying a Jewish moneylender in a positive light. In this case, he had the appearance of a miser – but it was all for show, as he was a most generous, kind, and benevolent being. It eased my worries to know that it was a comedy, as it helped to keep the spirits of the audience light. Following a serious Shakespearian drama would have created a stark contrast, which may have unsettled the audience; or made them think that our pantomime was nothing but trifling piffle, unworthy of being displayed on this very grand stage.

Since the incident with Mr. Johnston, I had been waiting reluctantly for the bitter retribution of Bella. She had been uncharacteristically aloof from me throughout most of the remainder of December. By no means friendly, she continued to be curt and rude – but generally ignored me. This should have provided me with some relief, but in actuality – I felt very unnerved by her behaviour. I knew that she was plotting something dastardly, and I had the feeling that this evening would bear witness to the culmination of my suspicions. As the performance was drawing closer, Bella Menage was working especially hard to try and unsettle me. Charlotte Bristow tried to shield me from her attempts through distraction, but to little avail as it seems Bella was determined to make my debut an utter misery. She had taken to call me 'Bandy', trying to make me feel insecure about my legs. I tried to avoid giving the indication that it bothered me in the least. If she wanted to resort to childish name calling, so be it. That was preferable to some of her other antics, and I was almost tempted to encourage this new nickname by looking wounded when she spouted the word – but I thought the better of it. Tonight - preparing in the dressing room, we were all in close quarters, forcing me to be in near proximity as she unleashed her taunts.

"Bandy – do remember that there will be a full house tonight. If you make a mistake, over three thousand spectators will witness it. Why, it may even make the papers. Mr. Sheridan would be most displeased. It would certainly place your employment in a most precarious position."

"All of our jobs would be at risk…" interjected the delightful Miss Decamp, rubbing coal smears on her face to get the appropriate downtrodden Cinderella look perfected. "Were it not for the full houses filled by your friend Carlo the dog."

I winced inwardly at Bella being reminded of her recent humiliation. I did not want her to fixate on that event as I felt it would certainly bode badly for me in the end. I aimed to change the subject, and I attempted to massage her ego sycophantically; yet somehow managed to twist things into a sly slight that I hoped could protect me.

"Thank you, Miss Menage, for your kind concern. But you have taught me well in rehearsals. Everyone knows I am indebted to your instruction. And if I failed somehow, I am certain that it would be no poor reflection on your teaching methods."

"Indeed Bandy, you are most correct. I think the blame would lie squarely with Mr. Byrne. People would say it was he who was foolish enough to hire you in the first place. On the bright side, the more amateur that you appear is the better I will look on the stage tonight. Don't feel bad about it when it happens. You are inexperienced. You must spend much more time refining your craft. One should not expect to arrive on the greatest London stage without treading the boards, honing your abilities in the provinces – or perhaps in one of the circuses. In fact, it makes one truly wonder how you managed to obtain a position here. Perhaps you have additional talents to offer gentlemen such as Mr.

Byrne and Mr. Sheridan that remain unseen to most of your colleagues here. In fact, I was just saying to Mr. Johnston the other day how you have such a fine figure – one that would be most greatly admired to its best effect in the horizontal position."

Aghast as I was by her shocking commentary - I ignored her hurtful retort, which implied that I had procured my place on stage through immoral means. Outrageous as her remarks were, I was determined to not let her undermine my special evening. I remained cautious, however. I was on my guard for the presence of a stray pin on my chair, her leg suddenly tripping me up or something even more unpredictable to throw me off my stride. It was so much for me to contend with, but I would retreat to the wise arms of Athena in my thoughts, giving me the strength to bravely soldier on.

The Jew was finishing, and the audience milling about to purchase baked apples, playbills, and song sheets for souvenirs. I was fighting the urge to look for my family in the audience. I promised Mother that I would concentrate on my professional requirements. I had a task to accomplish, and that required my full attention. Charlotte, Miss Decamp, Mrs. Mountain, Mrs. Byrne, and her little boys – they all took the time to wish me well. I was most touched that Mr. Grimaldi came to me and told me that he saw a great future in theatre for me; and that he would remember this evening as the début of that most magnificent dancer - Miss Searle.

We all took our places behind the curtains, in a scene resembling the magnificent heavens above. Seeing the delightful little Byrne boys relishing their impending moments of stage action helped to put me at ease. Mrs. Mountain was ready to take to her throne, replacing the fairy of the traditional version of the story as the goddess Venus. Miss Tyrer as the Nymph, the Byrne boys as Cupid and Hymen, and we three Graces were gathered round

Venus as she gazed upon Mr. Byrne, the fair Prince – a traitor to love that she would soon ensnare under a magical spell.

The light from the candles were in place on the moveable wings of the stage sets. There were in place a myriad of technical support workers on hand to help with the props and to work the 'tricks' that had been constructed, wick trimmers to see to the lighting, prompters to whisper lines to actors who had forgotten them. The curtains parted to the sound of the orchestra striking up. It begins! My heart was aflutter.

Gazing forward, I saw the theatre from a perspective I had not witnessed before. The auditorium was so brightly lit. There were at least five crystal chandeliers lighting up the whole audience before us. They were further enhanced by mirrored wall lights. All told, there had to be hundreds upon hundreds of candles, shining bright. Clever Argand lamps using oil lit the stage even brighter than daylight itself. I had to concentrate hard, so as to not be mesmerised by the dazzling brilliance before me. Mrs. Mountain expertly set about delivering her dialogue. It was interrupted by the sound of a horn.

"Hark! Hark! The glad sound!" exclaimed Mrs. Mountain - to which we all replied, "The traitor is found!"

Our dancing ensued, and aside from squeezing my hand too tightly, to the point of near pain – Bella Menage did behave herself. As the prince was transfixed by our movements, little Cupid pierced him with his magic love arrow. The conclusion of the scene was the final requirement for the Graces until near the end of the show. As we made our way back to the wings, Bella stomped on my foot – nearly sending me cascading and tumbling until I clutched onto her shoulder for support. Bella hissed back in a very audible whisper "Watch what you are doing, you fool! And get some singing lessons while you're at it – your off-key warbling is most off-putting!"

At that moment, cherubic Oscar Byrne, dressed as Cupid, drew his bow to his side and said softly and sweetly "Miss Menage, why are you being so unkind? I saw you step on Miss Searle's toes!"

The prompter gestured for us all to be quiet, and we continued to make our way out of earshot. I glanced and smiled at dear Oscar, as I made my way to a point far from Bella – but where I could glimpse a hint of the stage action commencing. I brushed thoughts of Bella aside as I felt the contagious enthusiasm of the audience. I was enthralled to hear the singing of the stout little 'Nymph', Miss Tyrer. She was blessed with a most sweet and enchanting voice. Hearing it in contrast to the equally splendid tones of Miss Decamp and Mrs. Mountain was like being in heaven itself. Watching the audience gasp as the clever tricks and transformations took place was a delight: Cinderella's kitchen table into a toilette, a pumpkin into a chariot, lizards into footmen and mice into horses.

Finally, we joined in with the chorus at the finale at the end of the second act, singing "For ever and for ever...". Concluding the proceedings with a dance, the applause rung through my ears. It felt how I imagined waves to be – nearly knocking one down with their power and strength. I happened to gaze up and caught a glimpse of my dear Papa – standing and shouting "Bravo! Bravo!" I did not succumb to distraction – as my Papa had taught me to maintain concentration. Besides, I had to be on my guard with Bella being around. She would be ready to cause me some injury if my guard were down. When it came time to take a bow, I was most fortunate that Charlotte somehow was in the centre of the three Graces – serving as a barrier between the wicked Miss Menage and I. This was not the way we rehearsed it, but Bella did have the opportunity of curtseying first – an ordering that she enjoyed as it prioritised her importance. Charlotte was next, then followed by myself. I looked to my family. Seeing them warmed my heart so, causing me to erupt in a beaming smile. I know not who was most excited – little Tom or my father! Mother and Aunt Harriet looked at me with such beaming pride. The admiration of the audience was splendid, but nothing could compare to my precious family's adoring approval. I knew this was what I was destined for. Thank you, Athena for delivering me this most wonderful gift - this unforgettable moment.

CHAPTER 10

Mr H. JOHNSTON
in the Character of Hamlet

Wonderful moments continued. The next evening was to be my second performance of *Cinderella*. I came early to prepare myself. That is the superficial excuse I made anyway. The reality was that I wanted to watch the comedy that would be performed as the first event of the evening. It was featuring the ever-wonderful Mrs. Jordan, and I wanted to ensure that I had a good spot backstage from which to view the proceedings. All well and good, one might say. That is until I relent and tell of my weak resolve. Nary four days into the new year, and here I was – observing Charles Merton, better known as the actor Henry Erskine Johnston, who was portraying him onstage in remarkably close proximity to my besotted eyes. There were several factors that helped my thoughts remain chaste. Firstly, Mr. Johnston remained fully clothed

83

throughout his performance (however he did still cut a most handsome figure). Secondly, the title of the play helped remind me of the moral action that one should aspire to. It was entitled *Marriage Promise*. I had to almost laugh at the messages the fates seemed to be trying to deliver to me. However, my mania for Mr. Johnston continued unabated.

This situation was further exacerbated by events yet to unfold. I took part in my main stage performance, alongside my fellow graces. Bella knew she had to be slyer and cleverer with her persecution of me onstage, lest little Oscar Byrne witness the transgression once again and decide to pierce her with his Cupid's arrow in my defence. Alas - I too was on my guard constantly in her presence. Charlotte, Bella, and I joined our hands and began our circular movements on cue. As we danced, not only did I have to convey grace and deportment with my every move, I also quickly became aware that I had to avoid her sudden high kicks aimed at my bottom. She took great pains to do this very surreptitiously. It only happened when she was coming to the rear of the stage, to make it less likely that she would be spotted. She only managed contact just once with her foot, and fortunately for me it did not deliver a full blow. After three unsuccessful attempts at her target, she suddenly changed tactics. Again, only when she was at the back of the circle did she attempt this. Additionally, Bella was very aware of the sightline of the Prince (Mr. Byrne, our choreographer) onstage. How she managed to get away with her next dastardly deed was almost like sorcery. She gave no indication to the audience of what she was up to and looked as graceful as ever. Her new ploy was to yank on our conjoined hands suddenly and viciously, so as to throw me off-balance. She tried pulling downwards, but I managed to stretch my arm sufficiently so as to ensure that it had no effect on our dance. The next time around she pulled her arm forward towards her so forcefully that I struggled to keep my balance. Miraculously, I managed to maintain my balance whilst not giving away my predicament to the 3,000 seated before me. I was genuinely terrified on the inside and feeling so very worried about what would happen next. Fortunately, our performance was coming to an end. We smiled and waved to thunderous applause from the adoring audience who were completely unaware of the tug-of-war that had just taken place before them.

Very rattled, I scurried backstage still holding on to Miss Bristow's hand. Looking back at her, I could see that she was equally distraught. Her face was drawn, and she looked more apt to burst into tears than I. Then to my amazement, I saw my Perseus before me. Henry Johnston was applauding – but it was an angry, slow clap and I could sense a volcanic rage underneath his false smile. "Well done, ladies!" Both Charlotte and I gave him a nervous smile. I glanced behind to notice Bella haughtily mouthing "Thank you!" to him for his most unexpected compliment. As the ongoing audience applause were still drowning out any backstage noise, Henry had the opportunity to speak his mind – quietly, but with frightening force and clarity with his full Scottish accent flowing forward unabated. "I wasn't talkin' to YOU! Wha' the HELL do you think you were playin' at? Green Room – NOW!"

Visibly shaken, tiny Bella tried to protest; but before she had the chance Henry was forcing her forward to the room by firmly wrapping his hand around the waist sash of her dress. Had she moved an inch her dress would have been torn – she had no choice but to be guided into the busy Green Room. I was so very shaken that I was going to avoid following. I was worried my presence would only have negative consequences for me, as Bella would take her vengeance out on me somehow. But I was still being held by Charlotte's hand, who seemed almost magnetically attracted to the unfolding drama in the emerald-coloured space ahead. Wordlessly she pulled me along with her. She was completely speechless as if in utter shock.

Henry still had Bella firmly by the waist as they entered the room, quickly followed by Charlotte and I. I think even Bella, bold as she was, would have been horrified at the audience in witness as this play began to unfold. As we had entered rather forcefully and abruptly, all eyes were immediately upon us. Looking around, I saw it was most of the cast from the previous, completed comedy. Some of Drury Lane's most prominent thespians were all there before us, including Mr. Pope, Mr. Bannister, Harriet Mellon, and Dorothy Jordan, amongst others. Henry announced in a big, booming Scots voice "Ah, let us all hear it for the three lovely Graces! They were magnificent tonight! Three cheers for the three ladies!" Everyone raised their glasses in a toast and continued with their convivial proceedings – some coming to congratulate us and place glasses of wine into our hands. I could hear Bella struggling next to me. She was trying to wiggle out of his death grip around her waistline, slapping him, scratching, and pinching – but all rather discretely as she fixed a smile on her public face. At her first opportunity, she whispered fiercely "Unhand me you knave! How dare you! Where is Nannette? Wait 'til she hears about this!"

"I think you'll be findin' that my wife is not present this evening." He stared straight into her eyes. "So therefore, I feel completely free to speak my mind about you as I please, you miserable little shrew!"

"You're drunk! Wait 'til my fiancé gets wind of this! You'll regret this, you cad!"

"Wha'? The painter? Is Mr. Sharp goin' to sort me out wi' a paintbrush in my face? A bit o' oil paint in me eye? I'm a quakin' in m'boots!" He laughed at her dismissively.

"Now I got somethin' to say a' you – you see these two fine ladies here - and unlike yourself, they ARE ladies… I consider them dear friends of mine. If someone goes messin' with my friends, then they are a gonna' have ME to deal wi'. Ya' catch me meanin'?"

"I've studied the dialogue of Scotch mongrels, so I can just about make out your words – but I have no idea what you are speaking about!" retorted Bella.

"Well let me make it clear t'ya. I saw you tryin' to sabotage the performances of Miss Bristow and Miss Searle this evenin'. I SAW ya'. Don't try and worm your clever arse way out of this one, you lyin' cow!"

Bella took her chances to try and make a scene and began to speak louder to draw in the attention of those around us. "Unhand me, you base fool! You have no right to be pawing all over me like some slovenly pig-man! Let go of me now you IMBECILE!"

"Oh, now Bella. You really don't wanna' be a makin' a scene!" By now, everyone was watching.

"You'll be wanting to be nice to me. And be a nice little girl to those around you. You see, we are goin' t'have a wee lesson tonight. You will now realise that when you humiliate my friends, you – mademoiselle, are gonna' experience something called consequences…also known as repercussions."

"You stink! You vile man – LET GO of me!"

Everyone looked on uncomfortably as Henry laughed aloud, then continued in a quiet, condescending manner. "Oh sweetheart! Bless ya'! You still don't get it, do ya'? Well – here it goes." Immediately, Henry spoke aloud to all in the room. "Ladies and gentlemen. For many a year, I have had the good fortune to work here at Drury Lane with some very amazing talent. Miss Menage here is no exception! A fine dancer. Passable actress… Yet in my time here, I have seen this little vixen bully and snipe at others with impunity. This evening… and I am sure none of you will be surprised about this…I witnessed her try to hurt Miss Bristow and Miss Searle. Onstage. During a performance. Now, I care not what grievance you have against a fellow performer, but we here as actors have a bond. We look out for each other. We help one another. If someone forgets a line, you help them out. You do not mock them before all of London to shame them. That is our unspoken oath to each other. As Drury Lane family, we are here for each other, so that when we fall – we have someone to pick us up and lend a kind hand. It seems as if Arabella has not taken this message in. Therefore now, in front of her fine colleagues here tonight – I want it known that we are all here for her. We are here for you Bella…to ensure that you do not misbehave. That you no longer try to make your fellow actors and actresses look foolish in order to make you look better. There is no need for that. You have beauty, skill and are capable of the utmost charm. Hone your good qualities Miss Menage. They will do you good in this world. We do not need a viper in our midst. You are capable of being so much better than that. And each one of us here will ensure that you go on the right path, Bella. It is our duty. So, if one of us sees you mete out unkindness and rudeness to another – I'm sure that we are all in agreement with this. We have had enough…and we shall call you up on your errant ways. Not because we are harsh and unkind, or seeking revenge. But because we all genuinely love and care for you. Frustrating as you can be, we are all a family here; and are responsible for each other."

Henry let go of Bella, who was sobbing inconsolably. Whether through shame or remorse, I do not know. "Would you care to apologise?" he gently prodded. She nodded and whispered sorry in my direction, then darted out of the room quickly. Smiles and looks of astonishment started to flow through the room.

"I sincerely hope I didn't overstep the mark!" Henry remarked to Charlotte and I with a wink. We finished our drinks and made our way backstage to join a sullen and contrite Bella Menage for the finale.

Cinderella was proclaimed to be a resounding success. Universal approbation was coming from all quarters, and the show was the talk of the city. The newspaper reviews were ripe with fulsome praise. Note was taken of Mrs. Mountain's most excellent voice. Likewise, the talents of Miss Decamp – demonstrating her accomplishments in the fields of acting, dancing and singing. One paper rather unkindly likened sweet Miss Tyrer as a more likely candidate for Mother Bunch than an alluring Nymph; but all was forgiven once they heard her mellifluous voice. The mightiest aplomb was reserved for the tiniest amongst us – Oscar Byrne as fair Cupid won the hearts of all witnesses who put pen to paper. The Graces had scant mention, reserved usually to "reasonably sustaining the action". However, to the delight of Charlotte and I, one paper did have a bit more to say – particularly about Miss Bella Menage. The review in *The Mercury* was several days later than most of the other newspapers. I suspect the author observed a later performance of *Cinderella*, as he felt compelled to give a rather sneaky rebuke to her in the guise of a compliment: "We must pay the tribute of a few words to the elegance of Miss B. Menage, more particularly as we thought we discovered her in the languor of indisposition – 'let not the Lily droop.'"

Indeed, I do seem to recall Bella being quite indisposed on the Friday evening performance. Although only our fourth performance of the production, she was seeming to find the dance routine most tiresome and somewhat beneath her formidable talents. She was making frequent forays into the Green Room, where wine was freely flowing, and we do suspect she was partaking. Uncharacteristically, she became more jovial when joining us to perform. Yet she was rather clumsy and clunky in her movements – lacking her exceptional poise. In contrast, *The Mercury* found "...the modest grace of her two companions was very pleasing to the audience." And that statement was most pleasing to both Charlotte and I.

No one mentioned the review to Miss Menage, and it

did seem to escape her self-centred attention. Her performances returned back to form though – the elegance and polished perfection returning. But it was apparent that Bella was thinking of the next opportunities, and new roles to be had. She now was just going through the motions of performing what was required and expected – with little enthusiasm or relish. And with that lack of interest was a decline in antipathy directed towards me. She seemed to be mellowing somewhat. Perhaps this was due to the attentions of one particular Mr. Michael William Sharp. Mr. Sharp was apprenticed to the well-known portrait painter, William Beechey. He was making his appearance in the Green Room with increased regularity, often keeping Miss Menage amused with his company. As he was also Sarah Siddons nephew, Miss Decamp could keep us informed on the latest news regarding that relationship. Charles Kemble was privy to the disapproval his sister Sarah was feeling towards this ever-blossoming romance. But if this helped to keep Bella distracted, I was all for it.

The performances of *Cinderella* continued with remarkable success. Night after night, the auditorium would fill. And dare I say it? The main performance changed with frequency, but we remained a steady staple. Audiences would even skip the main performance, turning up to see the afterpiece sensation that was *Cinderella*. *The Marriage Promise*, *The Rivals*, *As You Like It*, *Beaux Strategem*... I began to feel some degree of pity for all those performers having to constantly learn complex lines of dialogue for a string of plays, whereas I could gaily prance about the stage; entrancing the handsome prince to distraction, night after night.

Pay day, however, was a much less enjoyable undertaking. As Charlotte Bristow had warned me, Mr. Sheridan was not the most punctual in paying his employees. I had received my 15 shillings every week of December, due in some part to the success provided by heroic Carlo the dog in *The Caravan* filling the theatre seats with regularity. But it seemed that Mr. Sheridan was resolved to avoid all creditors throughout the month of January. I joined in with the backstage crew of painters, carpenters, and minor players in waiting for hours outside his office in the hope that Mr. Sheridan would arrive with our pay. It was very tedious, but it did provide me with ample opportunity to get to know those who worked so diligently behind the scenes. Everyone had their own tales of financial woe, all due to the inconsiderate Mr. Sheridan. To my great dismay – I had gone three weeks without payment. When I did get paid, it was only for the week at hand. I was given a promissory note for the arrears that I was due. Needless to say, this was causing havoc with my family's finances. Father was losing clients due to his continued inability to carry out any work. Propriety dictated that Mother would be unable to fulfil any lessons with his clients, even with his female pupils. She continued to work hard at her sewing, but the recompense for this effort was minimal.

I confessed my distress to Miss Decamp one afternoon, who informed me that the great actor and theatre manager John Philip Kemble left Drury Lane being owed well over £1,100! He was becoming angry and stressed to the point of illness at having to deny loyal, hard-working staff their salaries when he was serving as theatre manager at Drury Lane – all due to the financial misdeeds of haughty Mr. Sheridan. His frustration eventually led him to become part owner and manager of Covent Garden Theatre – Drury Lane's great rival amongst the Royal Patent theatres of London. Miss Decamp was exceedingly kind and gave me payment in exchange for the promissory notes I had collected. She assured me that as a well-paid performer in high demand, that she would easily be able to persuade the management to re-compensate her for this generous outlay. Furthermore, she would try to shame them in order to ensure that such injustices did not happen to me again in the future.

And so, the performances continued to overflowing audiences. An evening of note was on a Friday, the 20th of January. Mrs. Jordan had just performed *The Inconstant*. She was watching our act in *Cinderella* from the wings. As we three Graces departed from the stage, she invited us all to the Green Room as we had considerable time before our stage presence was needed again at the finale. She stated that the room was far too masculine at the moment, and she would appreciate the company of her theatrical sisters. As we entered, there was an air of joviality about, no doubt aided by the wine that was on offer to all and sundry. There seemed to be a celebration of sorts taking place, but what it was exactly I was never able to determine. Mr. Bannister was there, as were most of the cast from the now completed comedy that had been performed earlier in the evening. Dora Jordan pulled me along and whispered in my ear.

"I think it may be important for your career to mingle a bit. The most important people to ingratiate oneself with are the theatre owner, the manager, the stage manager – and perhaps the playwrights and composers as well. They are the key people involved with casting. If you are not constantly at the forefront, trying to promote yourself – then you may well be forgotten and left to the chorus forever. Have a look over there – see Charlotte speaking to Mr. Barrymore? It is all well and good, speaking with this fine young actor chum; but it will lead nowhere as far as career progression. Now may I point out Bella – she instantly has headed for Michael Kelly. I suppose she is congratulating him on the success of his score for *Cinderella*. Take notice of her demeanour. Flirtatious...complimentary."

Mrs. Jordan continued to watch Bella discretely, occasionally directing her eyes in the direction that she wanted me to cast my gaze upon as well.

"He offers her wine – and she accepts with a bit of a false protest at first. But wait – here it is! The laugh and hand placed gently on his arm. This is no criticism of her. She has the game completely right, and she knows exactly what she is doing. Making men feel important and admired, yet capable of keeping them at bay should they get too close. Take note my dear. These are the ways of the theatrical world. If you want success, you will have to fight for it."

She smiled at me, then led me straight to Mr. Sheridan. I really hated this situation. I felt insecure and completely uncomfortable. In my mind, I epitomised 'Bandy', the scrawny legged child that Bella thought me to be. Who was I, to be in the midst of these important people?

"Richard, have you had the opportunity to meet our newest dancer? May I introduce to you one of our delightful Graces of the stage - Miss Elizabeth Searle."

"Why – I don't believe I have. Tell me Miss Searle, how are you finding it here with the Drury Lane family?" Mr. Sheridan seemed only half-hearted in his interest, and he was far more interested in looking at me up and down – from head to toe, than he was in listening to my reply. I felt as if he was getting the measure of a fine racehorse that he was considering the purchase of. It made me feel most uncomfortable, as if he were undressing me with his eyes.

"Oh...fine, sir. I mean to say...I...I... absolutely love it here. Everyone has been so very kind, and..."

"Yes, yes. Now do tell me...I have seen you dance, and Mr. Byrne assures me that you are quite accomplished and skilled with this – even at your young age...which is?"

"Uh...Fourteen, sir." I was feeling so tongue-tied, as if English were not my native language.

"And how are you at memorising and reciting dialogue?"

"Well...I've had little experience...you see, this is my first time upon the public stage."

"Good God! Your first time on stage, and it is in front of a throng of over three thousand people! You certainly are a plucky young lady!" He gave me no time to respond. "And how are you in voice? Can you sing a fair tune?" Before I could answer, a gentleman abruptly butted in – offering Mr. Sheridan a glass and pulling him by the shoulder as he guffawed something bawdy into his ear. This short, balding man was looking at me leeringly; causing me to feel a great deal of discomfort almost immediately. I apologised and made my way over to the familiar safety of Mr. Bannister with the intention of asking about the well-being of his dog, for he was owner of one of the 'Carlo' dogs who swam upon our stage last month. Before I could get there, I was intercepted by Miss Menage, accompanied by a distinguished looking gentleman. I was most taken aback by her polite approach towards me. Certainly, under most normal circumstances I would expect a dressing down, belittling comment or a surreptitious kick to my shin. But she now was introducing me as if she were the most gracious hostess, instead of the truly reprehensible cow that I knew her to be.

"Oh Miss Searle, may I introduce to you Mr. D'Egville. He was my ballet instructor in my youth. I owe all my talents to him!" She looked at him with a most genuine-looking smile of fondness. "Oh, please do excuse me James. I have just seen your brother George and I must say hello." She smiled at a similar looking gentleman across the room and waved gently. "I will leave you two to talk. Miss Searle is an exceptionally fine dancer. You both have something in common!"

James D'Egville chuckled, grinned, and then looked at me directly in a most charming way. His large brown eyes seemed kind, framed by his rounded face. He was lean – having the build of a ballet master. As with many others in the room, he was exquisitely dressed; but he wore his clothing with particular aplomb. His sharp white starched collar and cravat were held down by a beautiful black velvet jacket which featured glimmering golden brass buttons.

"Miss Searle – I am delighted! I had the good fortune of watching you perform with your fellow Graces last week. I was most certainly taken aback by your elegance and charm. It was simply magical to witness!"

"That is very flattering Mr. D'Egville. Forgive me for asking, but your surname seems quite exotic. Are you French, by any chance?"

"Well, my father was. His name was Pierre and he was ballet master here at one point, as well as at the Saddler's Wells Theatre. I suppose I have followed in his footsteps slightly, as I am currently the ballet master at the King's Theatre in Haymarket. Although I have performed at the Paris Opera many years ago, I'm afraid that I am about as French as the jolly Mr. Grimaldi is Italian!"

Mr. D'Egville then chuckled in a most amiable way. I was a bit startled by all of this. Had Bella Menage done me the most profound favour? The season at The Haymarket ran during the summer months, after Drury Lane and Covent Garden were closed. I would be seeking employment for those months, and here was an opportunity with the ballet director of that theatre. It was the most prestigious dance venue in the nation, if not all of Europe. Perhaps he has a place that needs filling amongst his dancers. Maybe he would offer me the chance to audition for his company. Why, did he not already express his admiration for my skills? I was most eager to make the most of this opportunity. I was trying to not get carried away with my excitement at the potential prospects. I knew I had to concentrate and see what could be made of this. I was soon to discover that my efforts would not be needed – I was to be offered a gift on a plate.

"Miss Searle, I hope you do not feel that I am impertinent for bringing this topic up. Miss Menage happened to mention that you and your family are facing straightened circumstances due to your father's indisposition. I am most sorry to hear of your troubles and do wish your father a speedy recovery. However, if there were possibly something I could do to assist you in resolving your predicament..."

I was most taken aback that Bella would even speak of me to Mr. D'Egville, and it seemed almost inconceivable that she would be trying to do something to help me when I had always been the target of her vindictive hatred. Perhaps she was just gossiping – saying unkind things about my situation. I had no idea she was even aware of the goings on in my household. Nevertheless, here before me was a stroke of good fortune. Perhaps kind Mr. D'Egville heard Bella's cruel jibes and felt some degree of pity for me.

"Oh, please don't worry, Mr. D'Egville. It is most kind of you to take an interest in my affairs. You must understand that it is not in my nature to ask for charity. However, if there were opportunities to provide a greater deal of comfort for my family by garnering employment – I would find that of great interest."

"Ah! Splendid! I am most pleased to hear that. I..." He hesitated briefly as if considering something very carefully. "I do believe I may be in the position of helping you to secure a very lucrative... engagement. I can imagine you being very much in demand. An instant success, no doubt!"

I was finding it difficult to believe how well this was all going. He continued "I will be meeting with some...some of my benefactors. We could call this an audition of sorts. Tell me would you be available in the evening on the 30th? That is on a Monday. I do believe that *Cinderella* is not being performed that evening. I could arrange for my carriage to pick you up. The event will be at Earl Craven's residence. There will be dining, and - dare I say? A fair deal of dancing! The Earl is fond of merriment; I do believe there will be musicians, singers..."

"Oh, that sounds most exciting! But please...I must say

that I do not know what to expect of such an event. What should I wear? And I should expect that I need someone to accompany me."

"Now don't you worry yourself about such trifles, Miss Searle. I will arrange for suitable clothing to be delivered to you. In fact, I can imagine the perfect outfit that will display your fine figure to its greatest advantage. Tell me, are you fond of silk?"

"Why...Mr. D'Egville – I could never afford to wear an item of silk! I've never worn such a thing!"

"Well, now that will be something you can tick off your list. Tell me, do you like the colour red? I believe that would be simply stunning on you! It would offset your fine fair complexion most exquisitely." Mr. D'Egville had his hands raised – as if he were some sort of musical conductor. Both of his arms opened outward as he grinned, apparently admiring the feminine beauty before him which was in my possession.

"I... I don't know what to say!"

"Your address, mademoiselle. That is what you need to say – you need to tell me your address forthwith, so that these arrangements...can be arranged!" Mr. D'Egville smiled at me and was speaking in the most disarming manner.

"Uh...it is 35 Hart Street. In Bloomsbury, not the Hart Street near Covent Garden."

"Of course not. Why, that area is the haunt of fallen women of the lowest order. Whereas you – you are something altogether rarer and more precious! A rare jewel to be treasured! Are you near St. George's then? Near Bloomsbury Square?"

"Uh...yes, sir. Indeed. It is located between the two, on the same side of the street as the church." I replied to him with a slight hesitancy, as I was trying to digest and interpret his comments towards me. Were these statements complimentary? Being more precious than a Covent Garden whore was no real commendation. Was he being a bit flirtatious? And what of this dress? Was he actually going to procure me a fine red silk dress? I was very puzzled, but I wanted to give an air of assured self-confidence and was determined that he would not discover my true bemused state.

"Well then...that is settled. I will be having Mrs. Jones – a most capable dressmaker, calling at your home. She will see to it if there are any alterations that need to be made to the garment."

"Mr. D'Egville, I honestly don't know what to say..."

I was very taken aback at what happened next. Mr. D'Egville had the audacity to place two of his fingers on my lips accompanied by a quiet "Shush!". It was done most gently. But I was rather shocked at his very forward, presumptuous behaviour. My eyes widened, and it felt as if they were popping right out of my head. He shook his head and started to speak in what I was beginning to think was a condescending tone. I flinched slightly as I felt his hand wander across the small of my back, then delicately drift away as he spoke.

"Miss Searle...really! There is no need to express gratitude! Your presence amongst us is a gift sent from the heavens! A Grace of unequalled beauty that we are blessed to behold. My benefactors will be astounded when they lay eyes upon you. And let me assure you, they are gentlemen of the highest rank and quality. There is no chance that you will be encountering any course manners on this occasion."

"Mr. D'Egville...forgive me, just a few questions to ask - if I may?"

"Most certainly." He smiled confidently after his reply and raised his eyebrows expectantly.

"Are my dancing skills to be tested?"

"I would expect that they may well be."

"And will there be a need for me to recite dialogue? Or sing perhaps"

"Not unless you feel the need to do so..." He was a bit

slow and hesitant in this reply. Mr. D'Egville looked at me as if I were completely daft for asking such an odd question.

"And I presume that there will be other ladies present...that are...auditioning??"

"Oh... um, yes. Yes. Certainly, there will be many ladies present. Many highly experienced professionals, and a few that are new I suppose. But Miss Searle, I do expect that you will be in the finest, most enviable position. I have no doubt that all eyes in the room shall be cast upon you. Of that you can be most assured. There really is no need to worry! I know that this may be a bit of a daunting step. Perhaps this is not a career that you expected to be in, but for a young lady this can be a rather lucrative way to garner some independence and financial security. Rest assured, I will ensure your well-being – do not worry that pretty, little head of yours! I see a very stellar future for you!"

With that, he wished me well until we met again at Lord Craven's, but not before placing his lips on the back of my hand – sealing a kiss firmly atop of it. It truly was a most peculiar encounter. My head was spinning a bit, I must admit. It did seem as if I were truly on my way to garnering a position as a dancer at the Haymarket. I kept wondering though...how could he be so very sure and certain of my dancing abilities? Yes, I gave my performances at Drury Lane my utmost effort, but they were, all in all, quite brief and were scarcely the fullest showcase of my talents. And I did not quite know what to make of Mr. D'Egville. At times charming, somewhat condescending, generous, and odd – all in equal measure. But I really had no time to dwell on this, as I was pondering upon whether I should thank Bella – or just pretend the incident never happened. I opted for the latter, as all the Graces made their way back to the backstage area in preparation for our duties.

CHAPTER 11

J. H. D'Egville, Esq.
Director of the King's Theatre

Mother and I had words. Angry words. I was so excited about my upcoming audition for Mr. D'Egville, but as soon as I relayed the information, she looked at me in horror.

"What exactly, pray tell, did this Mr. D'Egville promise you?" Mother emphasised his name with special disgust and disdain.

"Mother! Whatever is wrong with you? He is the ballet master for the King's Theatre! That means I could be dancing at the Haymarket this summer. I could have the possibility of work with the finest ballet in the nation! Think about what that could mean for our finances. We need the money, do we not?"

"Oh, I am well aware of Mr. D'Egville. He has a very fine reputation indeed. He is especially fond of collecting young girls and expanding their talents to incorporate some less than reputable entertainment. So, do tell me exactly – what precisely did he promise you?"

I explained about the audition that was due to take place at Lord Craven's, and about the dress that would be made for me. As I was relaying the information, I began to have the realisation dawn upon me that perhaps I was being foolish. I neglected to tell her about the two fingers placed upon my lips, or the hand drifting skilfully down my back.

"Lord Craven's residence? A silk dress delivered to you at your door! Are you simple? Stupid girl! Does that sound like a typical audition to you? I will tell you what you would be auditioning for...a gentleman who will have his wicked way with you! Strip you bare and use you!"

"Mother! How can you know that his intentions are wayward? He seemed a perfect gentleman...polite and kind. And I pressed him for details of what I needed to do." I sounded less and less convincing – even to myself.

"Really? Well, I do suppose that there is one way to clarify all of this. I think we need to pay a visit to Mr. D'Egville, where we can discuss your potential contract details."

"Mother, please don't embarrass me! I have to work in the theatres here. I don't want a reputation of being difficult."

"So, you would prefer the reputation of being a wanton doxy instead? No, I will not have this done to my daughter. They can know that you may not be difficult, but you do have a reputation: for possessing a fearsome, protective mother that is not to be crossed!"

I dreaded the walk the next day. Mother was adamant that we go to the Haymarket Theatre to meet up with Mr. D'Egville. Of course, we did not know if he would even be there – as it was off season. But Mother insisted that we would find his address from someone there or nearby. At the door, mother asked if Mr. D'Egville could be informed that Miss Searle and her mother were here to see him regarding contractual issues. The doorman immediately stated that Mr. D'Egville happened to be in and he would escort us to his office.

Wandering in the dimly lit interior, we followed the gentleman to a small office. The door was cracked open slightly, and I could only make out the back of the shoulder of a man writing with a quill. With a knock on the door, we were announced. "A Mrs. Searle and her daughter here to see you, Mr. D'Egville." The quill was placed in a stand, and the rather puzzled gentleman turned around. To my absolute horror and embarrassment, I saw that it was not James D'Egville – but his brother George D'Egville that was now standing before us and giving a slight bow as a greeting. "Good afternoon ladies. How may I be of service to you?"

Before I had the opportunity to explain to Mother, she launched into her tirade. "Well, for a start, you can explain to me what your intentions are for my daughter! What precisely is this 'meeting with benefactors' at Lord Craven's residence? And why do you feel that you have the arrogance – the outright rude impertinence to be offering my daughter silk dresses and rides in carriages without so much as asking her parents for permission? This seems to be a most immoral way of auditioning ballerinas. Now perhaps you may wish to show me the contract that you intended to offer my daughter. Or was to…" My mother trailed off her diatribe, very puzzled at first – but then becoming enraged to witness the laughter and tears that Mr. George D'Egville was trying his best to stifle. I was mortified.

"Do you think this funny, Mr. D'Egville? I fail to see any humour whatsoever in the ruination of a young girl's reputation! What a despicable man you are! I cannot find the words to express my sense of outrage! To think that you…"

"Mother please! Wait – there's been a terrible mistake!" I held my mother's arm back for I half feared that she would strike the poor man.

With a very charming grin, Mr. D'Egville spoke up. "I will be most happy to convey your sentiments to my brother James – who is the Mr. D'Egville that manages the theatre here. I do wish to apologise however if my behaviour seemed indelicate. For you see, I am only just now making the first acquaintance with your lovely daughter here. I do say that I have admired your delightful work at Drury Lane, Miss Searle. Allow me to introduce myself – I am George D'Egville. I am a composer and choreographer, although strictly speaking - I am not attached formally to the theatre here. However, I do lend my brother a hand from time to time."

"Oh dear, oh...I am quite embarrassed. I do apologise Mr. D'Egville." It was Mother's turn to look uncomfortable now.

"Honestly, there is no need! It is so very good to see a mother take great interest in protecting the virtue of her daughter. A highly commendable way to behave, and more parents should follow your lead, madam. I will be frank with you. I have no idea what my brother's intentions were, but as he is a man of sometimes...shall we say, rather libertine values, I will ensure that he alters his plans according to your wishes. I must add, and I'm ashamed to say this - I know that we are not looking for any dancers for the upcoming season, as far as I am aware."

Tears of frustration were starting to flow from my eyes uncontrollably. "I'm so sorry Mr. D'Egville. I feel foolish. I was just so eager to procure employment for when the season ends at Drury Lane. My family are very dependent on my being able to earn steady wages."

George looked at me kindly and said "Nonsense! There is no need to feel this way. This is all my brother's doing. Shame on him! Now, interesting that you mention that you are free this summer. Please take a look at what I am working on at the moment."

Mr. D'Egville folded his papers back to the title page. In bold, large script was *"The Wild Girl! or La Belle Sauvage"*. I could tell that the title was causing my mother a little bit of alarm.

"Do you remember the story of the French girl who lived in the trees as a savage? Mr. Cross, the manager of the Royal Circus has commissioned me to score the music for his new pantomime based on the tale. Mr. Cross is always looking for new talent. And the fact that you have been employed at Drury Lane will greatly increase your status and desirability. I'm very certain he would be interested in you joining for the summer. It is a beautiful theatre, recently refurbished – lots of spectacle. Performing animals, historical events portrayed in wordless pantomime, operettas and burlettas, dancing of all sorts. Oh, and John Cross is a very devoted family man, Mrs. Searle. Very trustworthy. I even believe your Drury Lane Cinderella, Miss Decamp, got her start there many years ago. If you would like, I would be happy to write you a letter of introduction and recommendation. I think you would make a remarkable savage myself!" He glanced over at my mother and to me with a mischievous grin.

"Mr. D'Egville, you are most kind. My daughter and I thank you for your thoughtfulness. I am terribly sorry for berating you so…"

"Never mind all that - it is in the past, and completely forgotten. I do wish you all the best, and just a bit of financial advice. I should hold out for £2 a week minimum with Mr. Cross…" George was brushing the plume against his lips before writing. "And the promise of a benefit night. A clear benefit performance will ensure that you take home the majority of the theatre's takings for that evening. A benefit night is also an indication that you are a performer of considerable importance. It will be great for your reputation as well as your finances. I should think that this all will be most acceptable to him, and hopefully it will go some way to helping out with the situation you are in at the moment. This is quite rude of me, but may I enquire as to the source of your current financial constraints?"

"My husband has taken very ill. He is a dance instructor. It has happened very suddenly, and we are not entirely sure how soon he may recover. Or even 'if'. I'm currently trying to sew costumes for the theatres as needed."

"Well, you may be in need of some summer work as well. I shall suggest that to Mr. Cross in my note here. If you wait just a moment, I will finish this letter for you in no time."

My innocence and stupidity could have easily led me down a wanton, wayward path. But fortune was smiling upon us, transforming awkwardness into opportunity. Mother and I heartily thanked George D'Egville for his courteousness and assistance. We immediately decided to seize the opportunity and make our way with the precious letter across the river towards the Royal Circus. I think Mother was a little stunned, as she did not say anything much as we wound our way down to Whitehall. We passed bustling Charing Cross, and then made our way beside the grand edifices of the Admiralty and Horse Guards. We walked briskly arm in arm – although I was depending on my mother for guidance, as I was not completely sure of where to go. The cold grey of winter did not penetrate as we were flushed with the warmth of this kind deed from Mr. D'Egville. Making our way over Westminster Bridge, I could see the bustle of the barge traffic below. People, horses, and carts spanning the river – going about their busy endeavours. I gazed upon each face I could see and felt the sense that here was yet another individual passing by – with their own lives and personal histories. Thousands of stories and tales whisking past as they got on with their busy day to day lives. And here was Mother and I, with our own unique fairy-tale story unfolding. It seemed that a new chapter was about to be revealed.

AN ACTRESS OF REPUTE

South of the river, the city had a most different feel to the area that I was most used to. Less developed and almost rural in parts, there was the impression that we were embarking upon a new frontier as we stepped off the bridge. I think I could count on my one hand the number of times I had ventured across the Thames before, so this was a rather unfamiliar experience for me. Making our way down the New Road, we soon passed the building site that would be the new Astley's Theatre; replacing the building that burnt down in a conflagration just last September. This was perhaps among the best known of the non-patent theatres, and the chief competition to the upstart theatre down the road that I was hoping to join. Offering amusements that did not require speech or dialogue was of key importance to theatres that were not officially sanctioned by the King. Plays at Drury Lane and Covent Garden were subject to approval and censorship by the government if the subject matter was deemed too political for the tastes of those in the seats of power. To skirt around this, the non-patent theatres enticed spectators in with promises of amazing horsemanship, tricks, and acrobatics. There was music on offer as well, with rounding choruses of patriotic tunes, and clever historical operettas that skirted past the dialogue ban by hoisting banners throughout the performances which described the actions taking place.

As we passed the Apollo Gardens, Mother began to tell me of the area's less than salubrious nature. The gardens were a rather down-at-heel version of Vauxhall Pleasure Gardens across the river, and she forbade me to ever enter there - lest I get myself mistaken for a girl who was eager to trade her body for monetary reward. She also pointed out the nearby Dog and Duck Tavern. A rather boisterous establishment with bawdy and base customers. I was beginning to feel slightly on edge and was pleased that she was accompanying me. At the big obelisk in the middle of the road, we stood near the theatre and looked at each other knowingly. There were cows grazing in the field opposite - adding to the sense of peculiarity that this area had. A strange mishmash of urban sprawl and agricultural idyll all in one odd package. Mother took a deep breath. With a positive look of eagerness as she faced me, we moved through the fine wrought iron gateway sporting three ornate gas lamps. We both looked to the steps of the theatre. She held my hand as she asked, "Shall we go?"

CHAPTER 12

The Royal Circus in St George's Fields.

The Royal Circus was a fine stone-constructed building in a Palladian style. Four fine white columns rising to hold a rather grand balcony. A triangular apex finished off the structure, topped with a magnificent statue of a Pegasus looking down upon us all. As much as my nerves compelled me to take flight, I took the winged horse as a secret positive message from my dear benefactress Athena. Indeed, the statue was reminiscent of the statuesque beasts I used to dance under on the porch of St. George's church. This happy thought put a smile to my lips as mother and I made the climb up to the door. Avoiding the Gallery door to the left and the Exit door to the right, we followed a carpenter carrying his woodwork in through the main entrance, enquiring as to the whereabouts of Mr. Cross.

Mr. John Cartwright Cross was a most amiable man in his mid-thirties. Thin, slightly balding and with a surprisingly heavy Scottish accent, the rather harried looking theatre manager kindly took the time to invite us in and asked us to take a seat in his small office just inside the grand, ornate theatre lobby. Mother introduced ourselves, stating that George D'Egville recommended that we should meet. He read through Mr. D'Egville's letter carefully and without hesitation offered us work to start as soon as my season at Drury Lane came to a close. In fact, he wanted me sooner, if possible. He was very accommodating, offering to dovetail performances to fit in with my obligations at Drury Lane. He was most eager to have a performer who could be billed as being from 'the Theatre Royal" on his roster, as this was good for business and helped to reassure the audience from the distinguished classes that he was hoping would attend. He stated that he would try to negotiate with Mr. Sheridan the possibility of extricating me from duties there – with the proviso that he would be working to build my status and stature as a performer in much the same way that Mrs. Mountain, Miss Decamp and Mrs. Johnston did back when they performed at the Royal Circus in the past. Just knowing that I too was following the same pathway as those fine ladies whom I had so much admiration for filled me with such pride and joy. As the theatre was much further from my home, he offered to ensure that my mother and I would be provided with a coach journey home each evening we worked – although we would have to make our way to the theatre before work ourselves. He was organising a number of coaches to transport his audiences home as well – helping to further placate those of a rather nervous disposition about the somewhat dubious location of the venue in Blackfriars. He also readily agreed to the salary request put forward by Mr. D'Egville. I could not believe how incredibly lucky I was!

Mr. Cross was a most prolific dramatist. He reeled off his plans for shows that he was planning for the Spring – all written by himself. He took time out briefly to show us the grand interior and discussed his intentions to try and rival the patent theatres. He spoke of the magnificent chandelier that he was planning on installing as a major draw to entice audiences. There was to be nothing like it ever seen before, he assured us. He had powerful, important friends, like the parliamentarian Sir Francis Burdett and William, Lord Craven (I almost winced at hearing the name – but fortunately Mother did not react) - who assured him that it would be possible to draw a higher calibre of clientele south of the river. By providing an elegant theatre with unmatched spectacles, he hoped to be able to outshine his immediate competition up the road at Astley's. I greatly admired his determination.

Mr. Cross very kindly said that he had heard exceptionally good things about me – particularly from Cinderella herself, Miss Decamp, who he was frequently in contact with. We had good news for Mother as well. He was very eager to get mother to work at the theatre immediately and offered to switch her position to help as a dresser once I started working – enabling us to work together closely. This was an offer Mother found impossible to refuse. She looked forward to drawing a regular salary; and would no longer be dependent on piecemeal work from the theatres north of the Thames. More importantly, she would be able to be my moral guardian; monitoring and protecting me from the dangers and vice that abounded in the world around me. Although I was less enamoured with the loss of my newly found independence, I tried to reassure myself that it could be useful protection should I encounter the likes of another Bella Menage here at the Circus. Mr. Cross bid us adieu and assured us that our contracts would be delivered to our home for us to sign and return. Mother and I held hands like little girls as we scurried down the steps of the theatre to the street below. Rushing around the corner out of any possible view of Mr. Cross, Mother hugged me with a squeal of excitement and a laugh. Heaven knows what any passers-by thought. We did not care! It was so wonderful to see that smile once again. It had been missing for so exceedingly long these past few months.

We walked briskly and excitedly back across the river, detouring to Aunt Harriet's to relay the good news to Tom and Papa. Along the way, we kept replaying the events of the day to each other; as if to reconfirm that they indeed actually did happen. Although our journey was long, the conversation made it seem like no time before we were strolling along the Queen's Walk, arriving at the gates of Aunt Harriet's idyllic farm.

CHAPTER 13

February 1804

*C**inderella* was continuing to be a magnificent success, guaranteeing me regular employment. With every appearance onstage, my sense of belonging at Drury Lane grew. None of Bella Menage's taunts could pierce my armour of newfound confidence. My performances were now second nature to me, and I no longer had a flutter of nervousness when stepping out in front of the adoring masses. I was further buoyed by the contracts for my mother and I from the Royal Circus. Mr. Sheridan readily agreed to an easing of my duties to enable my participation of rehearsals with Mr. Cross in March. He was looking to set a grand reopening of the theatre, aiming for maximum spectacle and publicity to ensure good audiences for my debut in April.

I took advantage of my sense of comfort by ensuring

that I watched my fellow thespians perform in the play before mine each night. I could not believe my good fortune to be able to see the full range of drama and comedy that the finest theatre in the land had to offer. I tried to observe the performers in detail – in order to try and absorb their techniques and expert ways. I felt that I was amidst the finest dramatic tutors in the land. And all for free! Each morning, I would face the cracked mirror of our house and try to imitate the poses that I witnessed, and to recite the dialogue that I had heard the night before. Out of all the fine performers of Drury Lane, of course my favourite was the incomparable Dorothy Jordan. Her talent and enthusiasm inspired my utmost devotion and attention. Her comedic flair was infectious – bestowing humour on even the most mundane and tedious of roles. The audience were simply compelled to adore her. I heard that she was commanding well over £30 a week – the very top ranking despite her being female. I felt she deserved every penny and more. She had earned my utmost admiration, despite her unorthodox living arrangements with her Duke. She was a strong, capable lady who had always shown me the greatest kindness. Even with her busy schedule, she would always be sure to take my hand and give it a warm squeeze by way of a greeting; or give me a warm wink and a smile whenever she saw me backstage or in the dressing room. These precious gifts can never be repaid, and I would treasure them always. Throughout my time at Drury Lane, I was always so very touched that she had made an effort to acknowledge me and make me feel welcome. Even though it cost her nothing, it was more valuable to me than if she had been handing me a bag of gold sovereigns.

And so, I watched Mrs. Jordan at every opportunity. Miranda in *The Busy Body*, the Widow Belmour in *The Way to Keep Him*, Viola in Shakespeare's *Twelfth Night*, and of course her most memorable role – that of Peggy in *The Country Girl*. And though there were other great talents onstage with her – such as the beautiful Miss Mellon, or the brilliant (but often inebriated) Mr. Cooke; I always had my gaze transfixed on my idol. One exception to the rule was on the evening of the 3rd. It was no fault of Mrs. Jordan's. She was adept as ever in her role as Belinda in the comedy *All in the Wrong*. The transgression was all mine, for I found myself staring helplessly at the character of Beverley. I was absolutely beside myself, as it was being portrayed by none other than the personification of male beauty himself – Mr. H. Johnston. To my great shame and embarrassment, I cannot tell you what the plot of the play was at all. I found myself studying his every move, trying to sear his lovely image upon my memory for all time; feeling all the more guilty in the knowledge that he was very much a married man. Yet any thoughts of his beautiful wife Nannette only led me to recall their argument in front of all the cast. How tightly he had gripped my trembling hand! The forcefulness of the anger and despair in his voice. And now, here he was before me – handsome, charming, eloquent, strong, and full of emotion. Try as I might, I could not stop myself from imagining being the source of his romantic inclinations. In my fantasy state, I could picture us being in lead roles together – I being Juliet to his Romeo. There would be much need for the practising of lines, and especially the rehearsal of the fair kiss. Yes – several times, this would need to be worked on to ensure perfection. And perhaps the need for me to run my fingers through his dark locks of hair as I gazed deeply into his warm amber eyes.

I found myself snapped out of this dreamlike state by the sudden waving of a fine masculine hand in front of my face. To my mortification, it was attached to one certain Mr. Henry Erskine Johnston, who had a beaming little boy smile - not unlike my little brother's. He must have spotted me from my vantage point behind a prop backstage, and he snuck over between scenes. "Yoo-hoo!!! Hello there!! You look deep in thought!" he whispered mischievously in my ear - so close to my ear that it felt a mere hair's width away from being a tiny delicate kiss. I could feel his breath caressing the back of my neck. I did not know what to say. I must have had the most surprised and dumbfounded look upon my face. Henry put his finger to his lips to try and guarantee my silence. He looked around to ensure that he wouldn't be caught out, then looked towards me with a most comical face imaginable. It was reminiscent of Mr. Cooke when he had drunk far too much wine in the Green Room. I had to put both my hands to my mouth to try and stifle the chortle that was fighting to emerge from my lips! I was tearing up, weeping as I gazed at him making one silly face after another to try and break my epic resolve. I held my hands to my chest – as I felt I could no longer breathe. Suddenly, he slowly waved a hand over his face and the character of Beverley re-emerged – only just in time for Henry to dart back onstage and deliver his lines. As he departed, he glanced over his shoulder and gave me a wink and a grin. I could feel myself beaming, and I knew that my cheeks must be flushed a rosy shade of red. I was savouring each moment of the encounter – lost in my own world, reliving each moment. I had a big ear to ear smile as I glanced behind me and noticed none other than Bella Menage looking at me like a sly fox as she delicately bit her lower lip. Without taking her eyes off me, she pursed her lips as if she had something wicked up her sleeve. I had a horrible feeling of panic start to well up in me. I took a deep breath and tried to compose myself. I thought hard and decided that I had to take the initiative this time and try to deliver a striking blow to Bella. What would she do? Would she try and find Mrs. Johnston to tell her of her husband's flirtatiousness?

I was certain that this was the opportunity that Bella was looking for. Nannette had taken on Maria Decamp's place in the role of *Cinderella* since the end of January. Bella had been working overtime to try and ingratiate herself with

Henry's spouse. She had two people to burn. Bella had not forgotten Henry's humiliating slights to her in front of everyone, and she always took every opportunity to make my life a misery. Somehow, I had to turn the tables on her. I was not absolutely certain of how I would accomplish it, but I had a thought of how to reveal her to be the evil, conniving creature that she really was. Unfortunately, time was of the essence; and I would have no time to try and refine my plan – or to think of the potential consequences. I swiftly moved back to the dressing room. I smiled and nodded to Miss Wentworth. This was her first performance as Venus, taking on Mrs. Mountain's part. She was busy undressing from the garb of Marmolet in *All in the Wrong* and starting to dress for *Cinderella*. I did not know what her impression might be of me after tonight, so I made sure to wish her well with her new role. Miss Tyrer was there as well – so one friendly face. Then Mrs. Byrne, and Miss Bristow – some more allies. In the corner I spotted her, wasting no time to disclose her gossip to a visibly shocked Mrs. Johnston. Steeling myself, I quickly made my way directly to the pair.

"Forgive me for interrupting, Mrs. Johnston, but I feel the need to have a word with this scheming, vile shrew that is bending your ear." I projected my voice loudly and confidently, for all to hear. I was trying to channel all my acting power, to pretend as if this were merely a role. Yes, here I was – Miss Elizabeth Searle in the backstage farce of *Who's in the Wrong*? I could feel the tension immediately. No one was used to hearing me speak in this way. I thought I could detect an audible gasp or two in the room. Whether Bella was feigning surprise or genuinely experiencing it, I know not which. "Why…what…?" she murmured.

"Miss Menage, I never had the opportunity to thank you for your kind introduction to Mr. D'Egville in the Green Room some time ago. For a moment, I thought perhaps you were demonstrating a rare moment of empathy or kindness. Mr. D'Egville relayed how he had heard of my family's unfortunate financial situation and my father's debilitating illness. As Mr. D'Egville is the respected ballet master of the King's Theatre, I presumed that he was going to offer me employment as a dancer at the Haymarket this summer. Now, do tell me Bella – and all the ladies here…when were you going to tell me that he actually was going to try and pimp me out as a whore?" I let the shock of that statement linger for a few seconds until the some of the gasps died down.

"The truth is you weren't going to tell me. You tried to set me up to experience the most shameful embarrassment imaginable. Thank goodness that my mother intervened, or I may have experienced a violation of my character that would be most unthinkable. Which could have stained my reputation permanently! How could you do such an unspeakable thing? I am young and I am having to support my family due to tragic circumstances. And you continuously play with my life as if it were a toy for your amusement. You should be thoroughly ashamed of yourself!"

Bella was very startled by my onslaught; but was feebly trying to regain her composure. "Why, Elizabeth…I had no idea! I was only trying to help. I had no insight as to what the intentions of Mr. D'Egville would be. In fact, all I did was introduce you. It was he who was making offers of support…"

Little Miss Tyrer piped up, looking incredulous and indignant. "You had no idea? No idea! EVERYONE in London knows that James D'Egville is a prime procurer and pimp – aside from his dancing duties. There is NO WAY that you can tell me that you did not know that this was going to happen. How spiteful! You really are a vindictive little…" Tutting and looking at Bella in disgust, she looked unable to find words that conveyed her true disdain for the lowly Miss Menage.

"It seems my husband may have been right all along." Mrs. Johnston interjected in a very calm manner. "Here I was, being kind and supportive when Henry was taunting you. Bella, I am beginning to think that you are not a very nice person after all. Oh, and do not try to bring up more of Miss Searle's supposed flirtations. I can see that she is a young lady who wishes to maintain her good virtue and would never contemplate transgressing the holy sanctimony of a marriage before God."

Nannette looked at me with an almost pious look of moral conviction. I had to work hard to maintain my composure through the intense glare of Mrs. Johnston, who was looking intently for any slight indication of guilt on my part. She certainly was no fool, but it seemed as if she was reserving the majority of her disdain for Bella at this point in time.

"I would suggest that you find more positive outlets for your idle time, Miss Menage – as gossip is rather tedious."

I was hoping that my feelings of underlying, hidden shame were not clearly transparent to all – for I know that a few minutes earlier, I would have been more than willing to cast virtue and sanctity aside in order to share a bed with her husband. Her gaze was meeting mine. We were making a pact – right here and now. Somehow, I felt that deep down she knew the truth. That Bella was truly a vicious troublemaker. And that this silly little girl fancied her potentially inconstant husband. But unlike Bella, I possessed a moral compass, and could be persuaded to follow the path of righteousness. How could I feel empowered and foolish at the same time? Yet I felt both of these emotions very strongly at that moment. Bella exited the room rather swiftly; but as she did, she cut me an icy glance on the way out. I may have won the battle, but not the war.

CHAPTER 14

Mrs SHARP,
of the
Theatre Royal Drury Lane.

Fortunately - for both my heart and my virtue, Mr. Johnston was now only rarely appearing in any productions at Drury Lane, due to provincial theatrical commitments. Nannette finished her engagement in *Cinderella* by the end of the week as Maria Decamp returned, thereby reducing my interactions with the wife of the man I had intense admiration for. There was a revival of *The Caravan*, in which she was engaged – but this time without her husband. Bella continued to be my regular tormentor. This was our routine. But she did seem to be a bit more guarded and wary of me than she had been before our dressing room stand down. Also, she was rather distracted by the attentions from her paramour Mr. Sharp. Mr. Sharp had been making increasingly frequent visits, finding most any excuse to try and be in the theatre in order to chance upon his betrothed. One afternoon, I saw him serenading her proficiently with an oboe in the orchestra pit. Another time, he was touching up backdrop scenery, and adding a likeness of her in surreptitiously. She was modelling for him in a love-induced languor.

Mr. Sharp was a genuinely nice man. One day, as I was idly eating some bread and cheese during a break, and he asked if he could join me and eat his lunch in my presence. As we chatted, he divulged to me his most embarrassing moment. He was serving his apprenticeship with the well-respected painter William Beechey at Windsor Castle, carrying out commissioned work for the King. In the midst of some detailed brushwork, he was startled by sudden cries of "Sharp! SHARP!!!" from the floor below. Unbeknownst to him, the word 'Sharp' was used as a call to attention amongst the King's servants. This was an alert that the King was imminently arriving, and all were to stand to attention. Thinking the cries of "Sharp!" were from his master Mr. Beechey - and thinking that he must be in a state of distress to be shouting so; he dropped everything in a hurry and started to scurry down the stairs. Low and behold, he smacked straight into King George himself and they both went tumbling down the stairs together. He reassured me (between our tears of laughter) that once His Majesty realised that his name was Sharp and it had all been a terrible mistake, he was most good-humoured about the incident. This self-deprecation and honesty endeared Mr. Sharp to me. I truly felt pity for him – he did not know what he was getting himself into. He was about to have a profoundly manipulative viper for a wife.

I took to calling Bella 'Bellicose' when she was out of earshot. She could not help but to spout off from her mouth – no matter who it was. I did take some comfort in seeing that she spread her bile wide and thin, with no regard to age or reputation of the recipient. One evening in the Green Room, an older gentleman actor, Ralph Wewitzer, was in attendance. Mr. Wewitzer tended to play relatively minor roles, but he was known chiefly for his ability to perform a myriad of dialects or accents. If you needed a devious Frenchman, a drunken Spaniard, or a stuttering Russian – he was a reliable choice. He was jovially divulging his observation to Mr. Sheridan – amongst several others, that very young actors seldom lived up to their potential promise once they had reached adulthood. Bella instantly quipped "Then, Sir, I suppose you were wonderfully great when you were a child…" and walked away smirking at her own cleverness.

In my case, she focused on taunting me about my lack of apparent roles at Drury Lane that were immediately upcoming. *Cinderella* was due to be winding down in March, and she had noticed that I did not appear to be any of the rehearsals for various other productions that were in the works.

"Bandy, are you feeling sad? I could not help but notice that you do not seem to figure in any of the new productions coming up. I am sure I could put a good word with Mr. Sheridan for you and get you a role as a charwoman, or perhaps a laundress. And you could always do those for real if your acting services were not required."

Although I did feel so tempted to boast about my prime roles coming up soon at the Royal Circus, I thought the better of it and held my tongue. I did not want to risk any chance of her scuppering my opportunities, so the less she knew about it the better. I was looking forward to a new challenge, and to working with my mother. *Cinderella* was a delight to perform, but my role was rather small, and it was starting to become routine. The thought of performing more complex roles appealed to me. It seemed that Mr. Cross had been busy creating a whole host of interesting dramatic operettas to perform. As these were wordless, it was to be very much a series of "dumb shows". On the positive side, it did not require me to memorise endless dialogue; something which I find very daunting. My performances would involve me conveying emotion through dance; or striking dramatic poses and attitudes whilst standing under explanatory banners.

One day in late March, mother and I met with Mr. Cross at the theatre as he had requested our presence. He was ready to have us start to work – mother helping with the costumes, and I to begin rehearsals. Mother was to be directly involved in aspects of the designs of the costumes in the productions that were planned for the spring and summer. Mr. Cross wanted to ensure that we both were very aware of the historical background and stories behind his dramatic pieces. He was a most intense man, and deeply passionate about his art and his theatre. He described his inspiration for the performance that I was to be in – *The Wild Girl! or La Belle Sauvage*. It was based on the story of Marie-Angelique Leblanc, a French girl who had apparently been living wild in the woods over 50 years ago. She had been caught stealing apples by local villagers. She could swing from branch to branch, and though she was dressed in rags and no shoes – she carried a club which she could use to deadly effect – killing the bulldog that the villagers set upon her. She could eat live chickens and rabbits with her bare hands. Mr. Cross had me elicit screams in front him and my mother, which caused me to giggle incessantly. He explained that Marie-Angelique had no form of communication, but she was well known for her piercing cries. Later, as attempts to 'civilise' her came into force, her health suffered. She became despondent, and the girl who could run as fast as the wind suddenly had no desire to do so. Mr. Cross wanted to spur our imaginations, and very kindly lent us books that would aid our understanding of the productions. I was given *An Account of a Most Surprizing Savage Girl*. We were also given John Gabriel Stedman's account of a slave woman that he fell in love with and married in Surinam. This would evolve into *Johanna of Surinam*, a show that Mr. Cross was developing for later in the season. I was enthralled to discover that I was to play the title character. Mr. Cross felt strongly that he must help to expose the evils of the slave trade, and he was eager to present a production that laid the crimes of slavery bare for all to see. And the summer season would conclude with *The Maid of Lochlin*, a Scottish romance set in ancient times that would no doubt showcase my ability to perform the hornpipe in front of an audience.

We made our way back to Aunt Harriet's after our meeting. Father has been steadily improving, and he has been able to take constitutional walks around the farm and Green Park. He has almost regained full speech, occasionally being at a loss for a word – only for a French replacement to sometimes spring forward. Yet I think Papa has been frustrated that he has not fully recovered. He is all too aware that he has not been able to carry out dance lessons, and perhaps thought that he never would again. We have all been finding him to be either a bit melancholy or irritable; despite trying to reassure him that we are so happy that he is still with us. For both Mother and I to be working has eased off some of the financial pressures, and we continually try to reassure him of that – so that he can focus on his recovery. But I sometimes fear that his low spirits will stagnate any potential progress. Seeing the sadness in my mother's eyes when they are together does nothing to alleviate my worries in that area.

Fortunately, my brother Tom has retained his cheerful disposition. His infectious laughter and enthusiasm for his farm chores have helped to buoy everyone who is in his presence. Great Aunt Harriet remains our rock and saviour, helping us through this trying time. So - all told, we have had many blessings. We sat down to a delicious stew and discussed all the happenings at the Royal Circus. Father sat listening with a soft, sad smile on his lips. Aunt Harriet reminisced "Oh, I do remember attending the old Circus – before it burnt down. And Astley's Theatre too! Such spectacles! Tell me Lizzie, will the audience even notice you? What with all the dog tricks, whistling siffleurs, prancing horses and tumbling acrobats?"

I laughed and relayed how I was to be the main character in each of the productions and listed prominently on the playbill as 'Miss Searle of the Theatre Royal, Drury Lane'! We then poured over the books that Mr. Cross had lent us, and Mother discussed her costuming ideas – how to turn me into a savage girl, a slave and then transform me into a Scottish princess.

Aunt Harriet begged, "Oh – do dance a hornpipe for us! I love to see you dance! There simply was not enough of you in *Cinderella*! I'd watch you any day over Miss Decamp!"

"Ugh! Here we go again!" groaned Tom.

"I do think you are terribly biased, Aunt Harriet...having worked with Miss Decamp, I've been amazed at her grace and..."

Suddenly there was a thumping on the table. I looked over to the source and saw that it was Papa, drumming out the beat of a reel with a delightful, mischievous glint in his eyes. I saw Mother clasp her hands to her chest in pure joy as she looked at Papa, and then to me. I stood up immediately and found the only clear space in the cramped little farm kitchen. Placing my feet firmly upon the dusty flagstone floor, I pointed my toe, lifted the hem of my dress – then gave a curtsy. On the next beat, I started to kick out the steps, moving my dress from side to side in time to the music – and giving a slight flash of my bare ankles in the process. Tom was giggling, and he stood up to perform his own clownish version of my dance beside me while clapping his hands. At that moment, a rare March sunbeam shone through the streaky windowpanes, focusing its warm yellow glow upon me as I performed. I felt myself flashing a huge smile uncontrollably. I could not remember when I last felt so naturally happy. Incandescent bliss!

CHAPTER 15

Westminster Bridge and Abbey by William Anderson

As March progressed to a conclusion, my thoughts were beginning to shift away from Drury Lane, and I began immersing myself into being the 'Wild Girl' of France. I began to take part in frequent rehearsals, as the finishing touches to the new Royal Circus Theatre were being put into place by busy workmen. I was pleasantly surprised to see a familiar face there. Mr. Male had been in the production of *The Caravan* with me at Drury Lane. He was practising scenes from the *Algerine Corsair* as I walked into the large auditorium. It was truly a novelty to be in a theatre with live horses in it. One of the animal handlers encouraged me to pat and handle one of the equine participants. There were many performers present. Mr. Cross was very organised and had us break up into groups based on which performance we were to be in. To my relief, I was not the only person that was new to the theatre. I discovered that I would have to be able to manage quite a repertoire of shows simultaneously. For the grand opening, I would be taking part in a pantomime – *Cybele; or Harlequin's Hour*. I was to play the main love interest, fair Columbine. And Mr. Male was to perform with me, making me feel a bit more at ease. I quickly got the impression that egos were not an issue here. Performers introduced themselves to me and stated how pleased they were to have me join in their company. Several had seen me in *Cinderella*, and they were very complimentary about my performance. If my insecurities had not ensured my continued humble modesty, I could have easily succumbed to developing an inflated ego here.

Until the season at Drury Lane completely wound down, I would be doing quite a bit of juggling. I had performances of *Cinderella* to still take part in, as the show was still very much in demand. There were also benefit performances to think about in support of my fellow thespians at the theatre in May and June before everyone went on their way to the provinces for the summer season. When not at Drury Lane, all my time would be taken up with practices and performances at the Royal Circus. I was so impressed with the professionalism and hands-on approach to the running of the theatre by Mr. Cross. It was such a contrast to the aloof and outright disrespectful approach of Mr. Sheridan. Mr. Cross wanted to ensure that the Circus stood up to comparisons with the Royal Patent theatres, and he was most eager to entice people of quality to this rather out of the way locale that had a somewhat dubious reputation. Every consideration was being reflected upon and addressed: riveting productions based on the most exciting stories of the time, sumptuous backdrops and rich costuming, plush interiors that were comfortable and had excellent sight lines to the stage from every vantage point, and even working to ensure that suitable transportation was available at the end of the evening for all the patrons to make their way home in safety. He demonstrated boundless energy and enthusiasm, and one could sense the great deal of pride he had in his theatre. His positive attitude was infectious, and rather than seeing the bickering and grumbling that was so demoralising at Drury Lane – all who worked at the Circus felt a vested interest and comradery that was truly inspirational. It was so very refreshing for me to witness, and it helped me to realise that theatre life did not have to follow Mr. Sheridan's model.

Despite my love for my new theatrical home, I did have to recognise the immense favour that being at Drury Lane had done for me. I had launched straight into the largest, most respected theatre in the land – one where most of the working actors in the profession would be desperate to be onstage at. Just being there, even for such a brief time in a miniscule role, provided me with a cachet of respectability and professionalism that most of my cohort at the Circus had failed to acquire – even after decades of working. Mr. Cross was using it to his advantage in promoting the new production in *The Morning Chronicle* announcements: "Miss Searle, from the Theatre Royal, Drury Lane, her first appearance on this stage." I could scarcely believe that anyone would have the slightest interest in this inconsequential young performer. But perhaps I should have a bit more confidence in myself. Mr. Cross certainly seemed to put his faith in me – feeling certain that I could shine as a key performer throughout the summer in several big productions that he had planned. If he believed in me, perhaps I should also? I have always felt hubris to be so very unbecoming. And yet a strong sense of self-belief propelled Bella Menage ever forward in her career. The women of the stage I admired so – Miss Decamp, Miss Tyrer, Miss Bristow, Mrs. Mountain, Mrs. Jordan - they all demonstrated a confidence that was unshakable from my viewpoint. Maybe it was time to side-line this self-doubt that wormed and niggled at me so. No good can possibly come of it. But still this one question haunted me. The question that I had put out of my mind for all this time until my insecurities start to take hold. What exactly did Mother write in that pleading letter to Mr. Byrne that made him decide to give this little girl a chance? And did I deserve it on my own merit?

This was a query that of course I could never bring myself to discuss with my mother. And besides – what matter would it be now? We both were in a much better position – the best that we had been since Father first fell ill. Mother had copious amounts of costume work to prepare. And she seemed to almost thrive in her return to the world of theatrics. I had noticed a blissful sense of joy in her that I had never before witnessed – even when Papa was in the rudest of health with numerous clients booked for his lucrative lessons. To be fair, a contributing factor to the positive outlook was that our worries about Father were reducing daily as improvements to his constitution were becoming increasingly evident. His speech – whilst slurred, was beginning to return to the use of wit and clever quips that we all loved so. With a walking stick at hand, he was taking more frequent walks about Green Park with Tom. Although uncoordinated on one side, his body was beginning to limber up. His appetite and strength were returning as well; and if he were unable to dance physically, we did hope that maybe he would soon be able to parley his instructions verbally to his students of musical movement. Luck seems to have smiled upon us through the dusts of misfortune.

Aside from Mr. Male and the well-known and respected Mr. Montgomery, there were some other notables from the theatrical world who were to be our partners at this circus of talent. Amongst the skilled horseman, dog-trainers, whistling siffleurs and acrobats was the elegant Madame Volange. She was the wife of a celebrated French comedian (and he the son of an even more renowned actor). She was due to have the prime role of Alzira in *The Algerine Corsair*. Gifted at all things operatic, and equally so in acting and movement – I found her enchanting and mesmerising in equal measure. She was very adept at the English language, which she spoke with a charming and elegant French flourish. Mother and I would sit and converse with her during costume fittings and adjustments. She was full of amusing stories of the Bon Ton and their extravagant theatricals. For some time now, it has been the fashion for those of great means to perform various dramas and musical pieces within their stately homes. This must give the opportunity for bored young ladies and idle gentlemen to channel their energies into something creative and purposeful. These spectacles would then be displayed in their own makeshift theatres or ballrooms in front of other citizens of wealth who had nothing better to do with their lives. Madame Volange and her husband would often be hired to coach the painfully amateur actors; or give vocal instruction and encouragement to the squawking, tone deaf chorus of unfortunates before their feted debut performances. Her recounting of incidents was absolutely hilarious and had Mother and I nearly weeping with laughter.

"Zey are dreadful! Woeful little beasts who zink zey 'ave some talent! Oh, my poor ears! What zey 'ave endured! And my 'usband and I – we must pretend we enjoy…I tell you, we only zink of za money and we smile…as if we enjoy. We imagine we are watching the amazing Monsieur Talma, or pretend we listen to Mademoiselle Rosine sing a beautiful aria. But ze reality is that it is all *merde*!" Her delivery of speech was an example of comic effect perfection!

"Ah, one time we perform for the Countess of Cork – in her home. What a name! Sounds as if she is from a bottle of the wine, no? And she likes to drink ze wine – indeed! At least she has good sense – no amateurs running about ruining things. Only my husband and I. We performed a play by Patrat, *La Resolution Inutile* – all in French, and we play all the parts. But she and the audience – zey all drink ze wine and 'ave no idea what is 'appening in ze play. No idea! Zey are all so confused, you can see from their faces. But zey say nothing. Only smile and then more drinking. They are so drunk! Just sit there – pretending to understand and to enjoy. Zey zink zey are so clever! Nobody knows. Incomprehensible! Imbeciles! And there is one particular man – so fat and disgusting. He drinks and he is talking all through our play. I hear him speak French under his breath…he is muttering something. It sounds French, but like a drunk man speak – it makes no sense to me. Only words – strange words. I think he try to recite something clever – waving 'is 'and in ze air as he speak, but it only sounds like stupid drunk man. After we finish, I ask someone…who iz zat 'orrible, strange man? I mean no disrespect – truly, but I must tell you who it was. None other than ze Prince of Wales!"

She held up her finger – pointing for dramatic emphasis, then sucked in air feigning shock. She clasped her hands to her chest, then to her cheeks. "I turn red – so embarrassing! I want to leave there at that moment. And the person looked at me – kind of shocked but also understanding. Because he know it is truth, zis prince is rather – umm, how you say…vile? But zis is the reason why we chop off ze heads of all our royals in France! It is a sensible thing to do, no?" She told all of this with such glee and merriment – even if we were fervent Royalists, we would still be enamoured so by the utterly delightful Mrs. Volange.

Final preparations for the grand opening on the 2nd of April were underway. Fine gold gilt was applied to the woodwork of the plush stage boxes and flowers were arranged decoratively around, providing a riot of colour. The lower boxes were festooned with a fine crimson satin cloth draped ornamentally over the sides. A circular vision of the heavens was painted on the ceiling above, complete with cherubic angels gazing down upon the audience below. Horses practiced their paces on the soft ground of the circus – ringed by the seating areas and stage. The skilled craftsmen were all industriously toiling to complete the mechanisms of the clever pantomime tricks. Exotic backdrops were being readied by the frenzied prop artists.

Mother was at work with the costumes, helped by other seamstresses and dressers. Musicians were in the orchestral pit practicing with the conductor, the talented Mr. Sanderson.

The actors and dancers tried to find space to rehearse as best they could. Fortunately, my role was a traditional Columbine. In most pantomimes, the primary requisite was for one to look especially pleasing to the eye. In this instance, I was to draw the attentions of Watty Wiseacre – played by the kind Mr. Betterton. Aside from being pretty, I had to occasionally be pulled along running by Mr. Betterton as we occasioned to escape some calamity or other – usually presided by one of Mr. Montgomery's numerous characters, or Mr. Ridgeway's Harlequins. A couple of opportunities to perform a pleasant dance, and my work was done. I spent the majority of the practice time trying to calm the nerves of the Welch girl. Miss Salkeld was performing onstage for the very first time and was a bundle of nerves. Also, she seemed to be in absolute awe of me for some strange reason. This left her frequently dumbstruck and almost incapable of moving. I had to constantly reassure her that I was a mere mortal, and not a miraculous, celestial being.

I felt for Mr. Cross at this time. Not only were there the worries of all the preparations within his own theatre to ensure all was ready. He was also very much aware of the competition for entertainment. Firstly, Drury Lane and Covent Garden were still offering performances – not yet starting the winding down of the season, which was marked by frequent benefit performances to help enhance the finances of the particular performer who had arranged the special entertainments of the evening in conjunction with their co-workers. It would be difficult to lure away from their pre-paid subscription boxes those patrons of quality that Mr. Cross was hoping to attract South of the river to the theatre he had invested so much into. Secondly, it was also the opening evenings for many of the non-patent rival theatres. To the North was the Sadler's Wells. The novelty it provided was the ability to recreate naval battles onstage in a huge pool of water. By comparison, it made the lake that Carlo the dog paddled in onstage at Drury Lane look like a mere puddle. No doubt many would be drawn in by the spectacle of witnessing the naval siege of Gibraltar in miniature form.

Closer by was our direct arch-rival: Astley's Circus. Replacing a previous version of the theatre, the new Astley's was a bright affair – with mirrored columns, sumptuous morocco leather seating, rich gilt ornamentation, and a most magnificent chandelier. Their entertainments featured similar thrills to offer the audience: horse tricks, clowns, and memorable music. They had the further advantage of being much nearer the river. Our audience would have to make considerable efforts to find their way to us. As if these competitors were not formidable enough, with improved weather our potential audiences would face further temptations as the pleasure gardens began to open. Vauxhall and Ranelagh offered musical entertainments and dining options, in addition to spacious natural attractions to lure potential visitors. All of this must have been daunting for Mr. Cross, and no doubt he must have felt the weight of anxiety on his shoulders; yet he did well to put on a brave face and carried on as best as he could under the circumstances.

At last, the day finally arrived. After a weekend of frantic last-minute preparations, the Royal Circus Theatre was as prepared as it was ever going to be – eagerly awaiting arrivals from half-past five. Mother and I set off a bit earlier than usual, packing a lunch of bread and cheese to eat somewhere along the way. It was quite warm and sunny for an early April day, so we decided to have a pleasant, albeit long, stroll to the workplace. Mother was concerned that it would tire me out or injure my feet, leaving me unable to dance. But I insisted that the walk would do me good – alleviating any opening night jitters I might possess.

Working together with mother was such a comfort after my struggles with a certain actress at Drury Lane. Our journeys to and from the Royal Circus brought us closer together. There were no chores or unavoidable tasks – just a destination and a time for arrival. During these times we reminisced about the past. Mother's past still seemed to be a closed book and I did not press her to reveal what she did not wish to share. But she was more than happy to speak about my childhood and the joys of child-rearing. Being engrossed in conversation served as a wonderful distraction from worrying about being a crime victim as we moved through the rather threatening neighbourhood of Seven-Dials. We could smell the delicious fresh loaves of the hot loaf man on St. Martin's Lane and immediately regretted having carried our own rather stale loaf from home along with us. Avoiding the doormat seller as we ventured past Charing Cross, we giggled like little girls while gossiping about the lively characters that were now our co-workers at the theatre. Walking past the grand edifices of Whitehall, we reflected on the challenging circumstances of the past year and how we appeared to overcome all the adversity that life was throwing our way. We discussed Papa's continued recovery and debated whether he should remain recuperating with Aunt Harriet or look to he and Tom rejoining us on Hart Street. I suspect that Father would greatly prefer the latter, as he desperately wished to enjoy his home comforts again. Before we knew it, we had arrived at the Westminster Bridge. Finding a good spot to huddle down into on the bridge, we unwrapped our lunch and ate while admiring the fine views.

To the North was the magnificent Westminster Abbey. Looking at Westminster Hall, we thought of the current parliamentary squabbles taking place. It was a great sign of Papa's improving constitution that he could enthusiastically report to us the latest political goings on, despite us having virtually no interest or comprehension of what he was speaking about. We laughed as we both professed to not knowing the difference between a *Pittite*, *Foxite* or *Grenvellite*. I could proudly say that I remembered the name of the Prime Minister – Henry Addington. Mother said that I should be prepared to learn a new name, for he might not remain Prime Minister for long.

Looking South, we admired the distant verdant, green hills. I pointed out a gently rotating windmill like an excited toddler. Mother pointed out the handsome red bricks of Lambeth Palace to me and wondered if the Archbishop were in, attending to all his bureaucratic religious duties – whatever they could possibly be. I clearly could see our circus rivals at the Astley Theatre and wished that we were as close to the river. But alas! We were not and we had to continue on with our travels.

As we moved along the Bridge Road passing cows grazing near fields that were interspersed with buildings that one was more likely to see in the city, I remarked to Mother how odd it was that anyone would choose this location for a theatre. As I spoke, I noticed an exceptionally fine carriage, complete with footmen and a driver, pulling up outside a rather grand building labelled as The Asylum. Out came two very elegant ladies. Mother said that the Asylum was a home and school for unwanted, orphaned girls; helping them to learn a trade and avoid a life of vice. The fine ladies were most likely benefactors who were coming to inspect what the proceeds of their charitable donations were resulting in. Finally, with the welcoming obelisk of St. George's Circus in front of us, we arrived at our destination.

Although only a few hours from opening to the public, the theatre was still frantic with the last-minute finishes and flourishes of the workmen. Moher bade me to follow her to the dressing rooms. She fetched a bowl of cool water as she sat me down on a stool, then undid my shoes. She lovingly placed my feet in the refreshing liquid and massaged them back into a revived state.

"There! That is much better, isn't it?" she said, with a rare loving look towards me. All my life, Mother had been so busy and harried that we never had such moments to share together. My eyes were starting to well-up from the sentiments behind this simple little gesture.

"I should be doing this for you, Mother!"

"Nonsense! It is a mother's duty and a pleasure! I've been bathing you since birth, so why stop now?" We both smiled at each other, as Mother continued. "You know, we are all so immensely proud of you Elizabeth. You have been our beacon of light in this darkest of situations."

I blushed from this rare example of praise from my most stern and critical parent. Papa was usually the one to liberally sprinkle me with praise with every little thing that I did.

"Just to inform you, Elizabeth – with all the competition out there for entertainment this evening, we as a family thought we should support kind Mr. Cross in the best way that we possibly could. And so, your Aunt Harriet has purchased tickets for tonight's performance. Papa and Tom were most excited, for they had heard that a most excellent dancer from Drury Lane Theatre would be performing tonight."

"Mother – how could you keep such a secret from me? How could you not let me know that Bella Menage was to be dancing at this theatre?" We both laughed heartily. I was so thrilled and proud to have my family share in this moment with me. I felt so very honoured. Drying my feet, Mother encouraged me to go and prepare – even though it was far too early to be doing such a thing. Giving her a big hug and a gentle kiss on the cheek, I made my way to transform myself into the most beautiful Columbine that London would see.

CHAPTER 16

I was going to have to endure a considerable amount of spectacle before I was to appear on stage. *Cybele* was to be the afterpiece, as my pantomime was to serve as a long-awaited finale to the evening's proceedings. I loved the spirit of camaraderie amongst all the performers. It felt like I was with family – so vastly different from the pit of back-biting snakes at Drury Lane.

The theatre did look resplendent as the audience began to trickle in. The beautiful painted ceiling, complete with cherubs gazing down upon us from the heavenly skies. It was still such a novelty for me to see such a huge empty space in front of the stage, all made of compacted soil – reserved for the true stars of the show, the performing horses, and acrobats.

Of course, amongst the first to arrive were my most

adoring admirers – my family. I made my way up to their seats and spoke with them for as long as I dared. Smiling and waving, I retreated backstage and continued to spy upon the proceedings. Although a healthy sized audience, by the beginning at half past six the auditorium was still by no means near full. A disappointment for Mr. Cross, no doubt. Perhaps the seats would fill as the prices dropped halfway into the evening.

The entertainment began with the expert horsemanship of Mr. McKene and his crew. Although I had seen the rehearsal, to see the event live alongside the audience was absolutely amazing. I was so impressed that the horses did not react to the shouts and applause from all who were watching. In fact, they seemed to thrive on the frenzied atmosphere, as did the riders themselves. Standing on the horses, jumping onto each other's, doing handstands. It was all simply enthralling! Then Mr. Belcher arrived as the clown to lighten the mood with his silly antics amongst the horses. All in all, this was an excellent start to the evening.

Next was the burletta, *Renegadoes or Algerine Corsair*. This was another of Mr. Cross's well-researched entertainments based on true historical events for which he was renowned. Berber pirates, kidnappings and battles on both land and sea; this story was compelling despite there being no dialogue. Horsemanship sustained the action scenes alongside a thrilling musical score provided by the orchestra. Sails and masts were hoisted onstage to give the appearance of being onboard a grand ship. The vocal talents of Madame Volange were enthralling and the most experienced actors in the troupe were at hand, lending their skills: Mr. Belcher, Mr. Male, Mr. Betterton, Mr. Ridgeway, and Mr. Bradbury amongst them. Their talents and cool, professional heads were needed – for I witnessed a most horrific tragedy take place. A certain Miss Taylor was playing the part of the soon to be aptly named 'Unfortunate Victim'. A piece of stage scenery – a background of the port of Algiers, suddenly snapped away from the rope suspending it from the stage. I heard gasps and a few screams from the audience. Fortunately, most of the cast were not near or were able to deftly move away from the falling object. But Miss Taylor was not aware of the unfolding danger and was struck squarely on the head. She went careening towards the pit. Mr. Slader, who was playing the part of a drunken ship's cook, snapped quickly to attention and was able to grab hold of her before she fell off the stage and prevented any further damage to her head.

To my shock, I was unable to speak. I caught a glimpse of some of the stagehands rushing to carry her backstage. My reflexes seemed to startle me into action. I found some linen cloth lying about. I quickly grabbed it and rushed to Miss Taylor. She seemed to be in a stupor. She was sobbing but did not seem capable of movement or verbal coherence. Noticing a gash on her forehead, I mopped up the streaming blood that was sliding down past her and dripping onto her neck. I was pleased to see that the wound was only superficial. Mother came and relieved me of my duty, assuring me that everything would be alright. She was speaking to Miss Taylor in a calm soothing manner as they moved her further to the back of the theatre, near an exit.

I was completely unnerved by this incident. Was it an omen or a portent of further misfortunes? I had expected that the show would be at a standstill. Perhaps all the performances would be cancelled for the evening. As I turned toward the stage, I saw a very terse, serious looking Mr. Cross barking out orders in a most assertive whisper. To my amazement, the cast continued with the play immediately. The whole commotion interrupted the proceedings for no more than a single minute. Everyone continued their roles in the most assured way imaginable. I saw Mr. Cross wipe his sweaty, furrowed brow with his damp sleeve. He looked so stressed. This was certainly not the kind of publicity that he wanted for his elegant new theatre. I decided to retreat to the Green Room to try and regain my composure.

The scene as I entered through the door was rather surreal. The room was mostly empty except for the female cast members of the third show of the evening, a pantomime by the name of *The Dwarf*. The ladies were already in full costume and make-up, ready to step on the stage when called to do so. Huddled together on a pink chaise longue and in tears, the women were all quaking with fear. Miss Dennet was a magical vision of beauty. Dressed as a sylph, complete with fairy wings, her tears accentuated her deep amber eyes which were framed by ample, flowing locks of curly brown hair. Miss Harrison, portraying a mighty sorceress, looked as meek as a mouse. Mrs. Helme, was portraying the daughter of the sorceress. This struck me as being most peculiar, as she was obviously older than the woman portraying her mother. Perhaps Miss Harrison was in possession of some time-altering sorcery. But then my eyes were trying to discern who the two tiny beings were in their midst. It finally dawned on me that one was little Miss Lettin portraying Cupid, and the other was Miss Johannet who was actually the dwarf for whom the show revolved around. It suddenly dawned upon me that this was the very first time any of them had ever been on the stage before. They all looked to me as if wise and experienced Merlin had entered the room. Little Miss Johannet was the only one who could muster any sort of communication.

"Miss! Miss Searle! What has happened? Please tell us! We heard screams and saw poor Miss Taylor! Is it safe? Will the show continue? What are we to do?"

The questions came in quick succession, preventing me from being able to interject an answer. And I must admit that I found it extremely difficult to concentrate on the content of the question, as the diminutive Miss Johannet spoke in a most peculiar, squeaky fashion. I am afraid to say that I was just staring at her tiny features, comparing them with the little 6-year-old Cupid bawling inconsolably behind her. Suddenly I realised that I was gawping in silence, as the questioning had finished, and all eyes were transfixed upon me. Quickly gathering my faculties together, I truly astounded myself with the conviction and maturity of the words that I uttered.

"Ladies, as you may be aware, there was a most unfortunate incident that has just occurred. It seems that a piece of scenery broke loose and has struck Miss Taylor upon her head." I was temporarily unable to continue as the women all began to wail hysterically, weeping and squeezing each other for comfort. I was beginning to find them all rather ridiculous. "Ladies, please gather your composure! You are professionals! The show is continuing now as we speak. Look out there now and tell me – do you see Madame Volange out on the stage weeping and panicking? Mr. Cross has told everyone to continue with the show. As far as I am aware, we will all be performing as expected, and you all will need to be on that stage, entertaining the audience who have paid money to have a good time."

I'm not sure if my words were having the desired effect. Miss Johannet again spoke up, in what I was now finding to be a most irritating, whiny drone of a voice.

"But what if more scenery falls? What if it hits us? We will die! Die like Miss Taylor! Oh NOOO!!! I don't want to die! Please don't let me die!"

"Miss Taylor will be fine. I wiped her head wounds myself. The bleeding was all superficial and…"

"BLOOD? Oh, she's gonna bleed to death! Poor Miss Taylor is bleeding! Did you hear? She's bleeding!"

Miss Johannet was whipping the others up into a frenzy. Little Cupid was crying – and I am certain that she did not understand why. The adult women weren't much better, to be honest. Here I was, not even 15 years old and playing the part of wise counsel. Athena – help me! I was starting to question myself. Was this a farce? Would the curtains open

AN ACTRESS OF REPUTE

for me to see that I was just playing a part in some improvised comedy?

I decided to change tactic. I was not awfully familiar with most of these ladies, having only met them briefly once before. But I did know Miss Dennet slightly better, for she was primarily a dancer and we had been practicing some routines together. She also seemed to be the one most in control of her faculties among this silly little group. I called to her to stand up next to me.

"Do you think Miss Taylor would wish for us to behave in this way? I am sure that she would want as little fuss made over this as possible and would beg us to carry on regardless of the circumstances. Now Mr. Cross and his crew will make every effort to ensure the safety of the scenery after this calamity. Miss Dennet will start to lead you all in a practice to ready yourselves for your performance. I haven't yet had the opportunity to see your show and I would be most excited to see a preview!" To be honest, I had no idea what Miss Taylor would have wanted from us and Mr. Cross may have been leading us all into a death trap like the Pied Piper for all I knew, but I certainly wasn't going to let them know that. Miss Dennet seemed willing, but Miss Johannet did not seem to want to let the misery of this tragedy to end.

"I…I…I CAN'T DO IT!!!" snivelled the wretched little being and my patience just snapped.

"Miss Johannet, you HAVE to do it. There is no choice! Pull yourself together! Now, present to me your performance!"

"But Mr. Betterton and Mr. Ridgeway aren't here. We can't perform the play without them." True, the male actors were all busy being Algerines onstage at that moment.

"Well just perform the parts that they aren't in."

"But they are in every scene."

"Well…" I suddenly remembered, "They don't have any dialogue! These are all dumb shows!"

"But they sing."

"Well, you will just have to sing their songs."

"But we don't know their words." Miss Johannet had an answer for everything. She annoyed me intensely.

Fortunately, tiny Cupid piped up and came to my rescue. "I know the words!"

"There you have it! Problem solved! Let us begin then, shall we?" I then had to watch a very miserable, wretched facsimile of the joyous pantomime take place in an ad-hoc fashion before my eyes and ears. Miss Johannet protested that they did not have the needed props and that Mr. Betterton would perform magic onstage as they danced; but with my reminder of the power of imagination, the rehearsal was able to continue. I was most relieved when the *Algerine Corsair* drew to finish around ten minutes later. As the actors began to trickle in, I wished them good luck, made my excuses, and escaped to the dressing room with my sanity just about intact.

I found a quiet corner and put on some finishing touches to my Columbine persona. Apprehensive thoughts were trying to creep into my mind as the words of irksome Miss Johannet seemed to worm their panicked way into my brain. I was pleased to see Mother return. She reported that Miss Taylor was shaken but more lucid. She was taken home where a night's rest may go some way towards restoring her back to herself once more. Mother seemed to be able to read my worried, anxious thoughts. She said that the stagehands were carefully inspecting the set pieces and scenery now before the start of *The Dwarf*. She made some minor adjustments to my costume and lovingly attended to my hair, ensuring that every strand was in perfect position. She enlisted my help in preparing Miss Salkeld and Miss Harrison with their costumes. They were quite rattled by the incident with Miss Taylor and needed reassurance. I found that the more I spoke, the more I began to believe in my platitudes.

I had a bit of a lump in my throat as the prompter called for all the *Cybele* cast to gather backstage. Mother gave me a big hug, put my face into her two hands and said "Enjoy it! Do what you do best – now go! Dance!" I smiled and felt as if I had wind bolstering my sails. Gathering together, I looked and smiled at my amazing colleagues who were breathing hard from their quick costume change. Indeed, for poor Mr. Ridgeway it was his third change this evening: transforming from a tent dwelling Berber to a Prince and now the mischievous Harlequin. He seemed to bear no complaints as he smiled back at me with a glint apparent in his masked eyes. To half-hearted applause, the orchestra struck up a tune and the show began. I felt as if I were transformed. Did Athena have a hand in this? As I stepped out, I was met by rapturous applause. It seemed that not only my family recognised me, but I did have other admirers as well. Mr. Betterton as Watty Wiseacre made lovesick, exaggerated glances at me as I pirouetted gracefully across the stage. I swear that I could sense gasps of enchantment from the audience. Perhaps it was a special energy emanating from the room. For me to hear subtle noises over the audience would have been nigh impossible. But that positive effervescence buoyed me immeasurably. It seemed but a fleeting moment before we were all gathered together to take our final bows. At that instant, I forced myself to drink in that moment. Looking out, I could see Little Tom, Papa and Aunt Harriet all on their feet and beaming with pride. My eyes moved around, and I saw that everyone I looked at seemed enthralled with the evening's entertainment. Although the theatre was not anywhere near capacity, my heart was full to the brim.

CHAPTER 17

April was a rather peculiar month. I felt as if I were not completely whole. Much of my time was at the Circus, performing as Columbine in *Cybele*. But *Cinderella* was still proving immensely popular, requiring my presence at Drury Lane once or twice a week. If Bella Menage knew of my new endeavours South of the river, she made no mention of it. I did press Miss Bristow to keep it a secret, if possible. But I had no idea if anyone, other than Mr. Grimaldi and Miss Bristow, were aware of my undertaking at the Royal Circus. But if any were to read the papers, they would certainly glance at the notices highlighting the appearance of "Miss Searle from the Theatre Royal Drury Lane". Just seeing that in print made me feel like royalty. Papa bought a playbill when he, Tom and Aunt Harriet attended my debut. I was taken aback to see it in a frame when I next visited Aunt Harriet's little cottage. They all anxiously waited to see if I would notice it on the wall. But as the framed parchment took pride of place above the hearth in the sparsely furnished cottage, it did not take long for me to spot it. Papa had a glint in his eye from my arrival, so I knew immediately to be on my guard. Although slightly embarrassed by the fuss, I did secretly enjoy the special attention.

But though I was treated with an air of admiration and deference at the Circus, Drury Lane would always bring any arrogance or pride on my part crashing down. I always felt I was a mere paeon. If ever I forgot, Miss Menage's hateful condescension was nearly always present to make me feel worthless and miserable. She always made a point to speak to others in my presence about her latest prominent roles and then to ask me what I was working on currently – knowing full well that I had virtually no other work on outside of *Cinderella*.

"I have to say, playing the part of Columbine in *Love and Magic* is keeping me so busy! It seems I am always on stage – I can't believe it is on almost every night this week. I'm afraid my legs will give out from all this dancing!" Looking in my direction haughtily, Bella then addressed me. "Bandy – I don't think I saw you there. Most odd, I thought you called yourself a dancer!"

I did in fact have a very brief pantomimic solo performance as a flower seller, dancing with a basket of roses for a few fleeting moments. It was actually very irritating, for often I had to perform, quickly race outside to an awaiting carriage arranged by Mr. Cross, and fly like the wind across the city to perform at the Circus. Mr. Grimaldi was playing Tycho the Clown opposite Miss Menage, but he was not in the scene following mine. He would always kindly escort me out the door to the correct carriage and bid me good luck, bless him! It really endeared him to me, this thoughtful brother-in-law of Charlotte. Mr. Grimaldi often had to be in two theatres at once – racing from Saddler's Wells to the West End frequently. I honestly do not know how he could cope with such stress. On arrival at the Circus, Mother would be waiting to quickly dress me then see me to the stage. In practice, his actually only occurred on nights where there were scheduling conflicts, but when this did happen – I was absolutely frantic.

"Bella, she's the flower seller – remember?" Miss Hicks unhelpfully reminded her. I think that this was purposeful and that she was in league with Bella to torment me.

"You mean on the street? Has she had to resort to that – it will be playbills or apples next, no doubt."

"No, No! You remember – lots of people come onstage and do their own individual little piece – Mrs. Grimaldi, and your sister Mary. It's when you have a brief break from all that performing, and you can have a costume change."

"Ah yes!!! That's right! I remember now – seeing Bandy run offstage and out the door in shame! Obviously, you must have embarrassed by your pathetic attempts at keeping in time to the music. Really Bandy, you are going to have to get used to these disappointments. People are going to tell you the truth when you prove to be an inadequate dancer for the stage. You mustn't take it to heart and run out the door in bitter shame and tears. I am certain that there is someplace where you will be appreciated for what you can do. Why, I am sure that I heard Mr. Cooke needs a charwoman. And you can clean up his vomit when he drinks too much. Now tell me Bandy, where do you scurry off to in such a hurry when you leave us so sadly?"

"I think Miss Searle has better things to do than respond to your wicked little taunts. Why don't you spend your time more productively? I am sure there's a spare mirror in the dressing room where you could stare at yourself and laugh at your witty insults. That should keep you amused for several hours I should think."

I turned to find the wonderful Miss Decamp had come to my rescue having witnessed Bella's relentless bullying of me. Miss Menage and her minion silently turned and withdrew without responding. Miss Decamp looked at me, smiled and winked. "Don't you worry Elizabeth. She'll get her comeuppance someday. Maybe sooner than she would ever expect."

That day arrived much sooner than I could have possibly anticipated as well. On the 23rd of April, it was a drizzly, rather dreary Monday morning. Mother and I had spent all day Sunday preparing the house for the return of Papa and Tom. It was going to be a strange readjustment as we attempted to move back to normality. We aimed to get Papa back in by the end of the week and were trying to make it especially welcoming for him. Mother found some old worded banners at the Circus which she brought back with the aim of draping a welcoming message for Papa – visible as he came through the door. As I was about to eat some bread with butter and jam, there was a knock on the door. It was a message from Mr. Byrne, asking for me to meet urgently at the theatre at noon. I was a bit worried as to what the concern could be, and promptly hurried down to the theatre as quickly as I could. Charlotte Bristow was there and could not answer my question as to what this sudden meeting was all about. As a trio, Rosamund Mountain walked in with Miss Tyrer and Miss Vining. We all huddled together on a bench in the pit. Bella Menage arrived, looking very perturbed to have to be roused to the theatre on a precious day off. Looking disdainfully around, she decided to siddle up next to Mrs. Mountain without acknowledging anyone in the room. In the distance, we could hear the church clocks striking noon.

Bella muttered "Come along Mr. Byrne – get a move on!"

James Byrne arrived and swiftly moved to stand before

us. "Sorry ladies, I shan't keep you long. Thank you so much for coming here on such short notice."

I looked towards Bella. She was giving Mr. Byrne a glare of disdain. He continued. "I am afraid we have a little bad news. Miss Decamp was due to perform this evening in the *Wags of Windsor* with Mrs. Jordan. Unfortunately, she finds herself in an indisposed condition…"

Bella interrupted "Who? Miss Decamp or Mrs. Jordan?"

Mr. Byrne replied "Uh…Miss Decamp…"

"And?" She looked at him impatiently. "What does that have to do with us, James?"

"If you could be so kind as to let me continue Arabella, I will inform you. It seems that Miss Decamp feels that she will be unwell for a couple of days at least. So, of course this will impact on all of you – as we need to organise a replacement Cinderella."

Miss Menage had a smug, conceited grin on her face as she anticipated that she would be the natural choice.

"Miss Decamp has requested that Miss Searle takes her place, as she feels that she would be most suitable to fulfil the role satisfactorily."

Everyone looked my way with congratulatory smiles, with one notable exception. I held my hand to my chest in disbelief as Charlotte gave me a warm hug. Looking over to Bella I could see that she was aghast. Lost for words, she was absolutely incandescent with rage. She looked directly at me with a shrewish air of contempt. It looked as if Mr. Byrne was completely expecting a temper tantrum and moved to cut her quickly before she started.

"So, Miss Searle, you know what you have to do. We will need to sort your replacement as one of the Graces."

"TWO replacements…" Bella hissed.

"I'm sorry. I don't follow…" replied Mr. Byrne.

"James, I think that Miss Decamp's illness might be contagious. I'm finding that I don't feel very well. I think it likely that I will be unable to perform tomorrow night feeling this way."

"Very well then. Be sure to notify Mr. Wroughton on the way out so that he can suitably dock your wages."

Miss Vining spoke up, helpfully – "Mr. Byrne, I think that Miss Boyce and Miss Taylor would be able to step into the roles quite easily."

Charlotte offered "Oh, and I can go over the movements and practice with them this afternoon – just to be certain. If that would be helpful."

Mr. Byrne continued, taking no notice of Bella who seemed in shock at being completely ignored and side-lined. "That would be most helpful indeed Miss Bristow. Thank you all for your kind assistance in this matter. I look forward to another magnificent performance tomorrow night. Good day!"

As we all moved to disperse, Charlotte took great care to try and manoeuvre me away from Bella as best she could. Bella would not let this go and began to protest. "Miss Decamp must be indeed unwell. Is she on her way to Bedlam? How could anyone think that Bandy would be suitable for such a…"

Everyone had left Bella to complain on her own. As the stage door shut behind us, I saw Mrs. Mountain shake her head and roll her eyes – then flashed me a grin. The ladies all giggled at the thought of Miss Menage being deprived of attention. I was still trying to absorb the incredible news. Tomorrow, I was to be the lead in Drury Lane's most successful pantomime. Rushing home, I arrived too late to tell Mother about my amazing good luck. I had no one to tell. Then I remembered the cracked mirror. I stood before it, then began to rehearse all of Miss Decamp's part in the play, going through it all scene by scene. At the end, I gazed directly into the eyes of my reflection then burst into applause and laughter.

CHAPTER 18

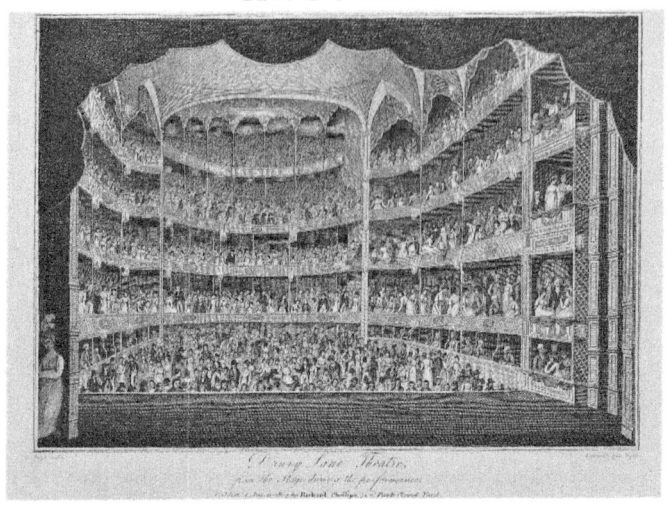

Mother was rather upset that she and the rest of the family would be unable to see me performing as Cinderella at Drury Lane on such short notice. She was on duty at the Royal Circus and it seemed a bit much for Aunt Harriet to organise at the last minute. However, my brother Tom did deliver me a bunch of gorgeous daffodils from the farm for my special evening. He shoved the blooms into my hand as he appeared through the door that morning. "Here – these are for you. From Auntie." He duly bypassed me and went to the kitchen to tear off a lump of bread which he then proceeded to wolf down. "I'm starving!"

"Has anyone asked for you to convey any messages to me, Tom? Aunt Harriet? Or Papa?"

"Oh yes. Right…They said good luck tonight, wish we could all be there. Except for me. I've already seen that stupid *Cinderella* show. Why would I want to see it again?"

Tom started prancing around with a broom from the floor. "Oh – where is my Prince? And where did I put that glass slipper? And is the audience still awake? They all know the story from the time they were babies." He yawned dramatically. I gave him a firm slap.

"Ow! What did you do that for?"

"Thanks for all the kind sentiments! You do know that I am working hard to keep a roof over our heads!"

"Your head – more like it. While I get to work with smelly farm animals all day long, shovelling manure." I could sense that tears were almost welling up in his eyes.

"So, do you actually miss Mother's schooling lessons every day?" I asked sceptically.

Tom took a while to respond. "I just miss home, I guess."

"It won't be long until we are all back together. Then we can fight and bicker every single day!" I grabbed hold of him and tickled his sides until he was sunk to the floor and having a fit of the giggles.

"Can I walk with you to the theatre? Then I have to get back to the farm to finish my chores. I've got to churn butter when I get back."

It was nice having someone to walk along with me. I sometimes felt a little vulnerable walking on my own – as if I were a lamb walking amongst wolves. I frequently had workmen and pavement sellers leer at me. They would make lewd comments and whistle at me almost daily as I tried to go about my business. I remember one swarthy character following me all the way down Bow Street making the vilest comments about what he would like to do to me and how much I would enjoy it. It was even worse at night after the performances. At that time, virtually the only women about were disrespectable tarts touting for business. There were frequently drunken men spilling out of the taverns and public houses that would make the assumption that I too was open for business and willing to sell my body for their pleasure. I would find myself almost running home to Hart Street, making no eye contact with anyone for fear that it may be misconstrued as an open invitation. It seems so unfair that women had to endure this mistreatment. But for some reason, with a little boy next to me it was as if I had a shield. There were no saucy comments or gratuitous hooting in my direction. It made me realise how often this really happened to me on a regular basis.

Waving Tom off, I went inside and prepared myself. I was most excited about the evening. Strangely, I think I was more enthusiastic about the absence of Miss Menage than the amazing opportunity of being in a lead role at the largest, most prestigious theatre in all of Europe. I asked Charlotte to confirm if it were really true – that there was no Bella this evening. Having confirmed this, I now could feel secure in the knowledge that I was able to savour and enjoy every single moment of this momentous occasion. What pleased me most was the wonderful words of encouragement and kind wishes of all the other performers. I first encountered the cast of *The Soldier's Daughter*, which was to be the first performance of the evening. Mr. Male approached me with a big smile, feigning surprise "Hey – didn't I see you as the beautiful Columbine at the Royal Circus? It can't be – because now you are Cinderella at Drury Lane!" We both laughed as he continued "Best wishes to you – and I look forward to playing mere Miller Meagre in your presence back at the Circus. I do have to express my eternal gratitude to you Miss Searle, for when you are on the stage – all eyes are upon your most beautiful self. It gives me an opportunity to have a little rest while the audience's gaze is mesmerised by your every movement."

"Well I am most flattered – and incredibly happy to provide you the opportunity of a much-needed break. I imagine you must need it, racing from being an Algerine bandit from one show to being a humble local working man just a few minutes later. It is like being thrust into another world. How exhausting for you!"

"What is exhausting is how we have to juggle work at two theatres. I shall look forward to the Summer season being in full swing – when we can just concentrate on being at one stage at a time!"

"Well – I am looking forward to working with you throughout the summer, Mr. Male. Thank you so very much for your kind words!"

I scarcely had finished speaking with Mr. Male when I turned and saw my idol walking towards me. Dora Jordan gave me a warm, friendly hug. She smelled divine – of expensive perfume oils. I wonder if it was a gift from the Duke of Clarence himself. "Look at you! Aren't you the accomplished, experienced performer now? Congratulations – it is so well-deserved! I *knew* you could do it! You have such a remarkable stage presence."

"Mrs. Jordan, coming from you – that is the greatest praise indeed! I have always held you in the greatest regard and esteem. I remember first meeting you – my admiration was so strong that it left me incapable of speaking! I do hope to be able to share the stage with you at some point. I feel that I have so much that I could learn from you."

"Now, I'm not looking for praise myself. I get plenty of that! But this is all new to you – so I want you to enjoy it! I'll try to have a peek at you from backstage if you don't mind."

I assured Mrs. Jordan that it would be the utmost honour and I thanked her heartily for all her kind words and advice since my arrival. I made my way to the dressing room and began to prepare. Mr. Byrne called me down to the stage just to briefly rehearse all of the show. He told me that he had every confidence in me – it was just to help me feel more at ease. To be honest, it all came to me naturally. He praised me and accompanied that with a warm smile. Unbeknownst to me, young Oscar Byrne had been watching the whole time and applauded heartily with a few whistles thrown in. Both generations of the Byrnes laughed and accompanied me to the Green Room. There was a most pleasant surprise waiting for me as I stepped through the door.

"There she is!" shouted Mr. Grimaldi while popping the cork off a bottle to rousing cheers. Mrs. Grimaldi and her sister, Charlotte Bristow, rushed over with glasses and thrust a full one into my hand. Miss Tyrer and Mrs. Mountain with their angelic voices sang the final phrases from the performance:

"Underneath the greenwood shade,
Lead him to a lovesick maid,
Make him bend the lowly knee,
She shall Cinderella be!"

"I don't know what to say! I have been so overwhelmed by your kind thoughts and words. It is just…simply the best evening ever!"

"Ah, but the evening is not over with yet. Lots of opportunities to fall down a trap door or to have some other calamity occurs…" Mr. Grimaldi was taunting me mischievously. "But no…that's not going to happen! Everyone, raise your glasses to the new Cinderella!"

I could not celebrate too heartily, for I had to keep my wits about me for the performance. I thought I would be nervous. It was a good-sized audience as I peered during Mrs. Jordan's entertainment. But as the music of *Cinderella* started up, I imagined myself before the cracked mirror of my home. I felt confident and professional, like I belonged. I was in my element. The applause at the end sent my spirits soaring higher than I think I have ever felt before.

CHAPTER 19

Benefit Night Ticket for the Johnstons

There was a palpable sense of the theatrical season winding down at Drury Lane. The contrast with the Royal Circus was most peculiar. The performers there were invigorated, heavily feeling the competition from Astley's Circus, Saddler's Wells, and the patent theatres. They were all competing for ticket sales. With greater choice, the audiences at Drury Lane began to dissipate and were beginning to thin more and more with each evening's entertainment offerings. Loyal box subscribers ensured that there were still numbers sprinkled about the auditorium. But there was no longer a scrum to secure the best places in the pit. The month of May often saw the theatre rented out by individuals for a benefit performance. This was an opportunity to secure a handsome bonus as the proceeds of the ticket sales went directly to the performer who organised the event. However, there was some risk involved, as the performer had to pay the theatre expenses – costs for hiring the theatre and all the crew to man the stage had to be met. And, with the odd exception of performers who may give of their time for free, the talent on the stage needed their wages covered as well. So, the benefit could actually result in an unfortunate loss of funds for the person for whom it was meant to assist. In most cases, the results went well –

and sometimes could result in a very hefty, handsome reward that far exceeded the person's usual salary for the entire season.

To my amazement, *Cinderella* continued to be performed. It seemed audiences did not want to let go of the magic of this pantomime. On the second day of May, I was due to take part in the 48th performance as Miss Decamp returned to the lead role. Another chance to see the consummate professional at work and giving me an opportunity to reflect and compare how had I done in contrast (although there really is no comparison with the irreplaceable Maria Decamp). The evening was a benefit for the actor Mr. Pope, whom I had not worked directly with. Again, I felt fortunate enough to be spared the presence of Miss Menage. The lovely Miss Taylor was joining Charlotte and I as a Grace. Many were gathering with Mr. Pope in the Green Room after the curtain fell. I gave my sincere thanks to Miss Decamp once more for her kindness, then made my excuses to leave as I felt I needed an earlier evening at home than usual. Papa had been back in the house for over a week now and he was very eager to hear any stories that I could relay about the latest theatre gossip. I do feel that poor Papa must have been starved of entertainment at Aunt Harriet's. It was so good to have him back at home and I was eager to have some time to chat before sleep.

On my way out, I happened to notice an announcement for Friday's performances. My heart skipped a beat suddenly. How did this fail to come to my attention? I must have been so preoccupied with the business of dancing at two theatres that I failed to notice that there was to be a special benefit that evening that certainly piqued my interest. Sometimes performers would pool their resources together for a benefit night that would reward both of their investments – splitting the proceeds equally. And this was the case with Friday evening – a benefit for the magnificent Mr. H. Johnston. Oh yes, and his beautiful partner Nanette as well. I was not working at either theatre that day. I knew at once that I had to go. But it might look odd if I were to attend alone. I hit upon the idea of rewarding a certain fan of the theatre to accompany me and took it upon myself to get two tickets for the pit – begging the clerk at the now closed ticket office to do me the kind favour of making this very late purchase.

Arriving home, it was so good to see Papa still awake and waiting for me. His speech and movement had greatly improved over the months and he was hoping to return to organising some dance instruction with clients during the summer. It would require him to speak commands more frequently rather than demonstrating moves – as he was more wont to do. He was hoping that this would be satisfactory amongst his clientele. In the mornings before I left for the theatres, he would practice a bit with me in front of our beloved cracked mirror.

"Elizabeth! So good to see you! Now, please tell me – how was Miss Decamp? And did you have to endure that awful Miss Menage? And how about Mrs. Jordan? Was she performing tonight?"

"All in good time, Papa. But first, I have a surprise for you! I am going to the theatre on Friday night, but I'm afraid I will need accompanying. Would you be so kind as to consider going with me to the benefit night for Mr. and Mrs. Johnston? Look! I have two tickets for the pit!" I held up two specially printed tickets with elaborate artwork of an intertwined couple in an embrace. I imagined that I was the model for this work of art, trying to not take note of the "Mrs." in the printed line: *For the benefit of Mr. and Mrs. H. Johnston.*

"Oh my! I would be delighted! How did you get these?"

"Never you mind! It has been a long time since we have had an evening at the theatre together. Much too long!"

"So, what is being performed? I want to know what I will be seeing!"

My heart sank a bit. I hadn't taken the slight bit of notice about those details. I just saw Henry's name in bold and the rest was inconsequential.

"Uh, I'm not sure. I was just given the tickets. I am sure that it will be wonderful whatever is onstage that evening. It will make for a nice surprise, won't it?"

"Indeed, it will!" Papa gave me a big hug and I wished him goodnight – with a promise to fill him in on the latest news of Miss Decamp and all his other queries fulfilled in the morning.

When Friday arrived, I wanted to ensure that we arrived at the theatre very early. I wanted to get a good seat and was hoping that my father would not get trampled in the scrum and melee to get a prime spot on the benches when the doors opened. But I had to ensure that we were able to get to the theatre in a timely manner. An acquaintance of the man who gave Mother and I rides back from the Royal Circus was able to pick us up and give us a ride to Covent Garden, sparing Papa the tiring walk. I prepared a meal for all of us early and ensured that some was left aside for when Mother returned from her work later this evening. Tom was miffed that he was left out of the evening plans.

"But Tom, I thought you didn't like the theatre. You always complain about going to my shows."

"That's because you're in them! I like to see shows that you aren't in!"

I was able to get Papa to the theatre early with a promise of a quick backstage tour. It was a ploy to get him into a good seat early, but I soon became worried that things would not go to plan. He was so in awe of the building and had so many questions about minor details. I had to crack the door of the Green Room so he could get a little peek but insisted we couldn't stay. It was a struggle to hurry him along.

"Oh, is that Mrs. Bland in there? Oh, and I think that's Mrs. Mountain, is it?" I had to make out that I would be in great trouble if Mr. Sheridan saw me bringing a non-performer backstage – especially on a night I was not performing. The other difficulty was that everyone wanted to speak with him when they found out I had my father on my arm. I was also dreadfully worried about who we would bump into. As I shuffled past the Green Room, I could see Bella Menage chatting with Mr. Dowton. The idea of seeing her truly filled me with fear. I hadn't seen her since taking the Cinderella role. The blood drained from my head when I thought I heard her speaking behind me.

"Does she not know that I should be Cinderella? ME! ME! MEEEE!!! Who does Miss Searle think she…"

I caught a glimpse of Mr. Grimaldi laughing hysterically and Henry Johnston in the process of using his best skills of impersonation and ventriloquy to throw his voice and see my face of absolute terror for their own amusement. I had to cover my mouth to keep from laughing and I gestured wildly for them to keep quiet as father looked bemused. Henry looked like a naughty, cheeky boy who was genuinely enjoying his mischief. As we walked past them, I explained that I was showing my father around. He was starstruck as I introduced them to him. I then wished Mr. Johnston all the best for the evening's performance. Hurriedly, I insisted with Papa that we needed to think about getting to our seats. Mr. Johnston suggested that we both should come to the Green Room after the performance. Papa's eyes lit up excitedly, but I was not sure this would be the best idea. I told Henry that we would think about it. Mr. Grimaldi congratulated Papa for having brought such a lovely, talented, and polite young woman into the world, while I began to blush from too much praise.

"And beautiful, don't forget that!" Henry said while looking into my eyes. Then he started up his silly Bella Menage impersonation voice. "And graceful too! Why can't I be that graceful? It's not fair! I'm going to kick her down the stairs and pull her hair!" Giggling in my direction, he gave Papa a pat on the shoulder and both made a move to the costume room. "Come Papa, we really must be going."

I was taking Papa on the stage, down the steps and through a little hinged doorway to get us to the pit before the audience started to rush in. We only had a few minutes, at most. On the stage we bumped into Mr. Byrne. I briefly introduced them, but to my surprise it seemed as if they already knew each other. Papa had a rather stern look of surprise on his face as James took his hand and shook it firmly and warmly while looking at him intensely.

"Tom! It has been a long, long time! I heard you weren't well. I'm glad that you are up and about again. Thank you so much for your care and instruction of this fine young lady. She is the most superb performer and she owes all her dance skills down to you, kind sir."

Father looked rather rattled, and said quietly "The pleasure, I assure you, has been all mine."

"She's lucky to have you for a father. She certainly could not wish for better. Lucky girl…" Mr. Byrne's voice wobbled slightly. It seemed from emotion, but for the life of me – I had no idea what the source of that was. He cleared his throat abruptly, then said "Enjoy the show! You had best take a seat. Here – let me help you." I could sense that Papa would have preferred that we would make our way on our own, but he had the wisdom to know that he could be unsteady on his feet still, and a tumble into the orchestra would not be a good start to the evening's entertainments. I thanked Mr. Byrne and we got a prime spot – centre stage front row. As we plopped ourselves down on the bench, Papa looked at me and winked with a grin. The crowds started rushing in to grab a good space, so I was not able to ask Papa just yet how he and Mr. Byrne were acquainted. I thought it odd that he had never mentioned it before, despite us talking all about the performers that we knew of whenever we attended the theatre. He put his arm around me and gave me a big loving squeeze.

I noticed someone near to us had a playbill. I asked if they could kindly let me see it for a moment. He looked a rather gruff gentleman and began to protest.

"Look here young, Missy; why don't you just go and buy yourself…hey! You! It's you! You were Cinderella the other night! You're Miss Searle! Why, here you go! Please have a look!"

He nudged his companions and pointed at me with eyes wide and an excited smile, explaining to them who I was in amazement.

"Oh look Papa! It's one of your favourites! *The School for Scandal.* That should be very good, indeed!" My immediate thought was how much better as a playwright Mr. Sheridan was than an owner of a theatre. Or being a decent human being, for that matter. "Mrs. Mountain is going to sing a new song. Oh, and Miss Tyrer too! You will like her Papa. She is short and a bit on the plump side. People give her such grief for that – it really is unfair. Because she has the most divine voice! That is really what should matter, but men don't think that way. Look, half of those men are unsightly to lay your eyes upon. Who are they to judge? You know, she is truly kind too. I so wish I could sing like her." I did not mention but noticed that Henry was to be on the stage very frequently throughout the evening. The more I saw him the better. I felt as if I could not get enough. I still felt a bit intoxicated from our backstage interactions, even if much of it was in a faux Mademoiselle Menage voice. Just seeing his name in print put me into a dreamlike state. I snapped myself out of my stupor and handed the playbill back to the gentleman who was now in a bit of a stupor of his own as he watched my every move gormlessly.

I was really enjoying this new perspective – looking at the stage instead of being on it for once. Papa and I felt as if we were in the centre of everything. We could see the boxes closest to the stage and tried to conjecture who of the Bon Ton was occupying the seats. The orchestra was literally at our feet. For the first play, Mr. Johnston was down to portray Charles Surface in the production of *The School for Scandal*, the good-hearted and most genuine of the Surface brothers. I loved that. Imagining him as the kind, fair lover of my dreams. Nanette was not in the play, so she was unable to spoil the fantasy that I would really be ashamed to admit to. I was there, close and gazing up at his most handsome face. And I am sure he glanced my way, delivering lines in my direction. I sat – mesmerised and feeling flushed. I found him completely enthralling. Mrs. Johnston came out to make a dramatic address after the play. She was absolutely beautiful. I wondered if she were more beautiful than I. Henry had said I was beautiful. And graceful too! Nanette couldn't dance. But she could sing better than I could. Which is more important to a man? To a man like Henry Erskine Johnston? If I were a man, I would find her mesmerising. Long flowing locks of curly dark hair. Azure blue eyes to melt in. I wasn't listening to her words, just gazing at her countenance. But her body seemed to be looking a bit thick. Perhaps that is from all the childbearing. It seemed that they had many children together. Therefore, it would mean that Henry was quite busy in their matrimonial bed. I did not want to think of them together. Frequently together in a passionate state. I rather preferred the arguing, bickering couple. I liked to think that she was incapable of making him happy. That is very cruel. Poor Henry! But I thought it might be true. Their arguing had been so bitter and aggressive when I witnessed it. How could she be immune to his obvious wit and charm? I loved everything about Henry. He was obviously perfection itself. If he were mine, I would love him. I was just starting to imagine Henry caressing me and stroking the back of my neck when I was startled out of my trance by the vigorous applause for Mrs. Johnston upon completion of her wordy dialogue. I belatedly joined in.

Father had been watching me and commented in my ear "Deep in thought? I thought she was most remarkable. How about you?"

Fortunately, I was saved by the sweet sounds of Mrs. Mountain singing a new Scotch ballad; the orchestra drowning out any reply that I could have mustered in response to Papa. Little Miss Tyrer followed, then the exquisite Mrs. Bland with more new Scottish tunes for the audience. And then, I had to draw a deep breath and grasp my hand to my pounding heart. Before me, I stared up to the most handsome soldier that my eyes had seen. Henry Johnston then began his patriotic address calling Britons to arms against the deadly foe that lies across the Channel. Fervent and imploring, his commanding words tore at the soul of all who were witnessing this moment (or so I imagined). And then, of this I was certain – he turned to me. He was staring directly at me as he continued. From that moment, I was a convert. I would willingly lie myself down and surrender to his will. Wherever he would lead I would follow. I had to call upon every ounce of self-control that I had to keep from standing up – to refrain from crying out "Yes! Together we must fight!" I felt as if my hands would move magnetically towards his outstretched arms. If I permitted it, they would conjoin and meld together, binding us into one living entity. I was trembling, and I saw my trembling hand move forwards and upwards. His impassioned pleas continued unabated, as I snapped my hand back to touch my quivering lips. I was almost not conscious of the tears of commitment rolling down my cheeks. He looked around to address everyone, then that stare returned. Beautiful, deep brown eyes seared into my very being – all witnessed by 3,000 pairs of eyes. Looking to the imaginary sky, the speech came to a sudden abrupt end. To thunderous cheers and applause, he suddenly turned and left me breathless.

Crashing down into my senses once again, I turned to

Papa. He was giving me a stony, grave look that instantly caused me much consternation. "Like that – did you?" he said, expecting no answer. There was no trace of his usual humour in his voice.

I felt myself turn red as a beet with shame. I had to think quickly. "It just made me think of all our poor soldiers. Unfortunate young men whose lives may be in danger. And yet their love of this nation enables them to do their duty and defend us against wicked Napoleon. It...moved me."

"Yes. I could tell that it did indeed." replied Father unconvincingly.

Feeling rather subdued and chastened, I tried to put all these thoughts to the back of my mind for the final of the evening's entertainments, *The Deserter of Naples*. I could continue to admire Henry, as he had the key role of the play. I was determined to be more on guard however and avoid the ridiculous lovesick trance that nearly overtook me just a few moments ago. I had to try harder to contain my urges, lest I become completely ridiculous and lose all my sense of decorum and sanity. I have found that a good cure for almost any positive feeling is to be in the presence of Arabella Menage, and she was an almost welcome presence with her brief appearances in the play. The highlight for her adoring fans was when she performed a hornpipe from *Corsair* in a rather unnecessary appendix to the proceedings of all the military-based actions of Naples. This did however give me an opportunity to objectively dissect her dance performance without worrying unduly about being the victim of some mishap orchestrated by her. And admittedly, she was radiant. Her shimmering red hair contrasting with her porcelain white skin. Her fine figure and form as she glided across the stage, skilfully kicking, and raising her delicate arms most gracefully. If I did not know her character to be so very ugly, one might say that she was quite a striking beauty. She certainly demonstrated almost perfect poise and elegance as she danced. I had never quite realised or thought deeply before about the power of dance. There were no words, but here was a performance that conveyed power and emotion, further embellished by an accompanying musical soundtrack. I could imagine her precious painter, Mr. Sharp, sitting in her audience. He would be lured in by her magical, hypnotic movement and trapped into adoring her. He would be as helpless as a fly ensnared in a spider's web.

My adoration continued unabated. Some of my favourite people were onstage with him: Mr. Male, Miss Decamp, Mr. Grimaldi, even cute little Master Oscar Byrne who seemed to be demonstrating an ever-growing, precocious talent for dancing every time he appeared onstage. But I was there for one person. I could not pretend. Oh, how very wicked I was. And a helpless hostage to deep emotion and feeling. I knew that I had to drink him in with my eyes – every moment, for I knew not when I would see him again after tonight. He would be always unavailable and never within my reach. A most cruel torture sent by Satan himself to torment me. Was I being overly dramatic? I did not care.

I was feeling some comfort in the act of wallowing in my pool of self-pity. It made me feel. I could feel emotion and the essence of being alive. Feelings and desires that I now could channel into my work. Before, as a naïve young girl I could only pretend to reflect these unfamiliar sentiments as my performances required them. But now I could draw upon experience. Thank you, Mr. Henry Johnston. Thanks to you I have felt unrequited love and heartache. I have known temptation and joyous frivolity. You have awakened feelings within me that I am most certain that you are unaware that you bear the responsibility for. You would think me most foolish if you truly knew my inner thoughts. I would be mortified. Yet, a part of me would be intrigued to discover if you shared this infatuation. How will I ever be able to contend with not knowing if Mr. Johnston could ever have feelings of affection towards me?

At the finish, I applauded him. I looked directly at him as I heartily cheered him with the utmost admiration – much more so than his many illustrious onstage companions. He looked towards me and with glee apparent in his eye gave me a wink and smiled. And then he turned and gazed adoringly at his wife Nanette as they moved together, conjoined at the hand, and took their final bow in appreciation of all the approbation being lauded upon them from the audience. Was it an act? Did he have the capacity to love more than one woman? Was he a knave who could just heartlessly trample on the hearts of the women that adore him? A talented Rake determined to sow his seed on any fertile ground that was visible? I could see that poor Mrs. Johnston must have to contend with these thoughts all of the time. Foolish pretty young girls such as I, fawning in a constant succession of availability to the beautiful man before them, full of that charm that he is blessed to possess and carelessly dispenses upon the guileless innocents so willing to acquiesce to his every wish.

I felt rather deflated as the crowd began to disperse. Papa could sense that I was feeling uneasy. He was tentative as he reminded me "I believe that we have an invitation to the Green Room. Shall we go?"

I wiped a tear forming in my eye, hoping that he would not notice. "I am so sorry. I think it best if we did not. I am a bit fatigued, and I have a busy evening tomorrow. Oh, I nearly forgot to tell you! I am singing with Mrs. Bland! Singing is not my forte. I need to ensure that my voice is in good form." I sighed. "Yes – a good rest is just what I need, I think. Too much theatrics will do me no good. And besides, I think horrible Bella Menage would be there."

"I don't care how pretty she is. I would throttle her!" Papa laughed and continued as we began to make our way out of the theatre for the late-night walk home. "A nice hot water with honey before bed will do your throat good. We shall see to that." He smiled at me. His smile was slightly crooked since his unfortunate health incident, but this was far more than I had ever dreamed was possible. I felt so incredibly happy to be walking arm in arm with Papa – even though I sensed that he might be toying with me. "I could not help but notice that you seem to have some affection towards Mr. Johnston. He seems to feel most at ease with you – to be able to tease you backstage in the manner that he did."

Father was fishing for more details. He was not easily fooled and no longer in an incapacitated state from his illness. His mind was fully engaged and probing me to divulge more information than I was willing to give.

"Oh - Henry is just like that. A playful little boy to everyone! You know, he reminds me of Tom in so many ways."

"I wonder what Mrs. Johnston would have to say had she witnessed the scene that I was privy to."

"Oh, Nanette is fine. We speak. We talk all the time. She is lovely, isn't she? I can see why Henry married her. So unbelievably beautiful and full of…"

"You wish it were you, don't you? You wish that he were your love."

"I would do nothing to break the sanctity of the vows of marriage. That would be unforgivable. There is nothing between Mr. Johnston and I. We are merely two performers on the same stage…"

Father chuckled. "Indeed! Are you to be Lady Teazle to his Charles Surface? Those happy endings in dramas tend to be in reality – a farce."

"I must profess that I have no idea what you are speaking about, Papa."

"Oh, you do. Save your embarrassment, Elizabeth. You know I am a particularly good judge of character. I can see the attraction. He is a most handsome man, very charming, suave... I really am not quite sure what to make of his true character though. There is something a little unsettling about him. He desires you."

I giggled embarrassingly, and rather unconvincingly said "Oh Papa! I think you are mistaken Papa. What would he want in me, when he has someone like Mrs. Johnston at home waiting for him? And they have children too. I am far too young, what could he possibly see in me?"

"I can feel it. I know men. You really must be on your guard Elizabeth. I don't want to lecture you. I know you know this. But I want you to feel that you can confide in me. I won't tell your mother any of this, by the way – so you need not worry. It would cause her far too much consternation. Now, my darling daughter. I know you have stared into that mirror of ours endlessly since it arrived in our household. What exactly do you see in that reflection?"

"Papa...please!"

"Gazing back is one of the most perfect examples of the female version of humans. She is gorgeous – both inside and out. A man would have to be blind not to have his head turned. Now, you profess in all innocence the relationship between Mr. Johnston and yourself. That's fine. You have my trust. But I don't know Mr. Johnston. And if he is not around, there will be many other fine gentlemen out there who will be most eager to meet your acquaintance. This is a most challenging world for a young lady such as yourself to be trying to manoeuvre in socially. I want you to know that I am here to proffer advice – sometimes it will be unsolicited for I cannot help myself. I will not judge, but I will be a level, wise voice of reason which you can depend on. Do you understand?"

"Yes Papa. Thank you. And you needn't be troubled about Henry. That is the end of the season for him and I shan't be seeing him over the summer."

"Well perhaps that will give your heart some time to mend. There will be someone who is right for you

Elizabeth. Be patient. It is a virtue, as they say. I want a good match for you Elizabeth. I think we both know that Mr. Johnston will never be that one. And so, you will move on. Difficult to imagine now, but it will happen. Oh – we are here already! Time flies when you are having awkward conversations with your father, right?" We laughed together and made our way inside.

CHAPTER 20

Charles Kemble

Somehow, I survived the vocal strains of *The Stranger*. I was very dependent on Mrs. Bland masking my deficiencies with her magnificent tones. I was rather intrigued that these beautiful sounds could emanate from such an unassuming looking woman. Short, stout with wiry hair and a prominent Jewish nose - if one passed her on the street, they would never suspect that they were in the presence of one of the finest voices ever to grace the stage of the Haymarket. I certainly could count upon Bella Menage in reminding me how weakly I compare to the talented singer. As Maria Bland and I made our way past Miss Menage and Mr. Byrne backstage, I could sense that a bitter quip would be hurled my way. I was not wrong.

"Well, *someone* was completely dreadful. And it was not Mrs. Bland. Tell me Bandy, where did you learn to squawk like that? It really hurt my ears so."

"Miss Menage, I think you'll find we need to be onstage – NOW!" Mr. Byrne firmly reminded Miss Menage of her duties.

Bella looked to me feigning disinterest. "Oh – yes! On my way! Off to singing lessons for you now, Bandy. Off you go! Goodbye!" She gave me a wave with a smirk on her face.

The following evening was Miss Decamp's benefit. I had the pleasure of knowing that Bella was not to be present for the entire evening. It was a joyful celebration of my kind ally, Miss Maria Decamp. Another performance of *Cinderella*, another opportunity to witness Maria breathe life into the character and learning from the master. Finishing with the piece again, I joined Miss Decamp backstage in the dressing room. She sat next to Nanette Johnston as they prepared for their roles in *The Caravan*. I took note of Mr. Bannister's delightful dog and was giving him lots of love and fuss before I dressed into my peasant costume to blend in the background scenes.

I overheard Miss Decamp proffering congratulations on Mrs. Johnston.

"Yes – this will be my fourth child now. I suspect it is a boy. He is very active and always kicking! He likes the orchestra when they strike up a tune."

"Oh, I envy you. I would love to start a family. It seems that Charles continues to be averse to confronting his family about our wedding. It is so frustrating! Why am I a secret from the Kembles? Would I bring such shame to them? What have I done? And what business is it of the mighty John Kemble or Sarah Siddons anyway? Who do they think they are? And the months continue to flow by – with only promises from Charles. I am growing impatient! My youth is ebbing away as we speak!" Maria looked very vexed about her continued state of matrimonial limbo.

"Well, at least you have time to reflect on whether you are making the correct decision. That is far better than foolishly rushing in as I did. Henry used to throw flowers onstage to me every evening from the auditorium – for weeks! Sometimes I think I just offered to accept his marriage proposal to make him stop all of his embarrassing demonstrations of infatuation." Nanette was revealing her early history with Henry of which I was unaware. I was intrigued but pretended to be engrossed with the canine licking my hand attentively.

"Aww…that is so romantic! I think that is so sweet!" Maria looked envious.

"I suppose. Looking back now, I just think he was obsessed. He was young, I was younger. What did we know about being in love and marriage? I should have stayed at the circus in Edinburgh. I could have been riding horses while dancing on their backs with my stepmother!" Nanette laughed, but there was a tinge of melancholy and sadness in her voice. Miss Decamp enquired how old they were when they married.

"Henry was all of 19 years. I was not yet 15. Whisked off by the whirlwind romance of it all. It felt like Romeo and Juliet! My father was not best pleased, but there was no way that I could be dissuaded. I think I was just eager to get away from my stepmother. And to have a chance to see more of the world. I thought that I had more to offer than just tread the boards of wee little Scottish theatres. Henry had the same drive and ambition. I think that's what really attracted me to him. His forcefulness and determination. Now I see it as a bloody nuisance! Oh, if only I had the chance to do it all over again." Nanette looked to her stomach and caressed the growing child inside.

"Really? Do you have regrets? He is such a fine chap – everyone loves him here!" Maria seemed rather puzzled by Nanette's revelations. I was hanging on every word – tuning out the bustle and the hubbub of everyone dressing for the fast-approaching performance so that I could get every piece of information.

"Oh yes! Everyone loves Henry! Isn't he the finest?" Nanette laughed sadly, looking at her reflection in the mirror. She discarded her brush onto the dressing table.

"You know what? I hate him. HATE him! He is so hot-headed. Signing his petition of grievances with other fools so that we had to leave Covent Garden last year. There I was with three children, not knowing where we would wind up. He is always wanting to manage some provincial theatre somewhere – Scotland, Ireland. Throw our money into the theatre pit – might as well burn it! Is that what I worked for? You must know from your fiancé's brother that it is no easy task and a constant worry running a theatre. But no. Our Henry likes to be the boss. But I put my foot down. I insisted that we were not going to leave London during the season. I bring in as much money as he does – if not more. He is seething with resentment about it. It just is something that is not up for discussion with me. I will not risk my financial future on some whimsical fantasy that he concocts about procuring a theatre. He can be such a stubborn idiot at times!" She took a soft brush to her face and vigorously applied rouge to her cheeks.

Taken aback, Maria Decamp replied "Well…good for you for standing your ground. Perhaps I need to take a firmer stand with Charles."

"Sorry, I perhaps said too much. Ugh!!! I just feel so frustrated though sometimes. No one to talk to that might grasp what I am going through. You know what? I think you should be firmer with Mr. Charles Kemble. If he is sincere, he will be subservient to your wishes and treat you like a queen. If not, then you can let him go and find a more compliant suitor. You only have one life Maria. Make the best of it. Don't waste it. Especially on a man. A self-centred man who only thinks of himself. Oh, not to say that Charles is that way. I rather like him. I think you can twist him around to your way of thinking, I'm sure. Let him know you are the boss! Too late for me. I have to live with my biggest mistake. It has a name – I call it Henry!"

"Don't feel down!" Maria looked at Nanette with concern.

"Oh, don't you worry! I will fight to the end of my days! I am stubborn and strong-minded. I am a bit like Joan of Arc – off to battle – impassioned!" Nanette laughed as she rose like a warrior. Maria did too. Then a curtain call came, and everyone rushed out. Except for me. I realised that I was still dressed as one of the 3 Graces. I frantically darted about trying to dress myself. One of the dressers saw me and gasped, helping me to quickly transform into a downtrodden peasant and rushing me to join the others – my head still reeling from the information that I had overheard.

CHAPTER 21

AN ACCOUNT OF THE SURPRISING

Savage Girl,

Who was caught running wild in the Woods of Champagne, a Province in France

CONTAINING

A true Narrative of many curious and interesting particulars, respecting this very wonderful child of Nature.

TRANSLATED FROM THE FRENCH

My thoughts and attentions were gradually focusing more on my work South of the Thames. *Cybele* continued to require my dance skills as the Columbine, but I was really spending more time in preparations for the opening of *The Wild Girl!* Mr. Cross decided to alter the story to tie it in with opportunities to throw in jousting and other equestrian excitements – making full use of the space and employing every living creature under contract to their fullest extent. He continuously was seeking an event to merit the label 'spectacle'. For me, I enjoyed the opportunity to try and convey a great range of emotion without speaking. One advantage in this particular show was being a savage raised by forest creatures was the substitution of screaming for dialogue. My rehearsals often dissolved into hilarity as John Cross directed me to emit a variety of blood curdling screams so that he could choose what would be most suitable for 'un Belle Sauvage'. This was a superb role for extinguishing any timidity or apprehension out of me. I was encouraged to nurture and develop my savage-like capabilities at every opportunity. I had to practice skulking across the stage in a most unladylike manner. I particularly enjoyed hissing in a most intimidating manner. As for my appearance, any sense of vanity would soon be extinguished with one look in the mirror. Coal dirt rubbed into my face was playing havoc with my natural complexion – being a nightmare to wash away at the end of an evening. And I wore the most hideous and threadbare of fabrics that even a rag merchant would be disinclined to acquire.

Perhaps the most challenging requirement of the pantomime was that my character was especially fond of a favourite lamb. I had to parade around the circus before the stage trying to keep hold of a frisky lamb in my arms. My experience at Aunt Harriet's farm did help me to feel more at ease with the creatures at the Circus, but even I found that lambs were quite difficult to keep hold of. And this grew to be progressively more difficult as the lambs grew to a more sheep-like stature. A rotation of runt understudies was steadily supplied until, I am afraid to say, the lamb was replaced by another creature altogether. A very docile little dog that would prove to be the Royal Circus version of Drury Lane's Carlo later that summer was fitted up in the skin of a recently dispatched little lamb whose final appearance was no doubt as a chop on some hungry person's plate. Unfortunate as it was for the poor baby sheep, it did improve my job immensely as I loved working with this most clever and obedient canine.

It is so odd to note that so little of consequence tended to take part at the Royal Circus. All the spectacle was for the audience. There was no evidence of confrontation backstage. It was refreshing to experience such a convivial environment. I grew to admire the hardworking performers, many of whom knew that they would never have the good fortune to appear on the stage of Drury Lane or Covent Garden. Yet no one displayed envy or jealousy to my face. We all worked together seamlessly as a theatrical family.

And having actual family onsite was not only novel, but it also helped me to feel safe and secure. I did not see much of Mother at work, but we enjoyed our travels together to and from the workplace. We also had much to talk about, knowing all in the theatre equally well; making for easier discussions without having to go into great descriptions and background to start our tales to each other.

More eventful were the round of benefit performances that I continued to be involved with at Drury Lane. For two nights in a row I was able to step back into the prime role of Cinderella. And to add further pleasure to the experience, Bella Menage had to perform in the background as one of the three Graces! To her great credit, she tried to keep her humiliation simmering under the surface without becoming incandescent with rage. But being Bella, she was not able to maintain this state of decorum at all times. She took every opportunity to hiss disparaging comments that were audible only to me: "I wouldn't get used to this, if I were you!" "Wearing rags really suits you Bandy. They complement your scrawny figure. Giving a little shapeliness to that flat chest of yours." "Thinking that you could be admired by a prince really tests the imagination of the audience." "You know – I think these are applause of politeness. The crowds have taken pity on your pathetic amateurish performance and didn't want you to leave the stage in tears tonight." "Miss Decamp was so much better than you. You must be so embarrassed trying to take her place."

I ignored everything she said. I did not respond to her in the hope it would eventually stop, but she was tireless in her campaign to undermine my self-confidence. I was determined to not let her win. Still – I found that her comments could sift their way into my subconscious, try as I might to repel them. It irked me that one vile comment from her could dissolve 100 kind compliments from others who were of far more importance. Why did her negativity have such power? I resolved to myself to be stronger and try to steel myself against her wicked verbal onslaughts.

Of much greater interest was the performance on the 7th of June. I had been a little dishonest with Papa when I stated that Henry Johnston's season was finished. It was certainly true that his attendance at Drury Lane was much more infrequent throughout the remainder of May. And as the castings came out only a week ahead, it was only several weeks after I informed Papa that our paths would never cross in the summer that I discovered they would, in actuality. This evening was to prove to be the very last opportunity I was to see him, at least for the next few months. He was playing St. Alme in *Deaf & Dumb*, which really was more of a showcase for Maria Decamp's talents. She portrayed a deaf boy named Julio – who could only communicate through the use of his hands in a range of gestures. Later in the evening I would portray a Grace to her Cinderella yet again.

I made my way to the theatre much earlier than usual. During the whole journey I contemplated many things in my mind. I was in turmoil. There was my vow to Nanette – unspoken of course, to respect the boundaries of her marriage. Indeed, I felt that the expectations of God were most definitely inclined towards the same conclusion. And Papa's earnest warnings. Furthermore, I tried to reason with myself, I may be imagining all of this romantic nonsense. Henry was soon to be a father again. Surely, he had taken no notice of me. That is, despite me being the same age as when he first threw flowers to his wife-to-be. I knew that Nanette was not working that evening. I now also possessed the knowledge of their unhappiness with their marriage. I had sensed it before, but now I knew it to be true – having come directly out of the mouth of Nanette. I was certain that I detected his distraught state of misery when I witnessed their arguments at the theatre. I was so confused. I yearned to be a comfort to him. I could fool myself that it was only the hand of friendship that I was extending. The truth buried within my soul was that I truly ached to be in the clutches of his embrace.

I was listless and restless at the theatre. There was little for me to do and Henry was not arriving early. I cursed myself for my foolishness. To my added regret, Miss Menage arrived early for once. She was there at the props room flirting with Mr. Sharp as he was trying to touch up some backdrops with daubs of paint. She suddenly noticed me after I wandered past them for about the fifth time.

"Bandy! My goodness you are here early! Surely you don't need to practice your Cinderella dance. You do realise that it is Maria who will playing Cinderella tonight."

"Oh, she's been demoted to being a Grace with you, Bella! Hi Elizabeth! So nice to see you!" Michael smiled at me, waving slightly with his wet brush.

Bella forced a giggle. "No – really though. Why are you here?"

I formulated a lie very quickly. "I heard you were performing Del Caro's hornpipe this evening. I was hoping to catch a glimpse of you rehearsing it as I haven't seen it before."

"Oh, aren't you the little Peeping Tom? Trying to steal my performance secrets, are you? How very astute of you. I mean, you really should learn from the best!"

"That would be great! I'd love to see it. I won't have a chance to see it from the audience tonight. Hey, why don't you dance it together? I'll go get a fiddler to come in – wait right there!" The enthusiastic Mr. Sharp put his paintbrush down and raced to get a musician. Bella's eyes conveyed her disgust over in my direction.

"Thank you so much Bella! If we are to dance it together, could you be so kind as to quickly go over some of the moves with me?"

"I don't know what you are playing at!" She sighed in despair then very quickly went over the rudimentary moves with minimal explanation. She was perhaps hoping that I would look inadequate and make many mistakes. Unbeknownst to her, I actually knew Del Caro's hornpipe quite well. I just decided to see where this encounter might go. She was on much better behaviour than usual. I supposed it was to fool poor Mr. Sharp into thinking she was a fun and carefree spirit, instead of realising the vindictive little shrew that she actually was.

With a violinist at hand and a small audience of a few crew and cast members, we started off. I could see that Arabella was rather taken aback by how quickly I had appeared to pick up the steps. It felt like a competition as we drove each other to display the dance to the absolute best of our abilities. The music stopped. There were applause and I noticed smiles all around, except for a miffed scowl from Miss Menage. I quickly bowed and half-heartedly thanked Bella. I saw Mr. Johnston laughing with Mr. Sharp as he pointed in our direction.

"Well that's something I ne'er expected to see!" Henry spoke with his full Scottish accent intact. I loved hearing it. It felt so exotic.

"And did you enjoy the entertainment gentlemen?" I directed my comments at both men so as to not arouse any suspicions regarding my intentions to gain favour with Henry. Unfortunately, I did not think that my actions could be considered a flirtation towards Mr. Sharp. Bella was full of jealousy and abruptly brushed past me.

"Come along Michael. It is time for me to get ready." She shot an evil looking glare in my direction as she marched poor Mr. Sharp down the corridor.

"Uh...I suppose the answer, Miss Searle is...aye! Indeed, I did find that most pleasurable!" I began to turn red at the flirtatious way he was speaking. I thought to myself that I could easily watch his every move forever. What was Nanette's problem? I would follow this man to the ends of the earth if he asked me to. At that moment, I realised I was in danger. I was completely susceptible to any suggestion he would put forward. I would happily be his mistress on the side. Anything, just to have those eyes continually gazing into mine. I discretely licked my dry lips. There was an awkward silence between us as we both continued to look at each other. I think Henry was taking some delight in trying to make me feel uncomfortable. I started to blush.

"I'm going to have to go onstage in a moment." He then started to gesticulate wildly and in an exaggerated manner, as if he were trying to communicate with the deaf Julio of his upcoming drama. "I…will watch…you dance…later…from backstage." We both laughed. "You will have some time before the finale. We can go to the Green Room together. You can bring your dear friend Bella if you wish…" He raised his eyebrows comically, then alternately raised and lowed both his brows. Who could possibly refuse?

"That would be delightful. Except for Bella accompanying me. That would be dreadful!"

Henry made his way, giving me a sheepish glance and a furtive wave of his hand, so as to not be noticed by anyone else. I took a deep breath and tried to compose myself. What was I doing? It was insanity! He was a married man, very nearly twice my age - with children and a wife. Perhaps not in the happiest state of relations with her, but married, nevertheless. I tried to reassure myself. He was just a friend. We would be in the Green Room with others around. Nothing will happen. He is a responsible, honourable man…I believe. Perhaps. Or was he a snake in disguise? It was best not to think too deeply about this. I was determined that it was going to be an enjoyable evening at work. Nothing more, nothing less. An evening at work where perhaps I could just run my hand past the stubble on his handsome, square jaw. And maybe I could trace the outline of his fair lips with my forefinger. Whilst my other hand would playfully run through the tousled, curly black locks of the hair upon his fine head. I snapped myself back to reality. What a hopeless cause I was! Surely, I was doomed.

In my helpless state, I could not keep away from watching him perform from behind the stage. I tried my best to do so in secret. It was not continuous. I would purposefully be moving about to get some vital piece of costume, an especially important hairbrush from the opposite direction, then returning to retrieve a most crucial piece of rag to mop up an imaginary spill. Each time catching a mere glimpse as best I could. Every moment was precious to me at that time. I was obsessed, without a doubt. Walking slowly in my trance-like stupor, I was holding a useless lump of used candle that had been accidentally dropped by one of the stage wick trimmers, still warm and gooey in my hand. I was nearly knocked off my feet by Bella Menage as she was rushing past, readying herself for the hornpipe dance performance. She looked at me up and down as if I were some gormless, wandering lunatic.

"What *are* you doing?"

Dazed, I just held up my sooty lump and muttered. "This. Someone…might trip, or slip. On this. I… I will dispose of this. Am disposing of this, right now. That is what I am doing. Please don't get hurt! We must all be careful…those careless wick boys!"

"Really? Are you serious?" Bella looked at me incredulously. She continued in a cross between a disdainful hiss and a whisper. "You are such an imbecile!" She shook her head and moved back to her task. Embarrassed, I decided to prepare for *Cinderella* in earnest now. I really did not need to give Bella further ammunition to humiliate me further.

Later, on the stage with my other two Graces, I felt almost as if I were some wind-up automaton. Going through the motions of our dance, I felt as if only Charlotte Bristow was on full form that evening. Bella was decidedly distracted. I think she was suspicious that I had set up some kind of elaborate trap for her. She seemed as if she were on the lookout for some slippery tallow on the floor that would lead to catastrophe. A further impediment to my performance was the knowledge that Mr. Johnston would be watching me from behind. Would he be lasciviously gazing at my silhouette as I moved? Would he see the outline of my nakedness contrasting against the bright glare of the stage lighting?

In reality, I suspect he may have had something more puerile on his agenda. As we came off the stage, there he was impersonating a Grace. He pursed his lips in the silly way that Bella did at times and fluttered his eyelids as if they were butterflies. Up on his toes, he did a clumsy pirouette and bowed gracelessly with his arms outstretched in a dainty, most unmasculine way.

Miss Bristow giggled and shook her head as she walked past him. Bella looked most annoyed and angrily whispered "You are really such a man-boy! I have really had enough of mingling with the gormless buffoons around here! You really need to think about ceasing your annoying, immature actions and acting as a man of your age."

"Uh...aye...I thought abou' it. I think I will carry on as I have been doin'." Bella glared at him with contempt. "Say hello to Michael for me!" He put his hands to the side of his tilted head dramatically, puckered his lips again and looked all dreamy eyed as if besotted by the very thought of Mr. Sharp. Bella walked slowly by, never stopping her squinty eyed scowl at him – even continuing to look at him with her head turned back as she moved slowly away in an attempt to express her deep disgust.

"Your friend is not much fun I have to say." Henry held out his hand to me. "Shall I escort you to the Green Room, M'lady?" Without giving me time to answer, he placed my arm underneath his and began a slow stroll further back into the building, as if we were promenading on a fine day at the park.

"May I say that you are looking lovely this evening. But then, you always look so very pretty!"

Blushing I thanked him, being unable to look him in the eyes.

"Miss Searle… It has been the utmost pleasure to get to know you this year. I have admired your tenacity at enduring that harpy of a dance partner of yours. We've had some good times, have we not?"

"Yes, indeed!" I was almost breathless. We reached the door. "Well, then. Shall we? Or…shall we do something else instead?"

"Uh…what do you suggest Mr. Johnston."

Henry looked around furtively. "Follow me!" To my shock, Henry pulled me outside and we walked swiftly to a group of fine coaches. "I've got 2 shillings for anyone who can take us around for a ride for twenty minutes."

A uniformed man called out "This way sir!" He opened the door to a rather splendid carriage and the man helped me in. For a moment, I imagined that I might be the victim of some kidnapping plan. But what a handsome rogue my captor would be.

"Anyplace in particular sir?"

"Just somewhere nice and back – we really must be back in time."

Off we set. Henry had a huge devilish grin on his face as we left. I looked excitedly out of the window, amazed at what we were doing. Then I looked down and remembered that I was wearing an odd theatrical costume. I looked as if I were some wood nymph that had stepped out of some enchanted forest. I burst into laughter.

"I look ridiculous!"

"Who cares? No one is looking in. And I think you look like…perfection!"

He looked at me intently. "I wanted to have a moment – however brief, to speak with you alone. Just the two of us, Elizabeth. May I call you by your first name? E-liz-a-beth. Like England's greatest Queen! Without the red hair and wrinkles of course!"

He could not help but to make jokes incessantly. My heart was nearly beating out of my chest. I was almost feeling ill. What had I done? What was going to happen?

"I hope you don't mind me sharing something with you. Maybe as someone…I mean, I talk to other men. But, as a… as a young woman, can you…"

"Yes?!" I tried to encourage him out of his fumbling for words.

"I've had a rather trying time. Marriage can be quite a challenge. Nanette…she gets very frustrated with me. And angry. Sure, we have some good times, but then we fight like cats and dogs." He was looking straight ahead with watery eyes, straining to get his words out. He sighed. "Then we make up and then it starts up again. Like a circle. Some shite circle…oh sorry!"

"No…no. It's ok. Please tell me more. To be honest, I…I could sense a sort of tension between you two…at times."

He grinned, but that was to fight back the sadness within. "Yeah. Umm…my friends tell me that I should hit her. Let her know who is boss and the like. I mean, they don't understand. I …I don't want to do that to any lady, much less my wife. The mother of my children. And you know Nanette! She wouldn't take that lying down, she'd tear a strip off me. She gives as good as she gets - if you know what I mean. Anyway, I wanted to ask you…because you are really a genuinely kind person and I don't think you would gossip and talk about this to others. I can trust you to keep this between us, right?"

"Yes…yes, of course! Absolutely!"

He sighed, the nervously chuckled before continuing.

"This is hard. But I need an honest answer from you. From a good lady. From someone genuine, who will speak…earnestly. I need that from you. May I ask you something?"

I nodded at him as he turned to look at me as he asked, "What is wrong with me?"

I must have looked extremely puzzled. He elaborated, his voice quivering. "I can feel that she does not love me. I don't know how to make it better. I try and then…I get grief in return. It seems as if I can do nothing right. So, I ask of you – as a woman…what can I do? How can I make her fall in love with me again? I want the girl I threw roses to onstage who returned my adoration. Instead of the woman who has betrayed my affections with her spitting and kicking out at me. Cursing me for coming into her life. How did that happen?"

I so wanted to tell him of the love I had for him. But I knew the best way to do this at this very moment was to be his support. To meet his expectations. It was quite a different outcome from what I wanted. I was preparing to be ravished by him in this coach in a frenzied state of passionate love. Instead, there was this. Perhaps it was for the best. Yes, I knew that it was best. But still – my poor heart. I did earnestly feel for him and the pain that he was going through at this moment. I promised myself before that I would do anything for him. Well – this is now what he has asked. Not what I imagined, but what he needed.

"I don't know anything of love, Henry. I'm just a young, inexperienced girl. But I do know this. You are a good person. Please know this. No matter how desperate things get, remember your goodness. Perhaps if you remind Nanette of your good heart. That love that still shines bright – maybe that can help overcome your difficulties. But please – never think that there is something wrong with you. We can all improve, surely. We all have our faults. But when I see you – all I can say is…you make me smile. I see you and I always think of you. Perhaps if you have had cross words with Mrs. Johnston – that stays in her head. Replace those bitter thoughts with kindness. Share in the love of the children you have together. That is such a bond! You both have created new lives. Lives that are dependent on you both – both being together. I do believe it is possible, Henry. Do not despair. Don't stop trying."

He smiled as a tear rolled down his cheek. He grabbed my hand and clasped it tightly with both hands. Oh, how odd this all felt. My emotions were all in a whirl. He brought my hand to his lips and kissed it with his eyes shut. "Thank you, my good friend. I am so sorry. I hope that I did not spoil your evening. I needed your kindness and your wisdom. I feel better now. Thanks to you. Oh look! Isn't that your father?" Henry pointed out the window. My heart was instantly in my throat and I reflexively dived down to the floor of the carriage. Looking up, I saw Mr. Johnston in fits of hysterical laughter.

"You cad!" I did not know what to think about this clown for a man. Perhaps this is what upsets Nanette so. Was any of this sincere? I thought it was. But was it all an act at my expense? I felt as if I were being played for a fool.

He could hardly breathe. "I'm sorry! So – I couldn't help it. I don't cope with serious reflections and introspections very well and a good bit of comedy to lighten the mood was just…hey. Elizabeth – whatever is the matter? Oh please. I did not mean that to hurt your feelings. I just had a stupid, funny thought pop into my head."

"Mr. Johnston, you asked for my sincerity, now I will ask you for yours." My anger was giving me a tide of courage to say and do things I never thought possible. Even I did not know where my swell of emotions would take us.

"Are you toying with me? Is this all amusing to you? I was willing to give to you…anything. Everything – do you understand? That is how much I care for you. Have you any consideration for me whatsoever? This is what I ask of you."

"Aye. I hold you in the highest of esteem Miss Searle. I assure you. Please believe this. I feel too much for you, if you must know. I feel my desire for my wife dissolve in your presence. I am FIGHTING it, not because I am an honourable man – devoted to my fair wife; but because you are far too good to be ruined by me. I will not despoil this precious treasure called Elizabeth and ruin her life with my cursed luck. You deserve more than I. You need someone better than me." He embraced me tightly. I was trembling, almost in a state of shock at this revelation.

"Elizabeth, believe me – I do have a deep love for you. This love I feel within is so intense…so strong that I know it could destroy you and I both. You deserve a good life. Do not settle for a life of turmoil. That is all I could bring, I know that. I KNOW that – and you should too. Now, my dearest friend – go, be happy. Do not settle for anyone who would treat you unkindly."

We arrived back at the theatre. "Elizabeth…"

"Yes?"

"You said that I always make you smile. Please let that continue. I don't want you to feel…uncomfortable in my presence. And I want to see your radiant smile. It is a most wondrous thing!"

I nodded in agreement. Stepping out, he told me to wait before going in. "We don't want any gossip about impropriety, do we? See you!"

I slipped in, looking to ensure that no one was seeing me. As I turned, I saw Henry walking away down Drury Lane, a lonely sad figure.

CHAPTER 22

Joseph Grimaldi

After my odd, emotional encounter with Mr. Henry Erskine Johnstone, I have to say that the rather mundane working conditions of the Royal Circus was a most welcome relief from the mercurial madness that I seemed to always experience at Drury Lane. I was struggling to fully understand what had actually taken place between Mr. Johnston and I at our last meeting. In the end, I thought it best to shut it out of my mind, at least for the time being, and concentrate on the busy theatrical events the Summer had in store for me.

My final night of the season at Drury Lane began promisingly and seemed it would be more positive than usual. I was once again taking on the key role in Cinderella. There was enough time for both Mother and Papa to come and see me perform. Of course, Tom did not attend because, as he said "Why would I want to see something I've seen before? Besides, it is sooooo boring!" I was so pleased that my parents were able to see me step into a prime role – having worked my way up to a most respectable position at the theatre in just a few short months. I could sense their great pride as we went together to the huge theatre. We stood outside for a moment, as they stopped to stare at the grand columns of the entranceway.

It was so lovely to actually see them together. It was as if they were courting from the beginning again. Father had a beaming smile as he gave Mother a gentle little kiss. She was glowing with happiness. I had not seen such joy in my family for a long time. Papa looked at us both and announced triumphantly, "Never in my wildest dreams did I imagine that my daughter would be on the stage – here. At the grandest theatre in the land! Replacing Miss Decamp as well!"

"Ah, there is no replacement for her Papa, I assure you of that!"

Mother chipped in – "And not just one theatre Thomas, but now to be seen at two of the most premier performance venues in London. You certainly have done well, my girl!"

"Playbills! Playbills! Oi! Sir! Would you like a Playbill of tonight's show? It has all their names on it…Hey! Yeah! Even her! You is Miss Searle, isn't ya'? Haha! I knows you I do! I've seen you around! Why I saw you get in that carriage over there the other night with Mr. Johnston I did! You still had your costume on, didn't ya?! A lovely couple you make, I'd say! Haha! Thank you sir, would you like an apple as well? A flower for the lady? Or maybe for Miss Searle over here!" The gap-toothed pamphlet selling girl made an easy sale. Both my parent's expressions changed suddenly with this little piece of information being revealed. I knew I had to make an escape immediately. Now was the time, when Papa was rattling with the coppers in his pockets to give to the mop-capped witness to my indiscretion.

"I'm sure you're mistaken. I really must go now Mother, I will be late. I will meet you here after the finish. And Papa, maybe I can get you into that Green Room after all! Bye!" I kissed Mother briskly on the cheek and my quick getaway whilst I could. I could hear the dim-wit girl continuing to prattle on.

"Oh, I ain't mistaken it! That were them, it were! They ran right past me. He was offerin' two shillings for a little ride. Oh, how lovely that were! I'd love to go for a ride with that gentleman, if you know what I mean! Haha! Oh, he is easy on the eye, he is! I can see that she is a lady with good taste! Haha! Have a lovely evening folks! Playbills! Playbills! Who wants a Playbill?" Charlotte Bristow saw me arrive in my flustered state. "Elizabeth – whatever is wrong?"

"I can't go into details now, but I'm in big trouble with my parents, I think. I need to distract them…put off the end of the evening as long as possible. Have throngs of people about to protect me. Escape to France… I'm joking – sorry! Not funny. Oh, what am I to do? Do you think I could get my parents into the Green Room after the show? I really need this – to do something, anything!"

"Uh, I'm not sure. You realise that this is the penultimate evening of the season. It will be quite crowded with some of Mr. Sheridan's favourites. Some particularly important people. I even heard that Mrs. Jordan has her Duke in the Royal Box this evening, and he is to come down afterwards. Let's ask Joe what he thinks. Joe!"

Mr. Grimaldi came over to us. "Elizabeth wants to get her parents into the Green Room tonight if she can. Do you think that's possible?"

"Oh…tonight, I really don't know. Of all the nights, this is a rather difficult one. It isn't up to me. I am not an important guy around here, Miss Searle – you know that! Let us ask an important gentleman. Oh look! Here comes one now!" Mr. Grimaldi gestured for Mr. Byrne to come over. I clasped my hand to my forehead as my brain began to ache. I could not believe what a farce this was descending into.

"James, James! Miss Searle…it is a special night for her. Her mama and papa are here to see her dance. It would mean so much to all of them if they could go to the Green Room to celebrate Elizabeth's achievements."

Bella Menage walked by and smirked. "What achievement is that? Stepping on my toes like a clumsy oaf on a regular basis? Oh, I know! Candle monitor! You've been promoted to supervising the wick trimmers! Well done you! CONGRATULATIONS!!!"

"Miss Searle – did you say your parents?"

"Yes – yes sir. Oh, it would really mean so much to them. Especially after all we have been through as a family this year." I really overemphasised my predicament for fullest dramatic effect. I am not sure how convincing I was. I hoped my desperation could elicit some sympathy.

Bella piped up – "Oh, and James – I just passed a smelly chimneysweep outside. Poor lad, I think his mum died of consumption and his father has smallpox. Can we get him into the Green Room as well, while we are at it?"

Mr. Byrne looked at her with a straight face. "Miss Menage you need to go and get ready to perform."

"Uh, no actually…I don't have to rush. We have plenty of time, don't we Charlotte? You see – our pantomime is the after show. That means second, we are the second show. And that is after an interval. So, in reality, we have hours before we need to be ready! And we are both just Graces. You gave the important role, Cinderella, to her. That one over there. And I don't see her getting ready. If she is not getting ready, I see no reason why I should…"

The vivacious, beautiful Miss Mellon now joined us, accompanied by Miss Decamp. "No reason to what?"

Bella started to explain "Oh Miss Searle wants to bring tramps and vagabonds into the Green Room tonight. I for one think it is a grand idea! Shall we go round some up right now?"

Mr. Grimaldi interjected "Oh now Bella – c'mon! It is nothing of the sort! Don't be ridiculous!"

"Ridiculous? I can assure you what is ridiculous is…"

Mr. Byrne took the opportunity of Bella's rant to steer me away to the side and speak quietly to me in a corner. "Miss Searle, is your mother here tonight?"

"Yes! And my Papa as well – you met him the other

night."

"Hmm…" He looked as if he was trying hard to think over the cacophony and mayhem that Bella was creating just a short distance away.

"Leave it with me – don't worry. We will get them in, no matter what. I promise you! Now you just concentrate on what you do best. You will want your parents to see you at your very top form tonight. I think it will be a most interesting evening for them." He then picked up his voice and spoke out commandingly "Cinderella cast - I need you all in the dressing room to quickly discuss some last-minute changes. Mr. Grimaldi, can you gather those who aren't here please. See you all in five minutes."

I saw James walk over to Mr. Wroughton – who seemed to be in a harried state. I saw him look over in my direction as James spoke with him. I decided to try and make my way to the dressing room as we were directed. Bella was continuing with her seemingly endless diatribe.

"…and before you know it, it is pandemonium – that is what it is. And another thing…oh, Bandy – Bandy! Come here!"

"That's not my name." I turned and continued to walk away.

"Oh right…Miss Sorrell. Tell me Miss Sorrell, what did James say? Are we having the vegetable sellers from Covent Garden market join us for some brandy? I do hope they bring some cucumber with them…I do love cucumbers so."

"I bet you do Bella!" laughed Joe Grimaldi. "Quick someone, get Bella a cucumber!"

Unbelievably, a workman from the props department happened by with a wicker basket of various fruits and vegetables. Within seconds, Joe had the cucumber in his hand and shouted out with mischievous glee "Miss Bella! Where would you like it!" There were rude guffaws all around, but Bella was enjoying the banter.

She responded saucily. "Well Mr. Grimaldi, I could think of quite a few places that you could stuff your cucumber!" She bit her lip and looked very coy as raucous whistling came from the amused male employees of Drury Lane Theatre.

"Why wherever do you mean Miss Bella?" Joe taunted, as he placed the vegetable in his eye, on top of his head like a unicorn, then protruding upright between his legs.

There were great peals of laughter all around, then the workman shouted. "Hey Joe! I've got to eat that cucumber you know!", leading to even more hysterics. All this madness proved a suitable distraction for Bella, and she mentioned the Green Room no more as we gathered to listen to Mr. Byrne's list of rather minor changes for the evening's show.

Throughout the performance of The Way to Keep Him, I kept thinking through how the scenario with my parents would unfurl tonight. It was very troubling, but at least I had some time to piece a plausible story together. Now if I only could think of a valid reason as to why I was entering a carriage alone with dashingly handsome, married man. My ideas were admittedly very thin.

I was feeling very miffed that an evening where at the very moment I should be feeling elation at reaching the pinnacle of my success that all that I felt was worry and agitation. This was punctuated further as I sang the lyrics of Cinderella's songs. They seemed to deliver a most poignant message directly to my heart. I had to try hard to keep hold of my feelings as the words sprang forth:

"Soft hours of childhood, how swiftly ye flew,
Sweet scenes of bliss, I must bid you adieu,
Thoughts that delighted,
Joys my youth plighted,
Mis'ry has blighted-
Hope leaves me too"

Mr. Grimaldi's Pedro brought me food, after the evil

stepsisters taunted me with their invitations to a ball that I had no chance to attend. In the back of my mind, I was associating this with the entrance to the Green Room this evening. The clever stage transformations then took place, as Pedro caught the magnificent dress falling from the heavens. The pumpkin transformed to a coach with footmen. The next scene at the palace, Mr. Byrne whisked me around the stage as we danced most elegantly. It occurred to me that he was quite different with me at this time in comparison to the other times I played Cinderella. I sensed he was harbouring much more feeling in his role. His stare was sincere and personal rather than theatrical, as it had been before. Perhaps this was due to some sort of sentimentality. As this was the final performance of a ballet that was an amazing success, he may have been overcome. Alas! The clocks struck midnight all around and chaos ensued. Very much a match for how I was feeling with my personal turn of events. Mr. Grimaldi demonstrated his comic powers to the extent that this minor role would allow. Trick wires pulled his fine clothing off, revealing Pedro's rags underneath. He acrobatically ran amok, leaping over tables of fine china and candles with deft precision. As he pulled a startled stepsister in front of him to protect his modesty to the great amusement of the audience, stagehands quickly used the smoke and distraction to whisk the ball gown off me, leaving me in humble peasant garb once again. As I ran across the stage, looking distraught and being sure to leave behind one shoe, I felt reminded that all of my success and achievements could just as easily be pulled out of my grasp and cast into history. Fortunes can wax and wane. I was staring at poverty and desperation at one point in time, and there I could return. Only fate could determine if, like Cinderella, this were to be my very own midnight.

CHAPTER 23

I did not want to give my parents an opportunity to question me about Mr. Johnston in private. I knew that being around others would delay the inquisition. Perhaps copious amounts of wine and being in the presence of celebrities would mollify them for the evening. Miss Bristow had previously met my father, so I pleaded with her to meet my parents and bring them backstage – with the excuse that I had to change out of my costume. Also, I was aware that I needed to check with Mr. Byrne if his assurances were indeed true and that we were allowed to enter. To my surprise, it was Mr. Byrne who came looking for me.

"Are they still coming?"

"Yes – I've just sent Miss Bristow down to collect them. Is everything alright? Am I able to bring them?"

"Yes, yes. I've cleared it with Wroughton. Pulled a few favours. I will tell Mr. Grimaldi to meet all of you at the stage door and bring you through."

"Oh, thank you! Thank you, Mr. Byrne, – for everything! For the opportunity to work here and to learn from you. Words cannot convey my gratitude…"

"Well, I think this evening will certainly be a night to remember. Miss Searle, it has truly been a delight working with you. I am not sure how many know. I have kept it quiet. The Byrne family shall not be at Drury Lane in the coming year. Rest assured; I am certain that our paths shall cross again. And I should be most delighted to work with you again or recommend your talents to any theatre company in the nation that has the good sense to consider placing you in their employ. So…I thought it may be helpful to you to have this." He pulled out a letter sealed with wax. "It is a letter of recommendation from me. It may prove useful in the future – who knows? In reality, I do not think you will need it - for your great talent, skill and beauty are apparent to all who take the time to observe you. Best wishes to you, Elizabeth!"

He smiled sweetly as he handed it over to me. I was so very touched that I embraced him, without a moment's hesitation. I was thinking I may have done something very wrong. Mr. Byrne was looking very reticent suddenly. Had I committed a faux pas?

"Uh…I was wondering, Miss Searle." He gazed intently at me. "Could I entrust you with this?" He pulled out another sealed letter, but this was addressed to an 'Elizabeth Siddenham', my mother's maiden name. "Would you be able to see that your mother gets this – in private, where it could not possibly fall into anyone else's hands? It is of a rather personal nature, you see, and I would think we would both be rather embarrassed if another party read the contents. The meanings of these things can be easily misconstrued of course. Especially if taken out of context and I mean to cause your mother no harm. So, can I ask you for your kind discretion?"

I readily agreed and assured him, reminding him that we had first met with the delivery of a discrete communication and now seemed to be parting in the same circumstances. I looked at the envelope and noted it was much more securely and heavily sealed with wax. Unlike my recommendation letter, there was no emblem on the seal to indicate who the letter was from (mine had a bold letter B for Byrne burnished onto the red lump of wax). As curious as I was, I was trustworthy and had no intention of letting him down. I was thinking much more about ensuring that my parents had no opportunity to get me into a private place to discuss about Mr. Johnston and riding in carriages. I had to get them into the Green Room quickly. Coming down the stairs from the dressing room, I saw they were having a pleasant discussion with Joe Grimaldi, his wife and his wife's sister Charlotte Bristow. Joe caught sight of me smiled and started to applaud. "Oh, and there she is! Cinderella herself – BRAVO! Well done!"

"And to you Mr. Grimaldi! Or should I say 'Pedro'? You had the audience laughing so tonight! Shall we go to the Green Room?"

"Ah yes, I was just telling Mr. and Mrs. Searle that it may be a bit crowded. Not just with people, but bottles of wine and nice things to eat. NO cucumber though, I assure you!" Joe winked at me and smiled, reminding me of his deftness at quick distraction techniques. If he could get Bella Menage off-topic, then he most certainly could divert Mother and Papa away from thoughts of my indiscretion. I was a true believer in Mr. Grimaldi's magical abilities.

Although a very sizable room, the elegant Green Room did seem small and far less grand when all the cast and their friends were present. And this evening was the fullest I had ever seen it. All of us had to squeeze through the door into the tightly packed room. We eased our way inside and I tried to steer my parents towards a table of drinks. They were mesmerised by all who were present. People only seen on stage or mentioned in the newspapers. There was pompous Mr. Sheridan chatting with the Duke of Clarence and Dorothy Jordan. Maria Decamp was with her supposed fiancée Stephen Kemble, the first time I had witnessed that. He was speaking to his nephew, Michael Sharp. Looking bored next to him was Bella Menage sipping on her glass and scanning the room haughtily with her eyes. Mr.

Bannister in a hearty discussion with Miss Mellon and Miss Pope, which seemed to have them laughing. I saw the little Byrne children giggling and dancing in whatever space they could find and stealing scraps of bread and pork pie from the tables when they had the chance. Mrs. Grimaldi and Miss Bristow whisked Mother away to introduce her to Miss Rein – our resident dress designer, having heard that my mother was talented in theatrical costume making. Wanting to distract Papa, I began to tell him of the letter of recommendation from Mr. Byrne. I pulled the envelope from my pocket. To my horror, I could feel Mr. Byrne's secret letter slip to the floor – only to be picked up by the bane of my life, Bella Menage. Mr. Grimaldi could read the terror on my face and with quick thinking, he pulled Papa away in the opposite direction. "Mr. Searle – have you ever met a Duke before? He really is not what you imagine – no airs or graces! He is so approachable! Come! I will introduce you!"

"Thank you kindly, Bella – that's mine."

"It is addressed to Elizabeth Siddenham. That's not your name. Can't you read? You do know that you have to look at the second name as well, don't you? Not every letter addressed to an Elizabeth is yours for the keeping."

I was looking around, aghast. Joe was keeping Papa occupied. I saw Mother in a conversation with Mr. Byrne. They both were looking a bit uncomfortable and speaking in a way that they seemed to hope was not apparent to anyone else. Bella was waving the letter in the air, keeping it out of my reach.

"Give it to me! It isn't yours!"

"Are you changing your name? Are you so ashamed of how dreadful you have performed in London that you are going to relaunch your career in the provinces with a *nom de plume*? Siddenham is a rather hard to spell, Bandy. You should have really chosen something a little simpler – to match your personality. Like Slut! Yes, I like that – easy to remember! Elizabeth Slut! And it still has the 'S' – so it wouldn't be that hard for you to learn to write it!"

She sucked in breath excitedly. "Or are you secretly married, Elizabeth?! Oh, you minx! Who would have thought you had it in you? Keeping secrets! Did you go to Gretna Green? I know who it is…it's that Chimneysweep I saw! He is a rather handsome little lad, I imagine. Once you wash off all that soot."

Bella waved the envelope in the air and called out "Miss Siddenham! Miss Elizabeth Sid…" I yanked on her arm pulling her slightly off balance. She was enjoying every moment of this.

"It belongs to my mother!" I whispered.

"Oh, don't be daft. I thought her name was Mrs. Sorrell – just like yours! Only with M R S in front. Those letters mean MISS-US. I can teach you all about reading sometime Bandy. In fact, shall we have a lesson now. Let's start with reading this correspondence…"

I pulled at the letter, trying to get it out of her grasp – to no avail.

"Oh dear…it is so tightly glued and sealed! It is as if someone does not want it to be easily opened! What could it possibly say? I cannot imagine…"

"Bella please…it really does belong to my mother, now give it back to me please!"

"Are you begging me? I haven't heard that you are begging me. Would it not be humiliating to have to bow down before me on your hands and knees, like some feral little dog. I think I would find that most amusing."

"Please, Bella! Stop now, you've had your fun."

"Why – if you say this is your mother's – and she is not really Mrs. Sorrell. Hmmm. Perhaps she is a bigamist and has two husbands. Or perhaps she is an unmarried woman named Miss Siddenham. BANDY! Oh Bandy, I knew it! You are a bastard! A dirty little bastard girl!"

"Just stop! Give it to me – NOW!"

"Now Bandy, being a bastard really isn't all that shameful really. It seems to be quite the fashion now – honestly. Why just look at Mrs. Jordan. Goodness knows she has pumped out about a dozen bastards for her Duke over there. Oh, isn't that your father over there talking to him? Maybe he is getting tips on how to avoid marrying the mother of one's children. Always good to learn from the best, I say…"

"That is enough." Miss Mellon snapped the letter out of the hand of Bella, catching her off-guard.

"Oh – it's the banker's wife! Oh – sorry, that was a bit premature, wasn't it? Tell me Miss Mellon, how is Mrs. Coutts these days? Bandy, do you know if the church can do a wedding immediately following a funeral? Poor Miss Mellon has been waiting ever so long to see her beau. She has to keep seeing him at the bank so he can help her with her accounts. Tell me Harriet, does he assist with deposits or withdrawals?" I was truly aghast at how Bella spoke to her superiors. It is one thing to slander Mrs. Jordan out of earshot, but here she was insulting Harriet Mellon to her face - one of the most celebrated actresses on the stage.

"I shall not descend to your base level of gutter-sniping Miss Menage. You are truly full of spite and must be desperately unhappy if you feel the need to sprinkle your misery around so liberally. Indeed, I have the utmost pity for you, for no one really cares to be in your company."

Bella laughed artificially. "Oh Miss Mellon! There really is no need to feel sorry for me! I quite enjoy myself really. By noticing the profuse imperfections of those around me, I cannot possibly feel low!"

"Go to your painter-boy now, run along! I do believe Mr. Sharp is feeling some admiration for Miss Taylor. They seem to be enjoying each other's company immensely! They make an attractive pair, don't they Elizabeth?"

"All this chat has made me terribly thirsty. It has been most pleasurable, ladies. Do try and have a good evening!"

Bella smiled sweetly, slowly turned as if she had not a care in the world, then rushed over to Michael Sharp as quickly as her feet could manage.

Miss Mellon handed the envelope over to me. She had never once looked to see who it was addressed to. "I don't know how she does it, but I always end up stooping to her low-level tactics. It is infuriating! I get so cross with myself! I always tell myself that I won't let her get to me, but she always manages to."

"Thank you so much for your kindness Miss Mellon. I really don't know what I would have done without your assistance. I don't know how she gets away with her shocking behaviour." This was perhaps the most I had ever spoken with Miss Mellon, as we rarely worked together directly. She was renowned for her beauty and great talent on the stage.

"I think Sheridan is fond of her. He doesn't have to endure what we have to. And there are many who are quite attached to her brother and sister. They are vastly different characters from her. Arabella has grown to be spiteful and vain. She is incessantly rude to me."

"Even to you? I thought her hatred was reserved for myself."

"Oh yes! At every opportunity she tries to shame me about my relationship with Mr. Coutts. There is an understanding between Mrs. Coutts and I. We are on friendly terms and I speak with her grown children regularly. It is…a unique arrangement. I don't expect everyone to understand. But most have the courtesy to keep their thoughts to themselves, Well, I do hope you have a good break away from Miss Menage over the holiday. I hear that you are engaged at the Circus?"

"Yes…they have been exceedingly kind to me. Mr. Male is there as well."

"Well, I wish you the best. Keep that letter safe now! I heard that Bella used to work as a street pickpocket. She will be after it again if you're not careful!"

We both laughed and I thanked her again profusely. It was interesting to me to witness the lives of some of these women I admired most. They seemed to sidestep the rules of decorum that society has placed upon us. They were strong, intelligent women – Mrs. Jordan, Miss Mellon. But it seemed they still had to remain within the orbit of powerful men. Was it ever possible to break free?

Papa grabbed me tersely by the elbow suddenly, making me gasp suddenly. "We need to go now."

Mother was frantically following behind, whispering loudly in an effort to remain discrete. "Tom. TOM, please. Maintain some composure."

Stepping outside the door onto the cobbles of Drury Lane, Papa looked furious. I had never seen him like this. He was the calmest, most mild-mannered gentleman I knew. He was marching up the road at such a pace, I could scarcely believe that this was the man who was so frail and infirm just a few weeks ago.

"Tom, tell me what I was supposed to do? You were desperately ill, and I did not know what was to become of us. I had to use the contacts that I knew to help…"

"To help place Elizabeth in that den of inequity when she was only 14 years old! And who did you entrust her to? Mr. James Byrne of all people! And look where it goes – she is riding in a carriage with a married man. After I told her to steer clear of him, she still contin…"

"You KNEW about Mr. Johnston? What has been going on? You accuse me of betrayals, and now you say this? Would someone kindly please inform me of what is going on?"

I tried to interject some information that I hoped may alleviate the situation. "I know that you will not believe me and that it looks most suspicious. But Mr. Johnston wanted to ask me advice on how to reconcile with his wife – that is all. Honestly! He has been a kind friend to me – he needed the perspective of a woman to know why his wife may feel so vexed at him and what he might do to mend their hearts. He did not want others to overhear this – that is why we were in the carriage." I was so very eager for this to be over.

Someone from one of the windows above shouted out the window. "Oi! Can you pack it in?! Some of us are trying to sleep!"

"Maybe I need the perspective of a woman. Tell me if you would – my dear daughter, why do you think Mrs. Byrne would come to me and ask if I could extricate my wife away from her husband's side? Why would Mrs. Searle allow Mr. Byrne to place his arm on her arm, as if they were well acquainted?"

"He was just leading me to the drinks table."

"And as I approached, he had his hand on your back. Tell me, did you need a push or a shove in order to get a bit of refreshment?"

"I cannot believe what you are implying here! After all that I…that we have done to keep us clothed and fed. To help you with your recovery…"

"By abandoning me to my elderly aunt? So that you could have an opportunity to dally with an old flame?"

"You KNOW that is not true! Not any of it! You have NO IDEA how worried and helpless we felt as you were lying there in your bed. We thought you would die! We prayed endlessly for your good health and did all that we could with the meagre resources that we had at our disposal. And I have no regrets – about any decisions that I made. Because they were what had to be done while you were in such an incapacitated state. I have not been unfaithful to you. Nor would I have the time or inclination to do so. Because I am devoted to you. You have my undying love and commitment and always have."

Papa stopped still in the street. He began to weep. "I…I am sorry. I feel as if I am easy to anger nowadays. I am not myself; I know that. I am incapable of doing what I used to be able to do …physically. I am not able to think in a clear manner as I did in the past. I cannot explain it adequately. It is as if my thoughts are lost in a fog and I have to work so hard to retrieve them. It makes me feel so frustrated. I…I am sorry if I take it out on you both. I feel so weak and useless at times. I should not blame you if you wanted to leave me for Mr. Byrne."

I took Papa by the hand and hugged him. "Please Papa, don't feel this way! We love you so. And be assured – I have been working with Mr. Byrne closely now for the whole year. He is a very devoted man and loves his children dearly."

Papa smirked sarcastically. "Oh really? Does he now?"

"Thomas, Elizabeth is right. We want you to know that we are a family. We are together in love, no matter what happens. We all have each other. Come now, don't be angry or cross. Let us put all our quarrels this evening in the past."

Papa sighed and nodded in reluctant agreement. We arrived at our door to be met by a groggy and grumpy Tom. "Where have you been? You've been out all night!" Mother rushed him up to bed and I kissed Papa goodnight, hoping that Mr. Johnston would never be mentioned again. I was most eager for this Pandora's Box to be firmly shut closed.

CHAPTER 24

With one palm of my hand outstretched dramatically and the other hand valiantly holding up a broom as if it were a spear, I gazed intently into the crack of my mirror with an earnest attempt to look impassioned. This was hard to maintain, as in actuality, I looked most ridiculous as I was wearing an upturned bucket on my head to replicate the feeling of a heavy helmet. I was trying to remember the longest dialogue that I had yet to recite onstage. Mr. Cross had suddenly thrown a script at me to learn the previous evening. Having thought that dialogue was not allowed at the non-patent theatres, I enquired about what this was. I did not want to run the risk of being arrested.

"Oh, it is fine, Miss Searle. It is not a concern at all. The censors never worry if it is all about patriotism and how wonderful the country is. They only get jumpy if they think there is criticism of the King or government in any way. I thought it may be novel for the audience to hear some words that had no musical accompaniment to them." He was always trying to push the boundaries to the very edge of what was acceptable to see what he would be able to get

away with.
And so now I stood here, with my loyal cleaning utensils, trying to drill the words into my memory. Athena ensured that I was transformed into a British Amazon, not a silly girl with broom and bucket. I began to recite my moving 'Patriotic Address':
"Citizens of Britain, I implore you to look to your hearts and souls – for our very freedom is at stake from…a…" I caught the glimpse of Tom behind me in the mirror. He was mocking me, mouthing the words in a most silly fashion, and holding up an envelope in the air. My heart sank as I thought it was the letter to Mother from Mr. Byrne. I hadn't the opportunity yet to pass it on to her in private.
"What is that?!" I snapped.
"Oh this? Oh yeah. You got a letter. You owe me a penny."
"They asked for payment? When did it arrive? Give it to me!"
"No…I just want a penny. I want to go to the market and buy something. It came a couple of days ago."
"What? Why didn't you give it to me? It could be important – foolish boy!"
He held it out of reach and continued to annoy me. "Just joking! It was this morning! Actually, it was last night when you were performing, but I just saw it in my room again this morning and thought I should give it to you. I tried to hold it up to the light to see if I could read it, but…" I snatched it out of his hand.
"Hey! Where's my penny?" I pulled my drawer open from a small desk in my room and took two ha'pennies out of my bag. I ceremoniously plopped them in his hand.
"What's it say? Who's it from?"
"You can go now." I pointed to the doorway. He shrugged and skipped down to the street whilst whistling with the coins in his grasp. I tore the letter open with a sharp opener, eager to see the contents.

Dear Miss Searle,

It has been troubling my mind incessantly since we parted. I have been thinking that I may have caused you much upset by my silly, prattish behaviour on the evening we last met. I often resort to playing the clown when confronted by life's serious questions.

I wish to reconfirm what I expressed to you. I was not being insincere at any point in time. The comical gesture was just a whim that came upon me suddenly and was not planned. I most sincerely apologise if it was in bad taste. I certainly do not wish it to trouble you any longer, so I do beg your forgiveness.

I do indeed value your wise advice and have taken note of your helpful suggestions. Daily, I do see some improvements in the situation and feel optimistic that it may continue. It is a great service that you have done for me, and I shall be forever in your debt. Whenever I am apt to feel low, I shall have a wonderous vision of Grace shining down upon me to lift my spirits once again. Know that it is with thanks to you that I am able to crawl from the dark clouds of despair and can see the light once again. And thus, I shall always be…

Your Humble Servant,
H

Inside were a few small, curly locks of his hair, a tangible, physical reminder of this man I had been so infatuated with. I held this precious treasure in my hand, dazed and not sure what to do. For the moment, I hid the letter and its contents away in a secure, safe place; hopefully hidden from the prying fingers of my brother Tom.

I was most pleased that my parents had overcome their differences, and all was peaceful at home once again. Even more pleasurable to me was that there was not any further mention of Henry Johnston either. As the days passed, I felt that his letter was quite a comfort to me. It heartened me to think that he was concerned about my feelings. And I had positive confirmation – a hint, of his true affection for me. And I could look at this small lock of hair and be reminded that I never did have the chance to touch any of it when it was actually upon his head. For some strange reason, that thought always made me giggle with silly delight. The most important result was that I felt I need no longer dwell on the matter. At this time, Drury Lane felt a million miles away. I had more pressing concerns, such as being a British Amazon.

Walking with Mother to the Circus that afternoon, I felt a bit awkward as I drew a secret communication from my sleeve. I almost felt as if I were betraying Papa in some way. I did not dare to think why he would be so jealous of Mr. Byrne.

"Mother, Mr. Byrne told me to give this to you in private. I do not know what it is about."

"Oh...oh...thanks. Thank you." Mother replied sheepishly. She never mentioned the contents of the letter I passed on to her, and I was determined never to ask.

"Is everything alright?"

"Yes, yes. I...I think this may be about all your fine work. Everyone at Drury Lane seemed so complimentary about you."

"Mother...I hope you don't mind. May I ask how you first came to know Mr. Byrne?"

"Oh...uh...I knew him from when I was dancing at Birmingham Theatre. So, in a professional capacity is how I knew him... uh, know him. When I was touring the provinces, we would work together sometimes. I saw him in Newcastle. Another season in Cheltenham. I think your father gets a bit jealous of Mr. Byrne at times because, and please don't tell him I said this, James is the better dancer." We both laughed nervously.

"You know, James has been the ballet director for many prominent theatres. He has had the opportunity to go to America. All the things I think Mr. Searle would have like to have had the chance to do. Instead, he had to tutor the miserable brats of the Bon Ton.

It is difficult, I know from experience. I've seen many of my colleagues move up the ranks. I was your age when Sarah Siddons first started at Birmingham. And I worked with Elizabeth Farren as well. Look at her now - the Countess of Derby! Why, even my very own daughter has achieved a level of success that I could only have dreamed of! I like to think I played some part in getting to where you are now."

"You played every part in it Mother! I would not be on the stage now had you not written to Mr. Byrne. And your rant at Mr. D'Egville actually resulted in my work at the Royal Circus!"

We both laughed heartily at this. It most certainly was the truth!

I spent a good deal of the summer in front of the mirror at home as I rehearsed my roles endlessly. I was most pleased to be involved with portraying some extraordinarily strong and interesting female characters. As the month of June wound to a close, the *Wild Girl!* would see herself transformed into a slave girl, fighting to be emancipated in *Johanna of Surinam*. Mr. Cross must have certainly saved a significant amount of funds on costuming for my characters. I went from the rags of a feral girl to the tattered cloth of a slave. And my skin was darkened further, moving from the patchy grime to the exotic, dark brown hues of the alluring Johanna.

Mr. Cross seemed to be able to pull in favours from all the papers to ensure regular glowing reviews. On our opening night, *The Times* reported on the most magnificent chandelier ever seen descending from the ceiling to great applause during the show. Much was written about the minute and accurate detail in the set design, based original drawings taken on the spot and 'new dresses corresponding to the costumes of the country' (which I can vouch as false, as my breasts were most certainly *not* exposed, as was actually depicted in the source material that I had seen). They were also impressed with the scene of the British landing and seizing of the fort. With all the horsemanship, firing guns and illuminations, it is no wonder why I never received a mention. People who did get mention were not employees of the theatre. They were the audience themselves. Mr. Cross worked hard to ensure that the names of the upper classes were frequently dropped into news clippings, such as the weekend performance when we had the Duchess of Rutland and Lord Bentinck attend.

And so, the month of July continued without any hindrances of note. The size of the audience was not as full as Mr. Cross would have hoped. It was not for want of trying. He engaged a performing dog to rival Drury Lane's Carlo, acrobats of all description, first-rate singers such as Mr. Terrail (who simply weren't quite first-rate enough to be at the Haymarket or Ranelagh Gardens). The heat of the summer amplified the smells of the animals and people present. With the candles of the chandelier ablaze, the theatre was indeed an accurate replica of the heat found in the jungles of Surinam. Adding further authenticity was the remarkable birdsong provided by Mr. Cuerton, a most talented Siffleur who could whistle up sounds as if conjured by magic.

There was one evening that proved especially memorable for me during this sweltering month. Mr. Cross had welcomed prominent members of the Abolitionist movement against slavery to attend a performance of *Johanna*. He permitted them space in the lobby to sell political pamphlets and other promotions to their just cause. Before preparing for my performance, I met briefly with some of the passionate members of this moral movement who strove to end the brutality and inhumanity of the slave trade. I was proud to sign up to the cause myself and pledged whatever support that I, a mere young girl, could muster.

After my performance, before I could slip out of my slave rags and wash the face paint off of my skin, I was called by Mr. Cross to come to the Green Room. There before me I saw a most beautiful dark hued woman standing before me wearing a splendid green silk dress of the finest quality.

"Miss Searle, Mrs. Davinier has asked specially if she could meet with you." Mr. Cross smiled and held his arm out in the direction of this striking lady.

"Miss Searle, I felt the need to come and thank you!" She spoke in the most elegant, refined fashion – as the ladies of quality that I served as a milkmaid at Aunt Harriet's farm. She coughed and was visibly looking a bit unwell.

"Please excuse me! I'm not feeling as well as I should be, but I did not want to miss the opportunity to see this performance. It brought back many thoughts about my childhood in the West Indies. I was a young girl when I left for England and have few clear memories of my mother. Watching your portrayal of Johanna moved me so. It made me think of the horrors and of the evils that my people endure every day. You are the conscious of this land. The torments that my poor mother must have endured. And what I too, would have endured had I not had the good fortune to be the daughter of the well-respected Sir John Lindsay. The feeling and emotions you conveyed…without words you expressed the indignities and the suffering of enslaved people. It is so important that all in Britain know are reminding everyone who partakes of snuff or has sugar in their tea – the true price of that commodity. It is human blood and the tears of a captive people. I wanted you to know that I could feel that this is much more than a mere stage role for you. I genuinely know this! I could feel the presence of my ancestors as you performed. I know that they were there supporting you and willing you to tell their story. Mr. Cross has always been a strong supporter of justice. And I think he has directed you well to promote the cause."

She took my hand and smiled as tears welled up in both of our eyes. I expressed to her how moved I was by her words and told her of my resolve to ensure that there was an end to the wicked trade in human cargo. I told her of my research into the role – reading the accounts of John Stedman and his Johanna. Then I suddenly looked at my hand and noticed the colour bleeding away from my skin and onto the palm of this elegant woman. I apologised profusely, embarrassed to be portraying a woman of colour when in fact I was an imposter. She reassured me that the message justified the methods. I sought reassurance that my portrayal was respectable and dignified – which Mrs. Davinier insisted to me it was. We continued to speak for a long time, joined by many of the cast and some of Mr. Cross's abolitionist friends. I was delighted to discover that Mrs. Davinier had been baptised at St. George's in Bloomsbury – my church with the Pegasus and old King George! We fondly bid farewell at the end of the evening. Had Athena arranged for me to meet this amazing woman to instil confidence in my performance? I was so grateful that I had the precious opportunity, for I was most devastated to hear that this amazing woman left her earthly body only a few days afterwards. It was truly shocking and most distressing to think how fleeting and tenuous our lives could be. In my heart, I dedicated every performance to the memory of Mrs. Davinier – in the knowledge that she had been so very moved by this burletta, and the part I had played in delivering the message to the audience. It was my resolution from that moment to strive for the emancipation of all men and women – to break free from the shackles of unfairness.

Back at home, in the world of mundane domesticity, Tom was feeling a bit disgruntled at having to take instruction. With my thoughts enmeshed in the brutal world of slavery every evening, I must admit that I felt Tom's troubles were trifling indeed, and I held out no sympathy or compassion for his predicament whatsoever. Agricultural skills aside, Tom's education had been neglected for the better part of a year now and he was in need of firming up the rigour of his learning regime. Papa, with the most free-time available, had now become teacher to my brother. He was getting drilled in reading and writing instruction, with an additional emphasis on elocution lessons. Papa was hoping to enable Tom to fool people that he was a respectable, well-educated gentleman upon reaching adulthood; instead of the penniless, annoying little toe-rag that he currently was. Papa also practiced his dancing instruction on Tom. This was something that Tom absolutely loathed, but Papa felt that he needed the opportunity to practice if he were to regain his dance lesson clientele. He had lost considerable confidence and unruly Tom certainly tested his skills of maintaining discipline amongst his pupils.

Little Tom tried to make as many excuses as possible to visit Aunt Harriet. He really played the part of farm hand best. I do admit that I was dearly missing our regular visits to my sweet aunt. It was nearly impossible due to my busy schedule. Sundays were free for all of us. Having a church only three doors away gave us little excuse to not be able to attend. Although I would say that we were not an overly devout family, I do believe that all four of us felt indebted to our Heavenly Father for delivering us from the catastrophe that we faced last autumn. Witnessing the sudden fate of Mrs. Davinier, I was very aware of how precious our time on this earth is. We had so much to be thankful for. I soon learned to find the services quite soothing. I enjoyed the music, the lovely, peaceful interior of the church and the opportunity to have an hour of time to daydream – letting my thoughts drift as I ignored the sermon. I often found myself remembering back to girlhood times when my mother would scold me for dancing on the grand 'stage' of the porch of the church. I think I would love to have a magic spell and be able to cast myself back to those innocent, carefree days of my youth. And perhaps even be able to right the wrongs of this wicked world and all the evil creatures who inhabit it.

CHAPTER 25

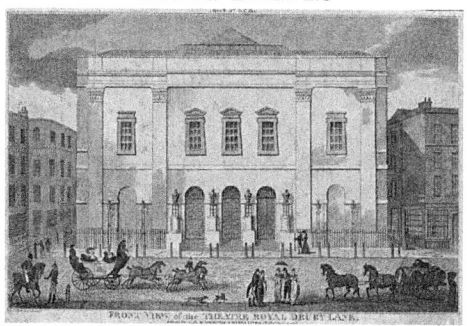

Mr. Cross very kindly spent all of four pence to purchase a cheap little chapbook for my edification. He gifted me Sarah Wilkinson's *Maid of Lochlin* to prepare me for my upcoming role in August. I became spellbound by the tale of Fingal, King of the stormy land of Morven as he meets with Starno, King of Denmark. Resolving to marry his beautiful daughter Agandecca, plans become thwarted by a wicked high priest who predicts doom for the state if the marriage proceeds. Of course, Fingal is so determined to marry the Maid of Lochlin that he invades Denmark. This would give Mr. Cross many opportunities for exciting horse led battle scenes. It all ends tragically as Agandecca is stabbed to death by her father Starno in order to prevent Fingal from whisking her away and living happily ever after. And I had many opportunities to express feelings and drama through movement.

As I carried on with being a slave at the Circus, I could see the grand sets being painted in time for this new grand Scottish spectacle to open in August. Mother and her minions in the costuming room fitted me up in tartan kilts and the clothing of a Danish princess. This was a welcome change from the humble cloth of my previous two roles! And the choreography was to feature my favourite types of dance – Scottish reels and hornpipes. There would also be moments for expressive ballet to convey events of tragedy without the use of the spoken word. Mr. Cross was determined to ensure the fine quality of the performance and hired the best choreographer he could enlist to his cause. So it was with great surprise that both Mother and I arrived at the theatre and found the gracious member of the D'Egville family, George, waiting for my arrival to go over the movements that he had in mind for the show.

I worked extremely hard those days, but with pleasure. I was invigorated by the strength of my character, the majesty of my painted backdrops, the elegance of my dresses and the sprightliness of the music I was to perform to. When one enjoys what they do, their work is not toil, but play. And that is how I felt precisely when I was at the Royal Circus. There was no drama going on behind the scenes. Mother expressed to me how exceedingly rare this was, and that the grief I experienced at Drury Lane was much more typical of the theatrical world. It made me feel a certain amount of dread for the summer to come to an end, as I had begun to feel so at home at this warm, welcoming theatre. My last performance of *The Maid of Lochlin* was the 15th of September. I had to bid my co-workers farewell until I was due to return one last time for my benefit performance in October. Mother was feeling sadness, as I would no longer be under her protective care whilst at work. Again, I would have to fend for myself at the competitive environment of Mr. Sheridan's crew.

At the end of September, all would be revealed, as the cast for the new season began to return to London from their summer engagements in the provinces. For some, it was a monumental comedown. Names associated with the patent theatres of London were lauded in the Provinces. The theatres of towns and cities from all across the land competed for big names that could draw in crowds and sell tickets. For many, the summer season was the 'bread and butter' to their existence. London only maintained their reputation – not their pocketbooks. For others, such as myself, it was a shorter journey back. We returned from the circuses – Astley's and the Royal, from the Saddler's Wells, or the most reputable King's Theatre in Haymarket. Perhaps even a few switched from speaking German at the Coburg and could ease back into speaking English once again. Or maybe returning indoors once again after a stint outside in the gardens of Ranelagh or Vauxhall. So much entertainment. And so very many entertainers all vying for the chance to be in the most special of all theatres: Drury Lane. I was one of the fortunate. I had my message from the managers, Mr. Bannister and Mr. Wroughton to come and meet all the cast and prepare for the year to come.

As I walked onto the steps outside the theatre at Drury Lane, I admit to having a feeling of excited anticipation as to what the new season would reveal. What would be performed? Would there be interesting roles for me to take part in? I had a new-found confidence since my successes at the Royal Circus in the summer. I was determined to continue to be bolstered by this wave of positivity. That joyous feeling was put to the test as soon as I entered the stage door for the first meeting of the cast. My heart immediately sank when the very first person I spotted was Bella Menage, speaking with her rather pleasant and benign sister. Her eyes were keenly fixed upon the door to see who was entering – there was no possible way for me to have entered without meeting her gaze. Her eyes widened with mischievous glee and her whole face immediately became radiant with animation. I was filled with dread. Whatever she was about to do – she was going to enjoy this.

"Bandy! Look everyone! It's BANDY! Oh Bandy, I have missed you so!" I was very startled and taken aback to find Bella embracing me and leading me by the hand onto the stage where the others had been mingling but now were looking at us with some trepidation. I did not for one moment fall for her well executed yet insincere mock greeting. I felt puny and insignificant almost immediately. How did she manage to do this? I felt as if I were suddenly the meek cornered mouse to her fierce Tomcat – toying with me just before the kill.

I feebly managed to mutter a "Hello Miss Menage...", trying to distance any sense of intimacy between us by addressing her formally. I almost immediately winced with embarrassment as I saw worried grimaces from the cast members around me and I noticed Bella beginning to giggle with pure delight.

"Oh Bandy! Where have you been – you silly little girl? How could you not have heard the news? I know that you keep company with the more mundane classes of peasants – but surely one of them must have had the ability to read a newspaper. As of 11th of August, I was transformed into Mrs. Michael William Sharp."

I stuttered out a meagre "Congratulations." Some of my sympathetic compatriots tried to distract her with cheers and applause at her matrimonial announcement.

"Oh, thank you! But speaking of congratulations..." As Bella addressed the assembly, I knew that I was destined for a particularly tortuous scene. "While I was performing leading roles at the King's Theatre this summer – we had our very own leading lady South of the river; didn't we?" Bella feigned praise through her fake smile. "Bandy was performing at the circus! Along with all the horses! I wonder if they mistook you for a mare?"

"I had my start at the Royal Circus. It is a wonderful theatre." Lovely Miss Decamp piped up in my defence, but Bella continued undeterred.

"Bandy performed a range of roles that were most suited to her abilities and experiences. Let's see if I can recollect them..." Bella affected a very exaggerated French accent. "First, there was 'La Belle Sauvage', a WILD girl! Haha!" Bella taunted me with purring cat noises and pretended to claw at me while laughing. It was so humiliating and demeaning.

"And then our little peasant Bandy played what? Oh yes! A slave – yes, that's it! Wasn't she a negress as well? Working in the dirty soil in chains. No need to wash for that role then – suited you perfectly!" It was all that I could do to hold back my tears as Bella cackled at me. I was determined that she would not see my cry, no matter what. But then she continued to comment, this time with an unbelievably bad Scottish accent "Then she was the Maid of Lochlin! Dancin' the hornpipe!" Bella danced a silly jig, like some imbecilic marionette.

At that moment, Mr. Grimaldi entered and interrupted the proceedings by gathering everyone together. As we moved towards seats, Charlotte Bristow came to me and took me by the arm to an area far away from the new Mrs. Sharp. She was about to say something comforting, but I knew I would not be able to bear it.

I whispered quietly "Please don't say anything…I will be fine. Thank you." Then took a deep breath as I sat down. I was seething with anger and humiliation. So much so that it was hard for me to follow what was being said by Mr. Grimaldi. I tried to envisage all of the people that mattered most to me: Papa, Mother, Little Tom, Aunt Harriet. Then for some odd, unexplainable reason I pictured the heroic, handsome face of Henry Erskine Johnston. I remembered his belittling of Bella in my defence. I imagined how he would have torn a strip off Bella, especially when she tried to speak like a Scot. There is no way he would have tolerated that insult! I found myself having to stifle a giggle, thinking of Carlo the dog trying to sniff at Bella's bottom. Bella was as vile and vindictive as ever. I could not deceive myself for a moment that she would be distracted by feelings of matrimonial bliss. She would continue to victimise me for her own pleasure, and I had to be prepared for this. I refused to let her turn my triumphs into debacles. I sat remembering that it was not Bella who was chosen to replace Miss Decamp for Cinderella. I was good... I AM good. I closed my eyes and a vision of my cracked mirror at home appeared before me. I could hear mighty Athena's voice reminding me – "Know your worth. Do not doubt! You are more than good!"

But I was a bit startled at the end of this comforting daydream, for I had a premonition of something. I couldn't quite figure out what it was. Something unsettling. A trial. An unexpected change. I could not quite fathom what Athena was trying to convey to me. I held on strongly to the message though – for some reason, the phrase repeated in my head over and over again. "Know your worth."

I tried to refocus and grasp what Mr. Grimaldi was speaking about. He had stated that Mr. Byrne was no longer ballet director. He, Mr. Grimaldi, was to act as temporary director until the named director was free from his commitments and could take up his position in full. I was so pleased for the talented but much underrated Mr. Grimaldi. He was kind, dedicated, extraordinarily talented and so hard working. It finally seemed as if his efforts would now be recognised by Mr. Sheridan and the theatre managers. Then someone asked aloud who the new permanent ballet director would be. I felt a sudden sense of panic as he responded. "It is a name that you will all be familiar with. A very resourceful man who has written a ballet that we shall perform this Autumn. The dance sequence is called *Terpsichore's Return*. One of many new dance performances from our new director, I'm sure. You will all be pleased to hear of the return of Mr. D'Egville. James D'Egville, just to clarify – there are so many dancing D'Egvilles around!"

There were a few groans from those gathered around. James D'Egville had a reputation for being a bit of a task master – extremely demanding of those dancers he directed and a bit full of himself. That did not concern me as much as his being lothario. I will never forget almost being lured in by him into a life of disrepute. He was untrustworthy and a snake, so unlike his brother George. I glanced over at Bella, who had a huge smile as if she were a cat licking cream. Then I saw her direct her gaze directly at me and nodded her head in a smug fashion.

All the actresses were asked by Mr. Grimaldi to head to the dressing room for costume fittings by Miss Rein and her assistants. As the ladies gathered in the crowded room, many were peering at a handwritten cast list of upcoming productions. I noted that Bella had taken a seat in a prime position in front of a mirror and table. I saw the matriarchs of the cast, Mrs. Jordan, Miss Mellon, and Mrs. Mountain glide past her in threesome – actively avoiding Bella, but I suspect that she was far too self-centred to notice.

Bella shouted at me disdainfully as I came into the room. "Bandy! The peasants are all to meet in the attic for a fitting – you don't need to be in here with the rest of us!" I was used to such insults from Bella, so I ignored her. I tried to look at the castings for the lavish production that we were dressing for, *Richard Couer de Lion*. Charlotte Bristow had a better view than I, and I noted a rather disappointed look on her face. She turned to me trying to put a more positive spin towards things, smiling and saying, "We are dancing in the 3rd act, along with Miss Vining!" Miss Vining came to my side as Miss Bristow moved ahead and whispered disappointingly in my ear "We actually are supporting dancers for Charlotte in the 3rd act. And we are also in the chorus of peasants." We looked at each other sullenly, then I was jerked away by my elbow to the dressing table by none other than Bella.

"You may wish to see Mr. Wroughton to check on your new salary. I'm afraid it isn't good news. But do keep in mind that I could always put in a good word for you with

Mr. D'Egville. I am sure he would be able to get you some extra employment outside the theatre."

I tried my best to speak at a noticeable volume, for I did not want Bella's sneaky bullying of me to go by unwitnessed.

"I have had quite enough of your disparaging, rude comments to me Mrs. Sharp! Unhand me as I have a benefit night to arrange at the Royal Circus. I think that shall keep me going financially without resorting to begging for favours from your pimp friend, Mr. D'Egville. Tell me, has he procured any non-theatrical clients for you? I am sure Mr. Sharp would be most interested. Unless, of course, that's how you both met!"

Bella slapped me across the face. It would have been hard, but it was almost comical for she was wearing a silk glove from her costume and it eased the sting of the blow immeasurably.

Grabbing me by the hair and drawing me close to her face, Bella hissed at me "Listen to me carefully – this is important information for you, 'Cinderella'. I shall never, NEVER allow you to be in a position to usurp any of what is rightfully mine – MY roles. Ever again! As long as you are here in Drury Lane, I will ensure that you stay in the miserable background where you belong. So, if you want more from your stage career, you had best learn to sing German at the Coburg Theatre or learn to walk the trapeze at Ashley's Circus. Get your adoring applause from the bakers, tailors and coachmen who frequent those places and save the aristocracy for us. You don't have your Mr. Byrne to protect you anymore. Mr. Sheridan doesn't care, and Mr. Grimaldi is, quite literally, just a clown. So, don't think that you can go cry and change things around. Your destiny is set. At Drury Lane, Miss Seale is forever delegated to the background." There was a silence in which one could hear a pin drop. Bella gave a tiny wave to me and quietly said with an exaggerated sad face "Bye, bye Bandy."

I stepped out the dressing room, walked out of the door of the theatre reeling and leaned against one of the massive stone pillars. Having arrived at Drury Lane this morning in a buoyant mood, I found myself leaving abruptly this afternoon in a most unsettled, distraught state. How quickly fortunes can turn. I let everything out that I had tried to bottle up inside in front of my colleagues. I sobbed inconsolably. To my surprise, I suddenly found myself in the arms of a passing gentleman, who just happened to be the kind Mr. Grimaldi. He tried valiantly to comfort me.

"Hey! Hey! It is going to be ok! It really is! Believe me, whatever it is. I have had awful things happen to me. Horrible things. My wife and baby died. I thought I lost everything. But I am still here. Look – here I am! And I manage to make people smile and laugh sometimes. You do that too! You're a great dancer! A fabulous dancer! Don't let anyone else say differently." His eyes were watery. I could tell he was speaking from his heart – from true experience. "Hey – do you remember that night you tried on the glass slipper? Remember always that you are a princess! Your wildest dreams can come true! You are young yet – don't let these little setbacks get you down! Here - look, I have something to cheer you up!" Joe took out the carnation flower that he had in his buttonhole in his coat. Why he had a flower on I do not know. But he held the carnation out, making me look at it. He sniffed the bloom's delicate scent, smiled sweetly, and looked to the heavens. Then looking at me directly – he suddenly made the flower vanish from his hands. I don't know how he did it. I found myself giggling like a little girl. Then, with his hand to my ear, he pulled out the missing flower and handed it to me with a grin. I gasped in amazement and had tears of laughter instead of complete despair. I mouthed the words "Thank you" as he made his way back inside. Smelling the fragrant flower, I thought of Athena's message again. "Know your worth."

CHAPTER 26

Richard Coeur de Lion

More heart-breaking than the actual event itself was having to disclose what had happened to Mother and Papa. Mother was incensed and ready to go and complain to the management – even Mr. Sheridan if need be. I wrestled an assurance from her that she would not. Papa seemed more resigned and tried to tell me that positives could result from adversity. It was hard to imagine being able to move to the forefront again. My part was so inconsequential. My salary had now been reduced to a meagre 12 shillings a week. How could I contribute to the family finances with a wage that was so paltry?

Mother focused me on the one bright piece of news that I still yet had remaining. I had a full benefit evening taking place at the Royal Circus. Set for the 10th of October, this was something that I could cling to and focus on to help me forget the miserable situation that I now found myself in. Hopefully, it would prove to be highly profitable as well. I had the great fortune to be sponsored on the night by Sir Francis Burdett. This meant that he was paying for all the costs of theatre hire and the wages of the employees on the evening. All the ticket sales would therefore go directly into my pocket, thanks to his kind generosity.

Sir Francis was a rather peculiar gentleman. Unlike most of the wealthy aristocracy, he seemed to be a man who championed the rights of the common folk. He had the good fortune to marry Sophia Coutts, daughter of the wealthy banker, and therefore recipient of her exceptionally large dowry. He had added fortunes on the passing of his grandfather, entitling him to become a Baronet. He used his money to purchase a parliamentary seat and to champion causes such as prison reform, ending the war with France and financially supporting the radical writer Thomas Paine. He was a good friend of Mr. Cross, a frequent visitor to our circus theatre and for some reason, I became a cause for yet more of his philanthropy.

I only recall meeting him once, and that was very brief. I was called to the Green Room after one of my early performances of *The Wild Girl!* Arriving through the door, I saw Mr. and Mrs. Cross, who introduced me to Mr. and Mrs. Burdett. Mrs. Burdett was especially taken by my performance in the play and asked me in great detail all about the character I portrayed and the methods I used to enable myself to transform into this feral creature. She was most impressed when she discovered my age at how I could pull forth such strength of emotion. Sir Francis was complementary, but in a very subdued way. After thanking me for my most excellent and moving performance, he explained that he and his wife felt compelled to speak with Mr. Cross as to how they could help support and nurture the great talent of this young performer. Upon hearing that I would have a benefit night, they insisted upon paying all the costs – including the cost of printing tickets and a few posters as well. And so, it is thanks to the kind Sir Francis that any risk involved in the running of a benefit night was swept away. He even stated that he would pay for advertisements in the newspapers.

They hushed me when I started my profuse thanks, stating that they were so incredibly pleased to be supporting such talent. They were looking forward to witnessing my progression as an artist, and they felt that they should in fact be thanking me for allowing them to play a part in my development. I was nearly speechless that anyone could be so generous and to be so touched by my performances. It was these thoughts and memories that I would need to cling to if times became challenging. It was extremely uncommon to have such a generous benefactor and I felt so incredibly fortunate.

I had to sustain these thoughts every time I approached Drury Lane for a rehearsal. I felt that my part was so negligible and forgettable. Yet to miss a rehearsal would result in my pay being reduced by almost more than I actually earned! I had to put aside the tears and be strong. As Bella had thoroughly decimated all my future opportunities, my mind weighed heavy with troubled thoughts as to what would become of me. Would I be destined to be some background performer – a piece of scenery to move around at a moment's notice? Would I be destined to fill the shoes of Bella's pleasant but rather unremarkable sister Mary – always there somewhere, but never really missed if she failed to be present? In rehearsals, I trudged around as a nameless peasant and later valiantly supported Miss Bristow's performance along with Miss Vining – barely noticeable as all attention would be upon Charlotte. I was now so inconsequential and unimportant that Bella no longer slighted me or put me down. She cut me dead completely, an act that I would have found most welcome in the previous year – but now, it was evidence that I did not even exist. I might as well have been an apple seller out on the street. I would likely command more attention in that role.

When the debut of *Richard Coeur de Lion* took place in October, it held no special joy for me. There was no excitement, no stage magic, nor was there any sense of awe. This assembly of doom held no merriment. I could not partake of any of the delights that seemed so apparent on the faces of the crowds in the pit. I had ample time to gaze at the glamourous occupants of the prestigious boxes. It mattered not one jot, for no one was looking at me – that smudgy faced peasant amongst the throng of other peasants. The best I could hope for was that one observant soul might glance around the stage and take notice, perhaps whispering to their partner "That girl – she looks familiar…was she not Cinderella? What a shame – now she is relegated to the chorus."

It was difficult for me to rise out of bed the next morning. It felt as if it were a coffin. But rise up I had to do and hope that I would be able to find the vivacity and charm needed to carry out the evening as the leading lady of the Royal Circus Theatre. My confidence was at the lowest ebb and I soon found myself sobbing and shaking. I was completely unaware of the peeping Tom at my doorway, taking in the entire scene.

"Hey! Elizabeth is crying! Mama, Papa!"

"Tom – please! Why can't you just leave me alone?"

"But you're sad! I don't want you to be sad! If you cry, your voice will crack and then all your singing will be like…" Tom grabbed his throat with two hands and pretended to choke himself. He made a wheezing, gagging sound as he crossed his eyes and made the most ludicrous face imaginable. I could not help to laugh!

"Well it looks like tears of laughter to me!" chuckled Papa. Mother followed in smiling and gave me a big, reassuring hug.

"It is natural to have jitters but remember that you will be absolutely amazing! This is your chance to shine. And you will be shining like a beacon, I know it!" Mother gave another loving squeeze.

Papa added "This is your chance to show those idiots at Drury Lane the big mistake they made! Why, I've had so many people come to the door and purchase tickets for tonight. I did not want to tell you in case it fed your conceit and vanity, but all have been so full of praise about you. Remember – they want to see you, my darling Little Liz! Half of London is turning out to see my talented daughter perform!"

"Not me. I can see her anytime. I'm going to see the horsemen performing! Weeeee!" Tom clambered on top of me and pretended that he was on the saddle.

"Tom – come away! You'll hurt her and she needs to be feeling her best today! I shall go get some breakfast ready. Tom, fetch the eggs from Aunt Harriet." Mother brought me my clothing to dress into. They all left on the promise that I would come downstairs soon. A little less miserable, I stood up, washed, and slowly dressed myself. I looked out the window onto Hart Street below. After days of grey, rainy misery there was sunshine beaming through breaks in the clouds. I hoped that this was a good omen, a special message from Athena. Then hearing the church bells of St. George's strike the hour, I felt reminded that my blessings might not actually be coming from a pagan deity. I closed my eyes and asked for forgiveness. I prayed for a successful performance without mishap. I prayed for consolation – relief from my misery at my current situation at Drury Lane. But I also remembered to give thanks, remembering what a dire situation we were in just one year ago. When all seemed hopeless, we were blessed with a miraculous deliverance through our tribulations. That reflection helped to buoy my spirits once again. I needed reminding that there was a path out of these bleak, dark events. I may not yet know where that road would take me, but I had to hold onto hope and continue on in faith. On my way downstairs, I looked at myself quickly in the cracked mirror. I curtsied and smiled at the reflection of the lovely young woman staring back at me.

CHAPTER 27

Vauxhall Gardens

I was feeling truly special this evening. Well-wishers came by in a steady stream as I prepared myself for the performance; Mother gathering the bouquets of flowers for me and messages of good luck. I made myself try to remember every detail of the night, should this prove to be the pinnacle of my career before a very swift decline. Mother was a great support to me, but I was eager that she join Papa, Aunt Harriet, and Tom in the special box that a friend of my Aunt had purchased the seats for this evening. They would be sitting amongst the well-known and highly respected – should anyone of that persuasion have decided to venture South of the river for an evening's entertainment on a Wednesday night. But I had a good feeling about it all. Even before the doors opened, I knew from Papa that more than half the spaces had been sold – a good number from our doorstep. This ensured that the evening would secure me over £100 at least, and more if sales were good at the door. This would go a good way to ensuring that we were financially secure this year as a family, and perhaps make up somewhat for the losses I would have from my reduced Drury Lane salary.

As I heard the 'clippity-clop' of the Taylor Riding Group's horses start off, I rushed Mother away to join the rest of the family. Teary-eyed with pride, she kissed me lightly on the cheek so as to not wipe away my feral girl dirt smudges on my cheeks. I finished putting on my ensemble of hideous, foul rags which was the favoured costume of the 'Wild Girl' I was about to portray. I burst into giggles thinking what joy Bella would have at taunting sad little 'Bandy' for her appearance. I took comfort in knowing that I would transform significantly as the evening progressed.

As I stepped out on the stage, screaming, and crawling as the half-mad little French girl, I was pleased to see that the auditorium was respectably filled – perhaps more than two-thirds full. In knowing that I was not performing to empty seats, I was determined to give my patrons the absolute best of what I had to offer. My screams had never been so loud and piercing, my savage dances never more expressive. This is what I was destined to do – I felt it so strongly coursing through my blood. I had to stop thinking about it too intensely, for I was apt to break out in embarrassed blushes, knowing that everyone was training their eyes upon me. They had come all this way, making a great effort to see Miss Searle before their gaze. I could scarcely believe it.

Savage duties complete to rapturous applause, I rushed backstage as a young boy dressed up as a soldier stepped out onto the stage for the very first time. He looked petrified as he was pushed on by his overeager parents, acquaintances of Mr. Cross, hoping this debut would lead to a glittering career for their budding little Garrick. I needed help scrubbing off the grime from my face and quickly changing into a beautiful Scotch costume left over from *The Maid of Lochlin*. I was hoping that the poor little boy before me at least elicited sympathy, if not entertainment. This was the portion of the benefit that worried me the most. I was about to sing.

I could hear the crowd murmuring and speaking amongst themselves in a rather jovial way, when Mr. Cross walked onto the stage to introduce the next act. I winced slightly as he spoke, enticing the audience to remember the well-known duet performed at Vauxhall Gardens by the acclaimed singers - Mr. Dignum and Miss Daniels. He then proclaimed that the audience would now hear the tune as interpreted by Mr. Terrail and Miss Searle. I felt he may as well have added "Please sit back and endure this second-rate version of a well-loved tune!"

To kind applause, I nervously accompanied the much more assured Mr. Terrail onto the stage. He gave me an encouraging smile from his rather chubby face. His green eyes expressed sympathy at my predicament. We had practiced this song throughout August, but I have always felt my voice had the opportunity to let me down whenever I least expected it. A duet was a fortunate choice, I felt, because I could always dip my volume down slightly to be covered by Mr. Terrail's more professional sounding notes. I pasted on a false, love-sick grin and gazed in pseudo-adoration of Mr. Terrail's thinning brown curls and his stout frame. Unnervingly, his looks of fondness towards me appeared that he was in complete awe of me. I half-expected him to lay down and worship me before a thousand pairs of eyes. I never stopped my stupid, insipid smile – even when not quite hitting the notes I wanted to on at least two occasions. I hoped desperately that it was only I who was aware, although I was certain that I could detect Mr. Terrail curl his nose in a reflexive wince each time it occurred. At last, my trial had ended. I bowed, to polite sounds of encouragement from the audience, then held my arms out pointing to Mr. Terrail. He took his bow to much more convincing sounds of approbation and made his way offstage.

I then posed, ready for my new Scotch dance composed by Mr. George D'Egville – a joyous sequence called *The Merry Highlanders, or Love has its Way*. Dance was my forte. This was the area of my greatest comfort and pleasure. When dancing, I had no fear of performing. I became so engrossed in my movements and the sheer enjoyment I was experiencing that there was simply no time or room left for insecure thoughts of inadequacy. At least I thought that nothing could throw my stride off until I turned and saw that my ballet love interest was none other than the choreographer himself, George D'Egville. He gave me the most mischievous wink and smile, as the music struck up and I was compelled to start. I tried to act as if nothing was amiss as he held my waist, lifted me and I danced – relying upon his strong arms to carry me along. It was certainly a surprise, but I feel that perhaps it had given the dance sequence some considerable measure of improvement by having this talented ballet director by my side. At completion, I took a deep breath and we bowed together. I saw George wave up to a box on the right. Following his gaze, my heart sunk as I spotted his brother – Mr. James D'Egville, sitting with an older gentleman in fine dress. They were accompanied by two beautiful women fluttering their fans. The ladies seemed much younger than their accompanying gentlemen and they seemed much more concerned with looking at the audience and giggling, than watching the performance at hand onstage.

I thanked George profusely as we headed backstage. He laughed and stated it was such a pleasure – especially seeing the look of shock and surprise on my face when he came to join me. Knowing that I had another complex costume change, he bade me farewell and promised to catch up with me in the Green Room later. I was readying for the finale, a hastily patched up pastiche of a burletta entitled *The Mermaid* – complete with my performance of the hornpipe from *Cybele*, which seemed to be an audience favourite and a crowd-pleaser. And so there I was, beautifully costumed as the Columbine, dancing opposite a masked Harlequin.

All things, both good and bad, must reach their conclusion. And so too with the end of my very first benefit evening. As I took my final bows, I was so touched by the rapturous applause, the flowers thrown onstage and the smiles of all those faces around me. Looking up and waving to my family I felt such a sense of pride. I, a mere teenaged girl, had helped to ensure the security of my family in the time of utmost need. I had accomplished far more than I had ever imagined that I could.

The time in the Green Room left me a bit melancholy. I said my goodbyes to the dear theatrical colleagues I had spent time with here. Mother would continue with her costume work, so I assured everyone that I would be back to visit. I was most taken aback to see Miss Harriet Mellon there, next to Sir Frances Burdett and his wife. She introduced me to the man accompanying her, who was none other than Mrs. Burdett's father – the wealthy financier Mr. Coutts. They all congratulated me on my performance and how much they enjoyed this spectacular evening. This brief encounter seemed to confirm to me Miss Mellon's assertion that there were special arrangements to accommodate her presence in this most peculiar family unit. I certainly would not judge one of my greatest heroines – both on and off the stage.

I was relieved to see that George D'Egville left his brother behind – bringing his wife to meet mother and I as he relayed the embarrassing circumstances of our first meeting. We all had an embarrassed laugh and it seemed it would be a tale that George would enjoy telling repeatedly. George had been key to our successful placement here at the Circus and we were so incredibly grateful to him. Indebted as well were we to the upstanding Mr. Cross, who nurtured and pushed my talents with strong roles to perform. Mother had ensured that all the books he had let us read for preparation in my theatrical roles were duly returned. He was such a dedicated, kind, and thoughtful man. I felt as if I had received a thorough education from him, whereas the staff at Drury Lane seemed to let me aimlessly drift and fend for myself.

I had hoped that the elation of my triumph at the Royal Circus would sustain me, but soon I felt the despondency of Drury Lane pulling my esteem down a deep chasm of depression. I did not think anyone was taking the slightest bit of notice of me skulking around the theatre, doing my bit parts, and keeping out of everyone's way. But one evening, the dear Maria Decamp pulled me to one side in the dressing room to speak to me in private.

"Listen Elizabeth, we never had this conversation, right?"

I nodded and assured her that no one would be aware we ever spoke.

"I have been very aware of your mistreatment here at Drury Lane. It is by no means a rare occurrence. As you know, I try to see my fiancée Charles as frequently as possible and I am working hard to win over his family into accepting me as a suitable wife to him. That is an ongoing process that is more successful at some times rather than others. Anyway, last night I had a long discussion with his brother, John Kemble. As I think you may be aware, he left Drury Lane quite embittered with Mr. Sheridan and at great cost as he continues to be owed thousands for all his theatre manager work here. That tradition of abuse continues at this theatre, as you well know. I often fill John in on the latest mishaps here. It helps to reaffirm to him that he made the correct choice in purchasing a share of Covent Garden Theatre and leaving this theatre for good. I think you might have heard that Mr. Grimaldi had not been paid the extra amount he was promised to take on the ballet directorship here. In fact, Mr. Sheridan is now professing that he made no such promise! The liar! For the moment now, my situation here is satisfactory. I have enough clout to ensure that I can hold my ground. But that is not the case with most that are here. You included."

I was not sure why she was telling me all of this, but it was heartening to know that I was not the only one to be misused here. I suppose misery does indeed enjoy having company. Miss Decamp continued her secret conversation with me.

"There is an unspoken agreement between Drury Lane and Covent Garden. It is exceptionally important and must be adhered to, or else things would get out of hand and become intolerably chaotic. The agreement is that one theatre must not poach the performer of another. No enticements are to be given; no tempting offers to lure prominent names away. This keeps a stable peace between the two rivals. So, Elizabeth, I must make this very clear to you. Having relayed to Mr. John Kemble about you and your current unfortunate position in the company and how your solid talents were going to great waste – well, let us just say that he was most sympathetic to your distressing situation. Of course, he is unable to give you any offer of work as you are in the employ of a rival theatre. However…"

Maria had a smile and a glint of promise in her eyes as she continued "Mr. Kemble assured me that should you ever find yourself out of a job, he would most certainly be keen to add a talented dancer onto his roster of performers. Do you catch my meaning? If you are no longer employed here…Elizabeth, I swear to you – I guarantee that you will walk into employment at Covent Garden."

"Really? Oh my…thanks! Thank you! But – what do I do? How do I go about this?"

"Well, I think if you just quit your post here then walked into a job with Kemble immediately, that might look a bit suspicious. Also, my future brother-in-law would never admit this, but I do think he enjoys a bit of chaos and disruption at Drury Lane. This helps to drive custom his way. But of course, it must remain our secret. Do you trust me? I think I have a plan that you may like, which could extricate you out of your contract very quickly. What do you think?"

Perhaps I should have discussed the proposal with Mother and Papa. But I felt time was of the essence. I was truly sick of Drury Lane and wanted out. I trusted Maria Decamp implicitly. She had always been one of my few champions there and if I could make use of her inside knowledge and connections to improve my standing, then I felt that it was a risk worth taking. I therefore agreed to whatever her plan entailed. Wednesday, the 24th of October would be the very last time I was to ever perform at Drury Lane Theatre. I could not wait!

CHAPTER 28

George Frederick Cooke

George Frederick Cooke was an innovative actor of great renown. He had a very engaging style of acting that made him wildly popular with the audience and a top draw, almost guaranteeing a sell-out crowd. His good height and aquiline nose gave him a commanding presence on the stage. The aging actor from Dublin had a very interesting rivalry with another well-known actor by the name of Charles Kemble. During the 1803 season at Covent Garden, the two would often vie for the prime role in each performance. The loser was relegated to a secondary, supporting role and would have to endure witnessing the success of their rival at close hand on a nightly basis. There was certainly no love lost between Miss Decamp's fiancée, a member of the mighty Kemble acting clan, and his competitor – the dynamic Mr. Cooke.

Drury Lane had secured Mr. Cooke for the season in a major coup. Mr. Sheridan felt quite smug in having manoeuvred a way to his theatre under the nose of his rival down the road. Mr. Cooke was doing well in his first role at Drury Lane, that of Florestan in *Richard Coeur de Lion*. Poor Mr. Cooke however did have a growing reputation for a problematic flaw that he possessed. One that was likely to reoccur at a moment's notice. It seems that Mr. Cooke had an extreme fondness for drink. So much so that he could find himself incapacitated and unable to perform. His contract with Drury Lane stipulated that he was forbidden to enter the Green Room in an attempt to prevent any temptation towards inebriation. Therefore, we became determined to deliver the Green Room to Mr. Cooke.

Miss Decamp had provided me with a fine bottle of Scotch whisky that she felt might prove irresistible to the all-important gentleman. My task was to ensure that he started drinking, for once he began it was a well-known fact that he could not stop. Mr. Cooke had a quiet corner of the dressing room and was trying to steer clear of the cast members of the first show. I began to set the wheels of the plan into action.

"Hello, uh – Mr. Cooke, Mr. Cooke sir, I am so terribly sorry to interrupt you…"

I moved towards Mr. Cooke's table with my cloth sack carefully held in my arms so as to not break the fragile contents. He had the pretence of studying his lines, but I could see full well that he had been napping before I woke him. Catching him off-guard, he was being especially amiable and polite to me, in order to cover his covert somnambulance.

"I…ummm…my name is Miss Searle. I am sure you do not know, but I am a member of the cast here and I have the privilege of working alongside you here at Drury Lane. Well, in the background anyway!" I gave a nervous giggle and a flirtatious look towards the awakening Mr. Cooke.

"Oh…my dear! I assure you the pleasure is all mine! I am most happy to make your acquaintance."

"I am quite embarrassed to be doing this but…I hope you do not mind if I beg a favour of you. You see, my father attends the theatre frequently and he is such a fervent admirer of your great theatrical skill and talent. It would be his greatest wish to meet you in person."

"Oh, but of course my dear. Not a problem!"

"I fear, Mr. Cooke, that there is a complication. You see, my father is not well. He has injured his foot and is unable to travel. But he told me of his greatest wish. He hoped that I would be able to stand in proxy for him on this occasion. His dream would be to raise a toast in honour of your genius and to share a drink with you."

"Oh...oh...well...um...I am not certain that would be such a wise..."

"And so, he gave me this bottle – I must confess that I am not familiar with strong beverages. My father assured me that this was the finest whisky he possessed – and he was saving it for just such an auspicious occasion!" I popped the top off the bottle, gave a little sniff and giggled as I passed it on to Mr. Cooke.

"Oh well now, that...that does seem to be a very nice whisky indeed." He smiled and looked powerless to resist the temptation.

I pulled out two glass tumblers that I had carefully wrapped in my bag, and began to pour – a minute, tiny amount for me and a most generous portion for Mr. Cooke.

"So, on my father's behalf, I wish to commend you – Mr. Cooke. The theatrical genius that has entertained my Papa so thoroughly. Cheers!" I clinked his glass and down the liquid went. Mr. Cooke gulped the liquid down, whereas my small sip was about to make me gag and cough.

"Oh...oh, that is nice! Thank you so much Miss Searle for..."

"Oh, but Mr. Cooke..." I quickly refilled his glass and dripped a small amount into mine. "That was only the toast from my father! I have to say that I have been witness to your great talents from close range and I am in awe! It would be a great travesty if I were not to toast to your greatness as well. Why, it would be most rude of me, don't you think?"

"Well, I suppose it could be seen that way by some..."

"So, kind sir! Raise your glass and do me the most gracious honour of accepting my accolades. To the finest actor since David Garrick – the incomparable Mr. Cooke!"

"To me!!" Mr. Cooke gave a hearty laugh. "Oh, it has been too long indeed, Miss uh…Miss…since I last was the recipient of such kind words of approbation! My throat has been quite dry these past few months and I do miss a good opportunity for…"

"For praise? And so you should have missed it, kind sir! You deserve far more praise! I think we have taken you for granted. So, let's make up for lost time, for you – sir, are deserving of another toast!" I filled his glass for a third time and was pleased that he did not take any notice of my own near empty receptacle.

Charlotte Bristow happened past and was nearly paralysed with a look of shock on her face. "Elizabeth! What in…what are you DOING! Uh, Mr. Cooke…I think it is time that you stopped with that now, shall I get you some water?"

Ah! Another beautiful woman has joined us! Miss…Miss uh…Yes! I think we need a toast – to beautiful women who are easy to the eye!" He smacked Charlotte on her bottom, making her gasp in horror. "And a delight to the touch!"

"Well if you are toasting us, Mr. Cooke, I think you need your empty glass filling – here you go!"

"Elizabeth, stop! Water! Mr. Cooke, please don't do anything until I get you some water!" Charlotte began to race off as Mr. Cooke insisted that he was not in need of a mixer as he drank his spirits straight. Maria Decamp quickly walked by, placing another bottle in my hands when she was sure that no one was looking. I popped the top and smelled the extremely sweet liquid.

"Now Mr. Cooke, I don't know anything about drink. This one smells nice! Quite different from what we just had. Pray tell, what is it?" I poured my glass full and handed it to him, making him a two-fisted drinker.

"Oh, now that my dear, is sherry! This is something that the ladies like to partake of. Usually in dainty little glasses, not big greedy bastards like this one!" He laughed heartily then apologised for his coarse language. "Here dear, try a sip!"

"Oh, but if you say I need a dainty glass then I must get one…"

"No! No! Stay my dear – here." He guzzled the whisky and asked me to pour a bit in his now empty glass."

"Oh, for me? Oh, thank you Mr. Cooke! Here – could you be so kind as to hold this bottle for me while I take the glass?" We both giggled as we traded sherry receptacles.

"I will do better than hold it my dear. It is in the way, so therefore I must drink it down!" He tipped the bottle up and drank the whole thing dry, tossing the bottle to the side." We both laughed hysterically. Everyone in the dressing room was now taking notice. Charlotte returned with the water and tried to pour it in his mouth, but he proceeded to spit it all back at her in a shower of drunken spittle.

Mrs. Mountain rushed over. "George…George! Are you OK? You must stop this now, right? You'll get yourself in a state! Miss Searle – you really should be most ashamed of yourself! I cannot believe that you would be plying Mr. Cooke with drink!" She scolded me fiercely, but then gave me a surreptitious little wink when no one was looking and handed me a fine pewter flask.

Miss Bristow was at a loss as to what to do. "Mr. Wroughton is on stage performing now! And Mr. Bannister isn't here tonight! Who do I tell? He isn't sober! He is in no fit state to go on the stage!" Someone suggested that she find Mr. Kelly or Mr. Barrymore, so off she went seeking help.

"Now Mr. Cooke…" I continued over his non-stop, drunken giggles.

"Yes…?"

I opened the flask. "I have heard of a most wicked drink called Geneva. It has been the downfall of many an empire I hear…"

"No, no!!! Geneva is good, my dear! My dearest Miss…Miss…What's your name?!! Hahaaaaa!!! Just give me the bloomin' gin!"

He gulped back a good amount, then tried to force me to sip from the flask as he held it. I feigned mock horror as if it were poison and giggled.

"Oh no! Not the evil drink Mr. Cooke! No! No! NOOOO!!! Hahahaha!"

"Noo, girlie! Gin good!! Geneva is your friend see?!" He gulped more back in a stupor, then tried to aim the flask towards my mouth – hitting my nose in the process! "Oh, I am most sorry, my young pretty, pretty little lady!" He slapped my leg clumsily and pulled me to his lap. Mr. Kelly ran into the room and I started to pretend to protest.

"Oh Mr. Cooke – please! Unhand me! Look – there's a glass of water over there!"

"You don't need water Missy! You need Geneva!!! GENEVA!!!"

Mr. Cooke clutched onto my waist then we both fell to the floor. Mr. Kelly tried to untangle us.

"George! George! Whatever are you doing? George get up!" commanded Mr. Kelly, to no avail.

I broke free and took advantage of the chaos to implement more mayhem. Bella was due to play the part of Laurette in the upcoming historical romance. If I could incapacitate another cast member, then the situation at Drury Lane would be dire indeed. Bella was a replacement for Miss Holloway in this role and was not accustomed to the costumes and routines – this being her first full performance in the role. This would require her fitting into Miss Holloway's costume and making last minute adjustments. Miss Decamp told me of a hiding place that contained the materials I would need to sabotage Bella's ability to ready herself for the show. I looked around the window seat where I was to find what I needed, but the box was nowhere to be seen. Mr. Grimaldi calmly walked by and kicked discretely at a box by a different window that I had missed somehow, looking back to make sure that I had found it. Finding a private place, I opened the box to look at the contents – then quickly went to work. The cast of *Richard Coeur de Lion* were all readying themselves. I quickly put on my peasant costume and tried to find a good spot to watch Bella dress where she might not notice me. In the meantime, Mr. Cooke was now comatose and Mr. Kelly was wondering desperately if any of the cast onstage now with *As You Like It* would be able to take Mr. Cooke's place, perhaps being given every line by a poor, overworked prompter.

Bella looked petulant as ever. She began the process of dressing with the help of some dressers to assist her. Fortunately, these dressers were all distracted by the antics of Mr. Cooke when I specially prepared Bella's costumes for this evening. First was the petticoat. I had sprinkled a few itchy, irritating seeds around it – just enough to be annoying but not enough to be overtly obvious. She put the garment on but struggled to settle and kept pulling at the petticoat, cursing at her helpers because they were obviously doing something wrong.

Next was a simple white dress that Bella was required to wear. Along the waistline was an adjustable band. It was there that I had placed a sealed pig's bladder filled with blood, in the hopes that at some point that evening she would lean back in a chair or move about in such a way as to burst the organ and release the offensive contents. The dress went on and she sat at the dressing table. She was still itching but no bladder problems, as of yet. Next, she slipped her feet into her slipper shoes. I could see her expression of shock and disgust as she realised that she had placed her entire foot and full weight completely into a shoe which contained a dead mouse. Bella squealed and screeched, again swearing at her dressers for their oversight in giving her vermin-ridden shoes. Bella leaned back hard against her chair as the ladies tried to quickly pry her foot away from the squished rodent. As she did so, the pressure on the bladder hidden in the waistline was too much and a gush of red liquid began to seep down to Bella's bottom.

I could see an already distraught Bella's eyes widen as she felt liquid down her backside. A female cast member shouted out "Bella! You're bleeding!" Bella jumped up in terror, screaming as she saw what she imagined was her own blood dripping onto the floor. The cast from *As You Like It* were returning, and the small changing area was complete pandemonium. Mr. Cooke was passed out on the floor and had just begun to vomit, much to the disgust of those trying to help him. Bella was stripping off her clothing and screaming like some deranged lunatic. Ripping at her petticoat, she was pleading for all around her – "Get it off! GET IT OFF!" As she was itching and stomping and virtually helpless, I thought I would be of some assistance. I pulled the undergarment right away from her forcefully. I am afraid that this did leave her in a state of considerable undress. Some would say that she was as naked as she was on the day she was born. I said very sweetly "There you go – all better now!"

Bella screamed even more which served the purpose of drawing more attention to herself. As she seemed to always enjoy extra attention, I felt that this was most fitting. She desperately clutched at her ripped and bloodied garments, trying to hold them up to provide a modicum of modesty. She was so mortified and traumatised that she could not find any words to hiss at me. She could only look at me with a deep hatred in her eyes and moaned a pathetic "EEEWWWWW!!! Ehhhh!" as she shook uncontrollably.

Mr. Elliston and Mr. Wroughton looked aghast at the

situation and tried to quickly get a plan of action together. Mr. Elliston offered to take Mr. Cooke's role onstage. He would be very dependent on a prompter and asked for Mr. Barrymore to scribble down the lines on scraps of paper that he may be able to hold and read from during the performance. Mr. Wroughton asked me to take Bella's role in the play, directing some of the dressers to find a suitable substitute costume for me.

"Well Mr. Wroughton, there is the case of my salary having been reduced. I don't think that someone on my salary should be performing such an important role as that of Laurette. I think I will remain being a peasant, thank you very much. It suits me at this moment in time."

"Miss Searle, I will see that your salary is increased to the previous rate. I assure you of that – you have my word. Now if you would please…"

"You know Mr. Wroughton, I don't really think I can completely believe everything that the management promises here. Why, Mr. Grimaldi was offered an extra £2 per week to take on ballet master duties, and from what I have heard – it seems that the theatre has reneged on that promise and not compensated him as promised. How am I to know that I can trust you? Perhaps if Mr. Sheridan were here right now and open up his pocketbook and pay me in advance, I might consider it."

Mr. Wroughton looked on in disbelief. He was speechless. After a few seconds he regained his composure and decided to take a stern approach. He began to give me a harsh dressing down. "Now you listen here Miss Searle, you have been directed to step into a role by your superior. I command you to get in that dress and get your little arse on that stage right now or you can find yourself another stage to perform at!

"Another stage? Why Mr. Wroughton – what a most excellent idea! By another stage are you suggesting that I find employment elsewhere? I should think I would like to do that very much! It would be quite a change from working in this piss pot of misery."

Mr. Wroughton was not used to being spoken to like this. I could see the intense stress building up in the veins on his face. He was getting desperate now and a crowd of my co-workers were watching to see what he would do next.

"Miss Searle…I…I am not bluffing; I will have you know! I shall fire you on the spot!"

"Oh, will you really Mr. Wroughton? That would be immensely exciting! Oh please – will you do it now?!"

"Uh…would anyone else be prepared to take on Miss Menage's place? It seems Miss Searle is unable to take on the part."

"No…not unable. Unwilling. And EVERYONE, is there someone to take on my little peasant role as well? Because Mr. Wroughton is going to relieve me of my duties. Oh yes, Mr. Wroughton – I also support with dance with Miss Bristow in the third act. You will need someone else for that as well."

"Uh, Miss Searle…I think you have made your point. You seem to have me over a barrel, and I am willing to meet you halfway here and…"

"Now Mr. Wroughton, you know that is no way to manage a theatre. Giving into the whims of arrogant, demanding performers. You know that will be a rod for your back. If I get away with it, then you will have lost control and respect from all the cast. You must be firm! Take a stand! Make an example of me! Listen, Mr. Wroughton…I am trying to help you here. This is an embarrassing situation. If you cannot handle it, I do suggest that you bring Mr. Richard Brinsley Sheridan here forthwith. Perhaps the theatre owner can fire me if you are unwilling to do so."

"Miss Searle, you may continue in your role as before. I will not require you to play Laurette. Perhaps that was a bit presumptuous of me to assume that you would be willing to step into that role. Please continue on as before."

"I am not entirely sure that I want to do that."

"I...I'm sorry?"

"I thought I enjoyed playing peasant girls for a pittance, then queueing up each week to beg Mr. Sheridan for my wages, but now I am beginning to think that it is quite tiresome."

"So, you are saying?"

"I am saying that I am not sure that I am what this theatre requires. I mean to say, not when you can have performers such as Bella Menage as an example of your requirements. Why would you want someone who is hard working and flexible? It seems that you prefer uncooperative troublemakers in your employ. If I were to stay here, I would need more practice with that. Would that be alright with you Mr. Wroughton – if I complained to you on a daily basis? Made your life a misery, like I imagine it is feeling right now at this moment?"

"Miss Searle, I have come to the conclusion that I never wish to work with you again. I shall arrange for your back wages to be at the office in the morning for you to collect. Please leave now. You have been fired from the grandest theatre in the land – you foolish little girl."

"Thank you kindly Mr. Wroughton, for the opportunity. It has been a most edifying experience. I wish you all the best. And I do hope that Mr. Sheridan does pay you what you are owed. He has bad form with that – just ask Mr. John Kemble." I did feel some sympathy for poor Mr. Wroughton, as he too was another of the underlings that Sheridan swindled out of their pay on a regular basis, totting up promissory notes until the realisation that Drury Lane is not a dream but a nightmare incarnate. As I gathered my things, there were smirks and smiles of admiration. Some congratulated me on the sly or bade me farewell with good wishes. Miss Bristow seemed most upset, but I thanked her profusely for her kindness and assured her that all would be well with me. I walked out of the door early that evening. I could hear the ensuing tumult and hisses from the audience inside as they were told that Mr. Cooke would not be performing that evening, nor would Bella Menage. No mention of the fired Miss Searle. I grinned with satisfaction. My work was done.

CHAPTER 29

I was most surprised to see that my back salary, paltry as it was, was indeed waiting for me when I came to collect it the following afternoon at the Drury Lane box office. I did not yet tell Mother or Papa what I had done. I wanted to be absolutely certain, without a doubt, that I had positive news to surprise them with to nullify the shocking revelation of my gross misconduct. The walk from the grand theatre at Drury Lane to Covent Garden could not have been much more than 300 yards. So within just a few short minutes – even walking slowly, I was there. I held in my hand letters of recommendation. I had not only my letter from Mr. Cross, but I had also received other letters of support by surprise – all delivered that morning in a bundle from Charles Kemble's address. I think Maria Decamp had been working in the background to provide this little ego boost for me. In my collection I had some fine commendations from good friends and colleagues. Thinking back on all the amazing talent I had the good fortune to work with, I now saw many of their names right here in my hand. I held my old letter from Mr. Byrne and my new letter of promised introduction from Miss Decamp. Recognition of my fine dancing abilities from the noted choreographer, Mr. George D'Egville. Glowing praise of my professionalism from the elegant Miss Mellon. I was astounded to see Miss Jordan's approbations, along with words of support from Mrs. Mountain. Mr. Male described my talents across the two theatres he worked alongside me. And there was a quick note, only for me from Charlotte Bristow:

Dearest Elizabeth,

I now know what you did – how remarkably brave! I had no idea! I forgive you for keeping such an amazing secret from me. I will be sure to inform you regularly of the misdeeds of Mrs. Bella Sharp. Please know that it has been a delight working with you from the moment I saw you standing, shivering outside that cold theatre door! I wish you the very best, my dear friend, and hope that our paths do meet again.

Your fellow Grace,
Charlotte Bristow

Holding this documentary proof in my hands, I could see the evidence of all that I managed to accomplish in one brief year. I had attained an admirable status. And even after what others might have perceived as my outrageous antics at the Theatre Royal the previous night, I knew within myself that it was indeed the performance of my life. I should always remember fondly my toast to Mr. Cooke and the thorough undressing of my nemesis, Bella Menage. A scene performed that rendered Mr. Wroughton speechless. I had achieved my aim. Success at two of London's grandest theatres, I was now truly an actress of some repute. Looking at the magnificent steps and portico of the opera house – I stepped forward to the door of what was soon to be the third great theatre of London that had the charming Miss Searle on their stage. A beam of sunshine illuminated my face as I looked back at the hulk of the Drury Lane Theatre. Turning the handle, I smiled confidently and pushed the door forward as I walked into the next chapter of my life.

BONUS MATERIAL:
THE REAL-LIFE INSPIRATION FOR
AN ACTRESS OF REPUTE

As a thank you for reading this novel, I am offering a bonus synopsis of the real Elizabeth Searle's life, and some information about the process of researching and writing this book.

To access this, please visit the following webpage:

www.ronanbeckman.com/bonus-material/

Best Wishes,
Ronan Beckman
July 2020